DAUGHTER

OF

STONE

J.R. MOLT

This is a work of fiction. Names, characters, businesses, places, events, locales, and incidents are either the products of the author's imagination or used in a fictitious manner. Any resemblance to actual persons, living or dead, or actual events is purely coincidental.

To my wonderful husband. The man who one day asked me what my dreams were, then never stopped pushing me to accomplish them.

Appear weak when you are strong, and strong when you are weak.

-Sun Tzu

So… I have just been shot. I know if I keep standing here, staring stupidly at the blood pouring out of the wound in my side, that I will probably get shot again. As everything moves in slow motion, I think back to a large Ukrainian man yelling at me.

"Pain clears the head girl. Keep your wits about you. Even if it hurts, you need adrenaline." I shake my head as I brace myself for what I am about to do. Gritting my teeth, I shove my thumb deep inside the bullet wound, just above my right hip. But everything starts to clear as a scream slips out through my dry, raw throat. *Man, this is really going to ruin my day.*

CHAPTER 1

Celeste

I stifle a heavy sigh and force what I hope looks like a smile. I try to ignore the gathering of sweat building on my temple from standing out in the muggy, insect swarmed suburban backyard of Denver Colorado. *Oh hell. Come on, Celeste. You have dealt with worse situations. You can do this.* I silently repeat this as the bead of sweat trickles slowly, almost mocking me as it slides down the side of my face. I check my watch and internally grimace. The last few hours at this boring barbecue could not have only been twenty-three minutes. I attempt another smile at a woman across the yard from me juggling two children in her arms; all while the third attempts to claim the rest of the poor woman's fraying patience. I smile at her just as the youngest of the three, the one cradled in his mother's arms, releases a volcano worthy amount of spit-up directly on the front of his mother's blouse. Only at that moment, the unfortunate and now vomit-covered woman decides to make eye contact with me. *Shit.* Now she definitely thinks I am laughing at her. The woman blushes deeply and ducks her head, dashing for the solitude of the air conditioner and the nearest bathroom. I decide to pretend that...whatever that was...did not just happen. I turn to survey the yard. *Beer belly, beer belly, receding hairline, way too tan, beer belly...ah, there he is!* I make eye contact with the, by far, most attractive man at the party; dark, crew-cut hair with his rugged yet charming five o'clock shadow covering his strong jaw. Dressed in khakis, and a light blue button-down shirt, it is a common look, but with his muscles, not even to mention his dreamy, piercing hazel eyes, he can really pull it off. *Yum.* He catches me staring and flashes a wink at me. *When did I become one of* those *girls who sits in wonder at how I got so lucky??* I softly laugh at myself as he says goodbye to his friend, beer belly guy number two, and makes his way back to me. *I really should have written down some names,* I think to myself as Keirion Harland, my dreamboat date reaches me, planting a kiss on my cheek.

"Would you like a fresh drink, Miss Bonaparte?" he flirtatiously bows in faux servitude.

"Well, don't you know how to treat a lady right?" I reply finally with a real smile, automatically relaxing in his presence.

"You would think by now he knows that you are nowhere near a lady!" A voice cuts through the crowd of suburban adults with the spirit of something that did not belong there. Only one person I know could waltz into a party knowing no one but me and announce herself with no hesitation. *Ridley.* I turn around to find her, which ended up not being difficult. As always, the flamboyant city girl is rocking the most insane trends not caring if they are ridiculous or a bit unreasonable. She stands nearly half a foot above all the others; tall, even aside from the ridiculous shoes she is wobbling around the lawn on. Dressed in her favorite neon, spiked wedges, matched with 70's style bell bottom high waisted pants and a Bon Jovi graphic crop top tee, she is definitely getting some looks from both the housewives and pot-bellied husbands. Stunning, sassy, and completely out of place, she was my first and last friend I made since moving to Lincoln, Nebraska eight years ago. We were both new to the city when we met. Her, fresh out of Manhattan, and I from London, together we got to explore the new city with her unstoppable energy and my Yelp app. We worked our way through restaurants, city attractions, apartments, jobs, and men. That is, until about eighteen months ago when our crazy twosome moved to Denver and were joined by the ever adaptable Keirion.

"About time you arrived!" I say, not nearly matching the same volume.

"Sorry, but not sorry, my darling! I was drawing out the inevitable." Ridley said, smirking. "Stuffy, suburban couples are not my scene and I had to self medicate before braving it." *That explains her even more than usual boldness; this is vodka cranberry driven.* Keirion and I try to stifle our laughter as we eye each other.

"Careful what you say!" Keirion says with a lighthearted tone, "We may be one of these 'stuffy suburban couples' that you are referring to sooner than you think!" Catching Ridley's right elbow as she stumbles on the freshly mowed lawn, my eyes widen. *What?? Were we actually at that point in our relationship already?* Although surprised, I find myself not repulsed, like I would have previously been. Maybe I would be cut out for a normal, quiet life after all...My friend snorts a laugh loudly, and the people around us shoot a displeased look in our direction before beginning to rapidly whisper conspiratorially with each other. I quickly turn back around and avoid eye contact before I can tell what they are saying.

"Don't let them get to you. Just ignore it." Keirion mutters to me, understanding shows in his eyes. *Hmm, they are more green than blue today...*I think, distracted for a second, and I lean in to peck him on the lips, breaking back into a smile. Keirion is the only one who knows I can read lips easily as a book.

"Dude! Can we walk or are you just going to stare at each other?" said Ridley, ever impatient. Keirion and I each hold an arm, trying to stabilize her as she attempts to wobble up the numerous deck stairs.

"Sorry, Rid. Let's get some water in you." I say, trying to gently lead her up the stairs.

"God, I am starving! Got anything to eat in this place?" she shouts at the nearest party goer. I grit my teeth and attempt to send a thought telepathically, hoping our years of friendship had at least gained us that talent. *Get it together Rid! I don't want to have to explain you to everyone.* After making it to the top of the stairs, she demands release to relieve her exceedingly full bladder. *Guess that didn't work.* I grimace and turn to face my boyfriend.

"Sorry Keir, I should have known not to mention it to her. It isn't exactly her scene." *Or honestly mine...*I think, then feel immediately guilty.

"Why don't you go get some real food in her, and make

sure she gets home safe?" He replies.

"How about I get her home, then come back to join you again?" I say, trying to make up for the internal elation that had subconsciously surged at the offer.

"I think you have suffered through enough of my coworkers for the evening." Keirion says, smirking and looking around. I lean in for a goodbye kiss and he whispers in my ear, " I did mean what I said, about this being us, hopefully soon." I snap my head back and look into his eyes trying to find a hidden joke or maybe even sarcasm. I sputter trying to find a way to reply, but Ridley mercifully rejoins us, and I am spared from answering.

"Bye babe, see you tomorrow!" I say instead as I turn to yank my friend out to my car parked out front. I walk away, missing the half-wave and hopeful smile that crosses Keirion's face, watching me go.

I wake in the dorms to sirens wailing, lights flashing, and my roommate's melodious voice yelling at me to get my ass out of bed. Thanks to my years of elite training I shoot up to standing, gun pulled from my pillow and into my hand, locked and loaded, before I can even take another breath. I

remember my classes, sweeping the room while I analyze what is happening. Efficiency, awareness, action. *I holster the gun and lunge for my go-bag once I note the room is, for the time being, secure.*

Pru beckons to me and mouths, "Must be drill night."

I roll my eyes and reply mouthing, "Oh you think so?"

To say Pru and I are not friends is an understatement. We are actually rivals. Our academy believes it to be character building to be placed with your biggest competitor. Something about teaching you to sleep with one eye open, mixed with the constant motivation to focus singularly on your schoolwork. Before we can try and decide what our next move should be, a tin can-like clanging sounds outside our door. What is that? I turn to ask; but before I can, a small cylinder bounces then rolls into the room. Smoke grenade. *Together we decide not to stick around to see who threw it. In our school, it is worse than detention if you get caught during a drill. We both turn and launch ourselves out of the only window in our room. Hands scraping on the brick exterior, I catch myself on an old eaves trough before I can fall 60 feet to the stone walk and the dark sweeping gardens that lie below me. I hear a whispered cursing and turn to see Pru has grabbed the rusted end of the eaves.* Well, that is not going to last long...*I reach for her, and panic begins to grip me. Realization flashes in her eyes. NO! Our eyes connect and we both know I am going to be too late. The fragile metal gives out, and with a terrifying scream; Pru falls to the hard ground.*

"Celeste!!! Wake up, sweetie! It is a dream. I am here. Wake up!"

I snap my eyes open and reality hits me. *You are okay. That was eight years ago. You are safe.* Keirion has one hand gently shaking my shoulder, the other holding a red and already swelling lip.

"I am so sorry, Keir!! Did I hit you again?!" I groan, sleep filling my voice.

"It's okay, your knee just caught me. I didn't know you could kick that high!" He says, trying to lighten the mood and my distress. "What was this one about?" *Crap...what did I tell him last time?* I rack my brain for a new nightmare. *Anything but the truth, unfortunately.*

"I um...was being chased by the Demogorgon from *Stranger Things.*" I make up, pulling from the first thing I could think of.

"Well, no wonder you were flailing so hard! Did you kick its ass?" He says, starting to laugh. I join him and force a soft giggle.

"Of course I did!" I reply.

"Coming from the girl who won't kill a fly...but I am sure you did CeeCee." He says lovingly and only a slight tease of sarcasm. *Don't cry. Don't cry.* I repeat to myself as he kisses my forehead and rolls back onto his side, already drifting back to sleep. I lay back down next to him, attempting to fall back asleep myself. Begging my brain for what seems like the millionth time to not dwell on the past. I finally fall back into the dark embrace of sleep.

My fingers tap a continuous stream across my keyboard the next day at work. I glance around the office space, mentally logging all the faces and emotions that I can see. *Bored, bored, hungover, bored...*I sigh to myself. Just another post-weekend slump at the office. I turn back to my work and carry on typing the description of the new item to be sold on the company's website. My job as a Content Writer is far from exciting. I stare with a glazed look at the logo for the company, stamped in black and red on my mouse pad. *ST&T; Survival Tech and Tools.* Anything you need for the up and coming apocalypse can be bought through our website, with free shipping on anything over $50. The newer company is a decent success! The best part?

No chance of running into anyone I went to school with. I shake my head trying to refocus on the latest survival knife the company is debuting; I reach for the unsharpened weapon resting on my desk. As I twirl it through my fingers out of habit, my mind drifts back to my nightmare from the night before once more. *That is the sixth one this month. I have got to pull it together.* I glance up at my computer screen, now with the screensaver bouncing around, thinking. I shake the mouse waking the console and the webpage flicks alive. I bite my lip. *What can it hurt? Millions of people Google every day!* I hesitate another few moments before I click the search bar. Then I begin to type: Amethyst Academy. With another glance around at my floor, confirming again no one is paying any attention to me, I close my eyes bracing myself, and with a deep breath, I click the button. *Here!* First on the page is what I am looking for. With an inner trepidation, I lock away the memories before they can begin to resurface.

"Not now brain." I mutter to myself. *How about when I am sleeping?* I think sarcastically as a half-smile cracks on my now tense face. I click to open the webpage to my old school. *Wow,* I think, slightly impressed, *internet-accessible now. You have come a long way!* I look at the homepage and its main picture. The large dark bricked building held more secrets than the world would ever, and *could* ever know. I brace myself and fight my resurfaced bad habit of channeling nerves into chewing my lip. I scroll down the page to where the description reads in an uncharacteristic bright, yet professional font.

"The Amethyst Academy *strives to provide intensely interactive and distinctly prudent courses to all of our specially selected students. All who achieve results in life that can not be put into words."* I snort with laughter, this time fueled by annoyance and humor. If people only knew how accurate that description was. *If I tell you I have to kill you...can not be put into words...same thing, different phrase.* I think, before clicking out of the web search window. Shaking my head again to try and dislodge the past that I, for some stupid reason, just decided to voluntarily delve back into. I return to my work. *This life is better. Remember that, CeeCee! Remember why you left. This is* your *choice. Quiet monotony over the risk of death any day.* Across the room, I see my coworker Janine waving her water cup at me and I grab my own to join in the walk to the break room. I walk away not noticing the light blinking next to the desktop camera; the signal that it was active and someone was watching.

CHAPTER 2

Celeste

"Oh my god, Keir." I moan with satisfaction as I stuff the pasta into my mouth. "You made this from scratch? Like from start to finish, not a box??" He smiles as I stuff another forkful into my mouth.

"My mom can make this even better!" Keirion bragged. "But, yeah, mine is not bad either. She used to teach me to cook on the weekends she had me, remember?" He looked into the distance with dazed eyes, lost in the memories. I nod in understanding, not knowing quite what to say. Keirion rarely talked about his mom; however, when he did you could tell, even all these years after her death, it continued to deeply affect him. He had never fully told me what happened to her; all he would say was that it was sudden and he had never gotten the chance to say goodbye. After she was gone, all he had were the fond memories he was lost in now; from the time after his parents had split.

"You okay?" I ask. He returns to the present, granting me a half-smile.

"Of course I am." He says, "I just was lost in thought! Want more pasta?" I snatch both of our plates away and shoo away his hands.

"You cooked, I will serve and clean tonight!" I bend over returning the smile and a kiss. I straighten up and hear the chime of my doorbell.

"I got it!" Keirion says, jumping off the couch and running for the door before I can stop him. As I dump another spoonful of food onto each of our plates, I hear the faint noise of his voice coming down the hall from the doorway. He is talking to someone, but it is not that fact that freezes me in place. The voice sounds familiar.

"CeeCee, there is someone here who says he knows you." Keirion sounds weird, almost jealous. No...protective? There is an edge to his voice and I can tell whoever it is at my door, it is making him uncomfortable.

"Be right there!" I shout down the short hallway and try

to calm my heart rate that has started to jump. I set down the plates I am carrying onto the counter before I accidentally tip them to the floor. I turn and walk to the front, trying to rack my brain as to who it could be.

"Hey, sexy! Long time no see!!" the stranger greets me as I come into the view of the door. *Wait...not a stranger. I choke on the words before they can leave my mouth. Naveen?! Holy crap. This is not good.* I grimace and glance wide-eyed quickly at Keirion.

"Hey V, what..." I clear my throat, feeling like I am gargling gravel. "What are you doing here?" My eyes convey my real question. *Umm...how did you find me?*

"You are acting like you aren't happy to see me!" He laughs and reaches across my scowling boyfriend to pull me in for an awkward hug. I make eye contact with Keirion who looks back at me with a grudging unease in his eyes. Naveen tucks me into his strong arms like he used to all those years ago, and I fight the urge to push him away. I feel his lips graze the side of my face and I tense with uncertainty and confusion.

"They are watching you." He whispers hasty and terse. I feel a chill trickle down my spine as what he says computes in my brain, despite the warmth of his breath on my neck. He holds me for a few seconds longer than would probably be socially acceptable, even if my boyfriend *wasn't* standing there watching in angry bewilderment. But I am thankful. With those extra seconds, I manage to pull my face back to nonchalance and make strong eye contact to let him know his warning had been heard and understood. My brain starts whirling a thousand miles an hour. *All my perseverance from the last eight years of uprooting my whole life… Do I give in and accept all of my past back? Do I have to become that person I ran away from all those years ago? I can't let Keir know about me and I can't let him know that A) I have been lying to him and B) that every second he knows me, he could be in extreme danger. I have to at least get him out of this.*

"It has been too long! We should for sure grab some coffee and catch up! How about tomorrow? Say, 0800 at the shop down the street?" I realize Naveen is still talking to me. Before I can nod, Keirion cuts in, misreading the panic plain in my eyes.

"Sorry buddy, she has a job." Keirion says, smugly. " I am sure she has your number and will reach out to you when she has some free time." He moves to close the door, but I stick my hand out, stopping it before it can shut.

"Eight works. I will see you tomorrow." Then I close the door as I see the smirk cross Naveen's face.

"Sorry, what?" says Keirion, with a look of surprise and slight irritation. "Who was that guy and why does he make me nervous?'

"He is just an old friend!" I say. *Too defensive!* I chide myself. *Relax.*

"No one I know talks to or hugs their friends like that." He takes a deep breath, taking my hands in his own. "But I trust you. Do what you have to do, okay? But know that you are mine." Shivers begin to tingle up my spine as he accentuates each of his last three words with soft kisses down the side of my neck. By the time I open my eyes again, he has let go of my hands and is back in the kitchen. The last few minutes catch up with me, with a rush, causing my emotions to swirl. *Naveen is here! And they are watching me...why? Who are* they? *Don't overreact until you know exactly what Naveen has to tell you. Knowing V, it could even just be a joke.* With a sigh, I rub my neck muscles and return to the kitchen, subconsciously already mourning the quiet peace of my life from just ten minutes earlier.

CHAPTER 3

<u>Naveen</u>

The second the door shuts in my face; I drop my facade. Taking a deep breath in I turn around and scan the street. I see a couple walking by look at me anxiously, and I realize my smirk from just moments earlier has now become a rather scary scowl. I quickly correct that back to a smile, and turn right to head back to the rental car I had parked down the block. I had spent the last two hours at a little coffee shop on the corner, that I had immediately fallen in love with while waiting and trying to decide how to best approach Celeste. *God, that was harder than I thought. And then to have that guy there with her… That should be me.*

Shaking my head to clear my unrealistic thoughts, I change my direction; turning left up the street instead. *I will do one more quick surveillance lap around the block and then I will go try to find somewhere to stay for the night.* While walking, I pull out my phone.

"Yes sir?" My assistant Belinda answers the phone in her usual chipper voice.

"Has the boss realized I am gone yet? I didn't have a chance to come up with a clever excuse before I bolted out of town." I ask, getting the worst question off my todo list.

"No sir, I may have misled Mr. Bently that you were busy with recon on the Terrance Corp. case and would be out of reach for a while." I crack a genuine smile and feel a surge of affection for the woman who has been with me ever since I first joined the company.

"You know I love you, Belinda, right?" I hear her laugh as I reach my car, my lap of the neighborhood coming up with nothing suspicious.

"Yes sir, I know you do. And because I love you, I have already arranged a hotel room for you at the Hilton Garden about five miles from where you are now."

"Perfect. I don't know how long I will be here. Do you think you can keep covering for me?" I ask, yawning while pulling out of the parking space and heading for the hotel.

"Of course, sir. I will take care of it. Be safe and I will see you soon." She responds before hanging up. I pull past Celeste's place, looking over just in time to see the man who was there for dinner finally leaving. *That must be the new boyfriend.* Gripping the steering wheel so hard my knuckles turn white, I realize that she is now alone. *Even though she is more than capable of taking care of herself, I can't fight the urge to protect her. Stupid urge.* I think, sighing and flipping the car around. *After all these years that is still there? Wonderful.* Pulling into an office building's empty parking lot across the street, I grin as I inspect the perfect vantage point of her street and house from this spot. I dig in my bag for one of my sweaters and ball it into some semblance of a pillow. I already mourn the comfortable hotel bed I had just decided to abandon. But I then realize that tomorrow morning I will get to see Celeste again and talk to her more. Suddenly the night's sleeping arrangements don't seem so terrible. *Maybe for a day I can pretend she is my CeeCee again.* With that thought, I relax back in the seat and wait for the minutes to tick away.

I join in groaning with my classmates as our Professor Aden finishes telling us where we were going. The bus

we are on lurches as it drives over the rough dirt road and I can see our destination in the distance. That doesn't look like a school. That looks like a hotel or some rich person's mansion. Our academy looks more like a military installation. *I can hear the other boys voicing the same opinion.*

"Why do we have to train with a bunch of girls. And from the looks of it, a bunch of snobby, spoiled girls." Tony, one of my halfwit classmates, mutters keeping his voice low enough that it didn't travel to the front of the bus where Professor Aden sat. Insubordination was not tolerated in the slightest and that included any negative comments and attitude.

"I'm surprised! I thought you would be happy about this, Tony." I say, full of sarcasm while rolling my eyes. "This will give you a chance to show us all those moves you have been telling us about. Those ladies won't know what hit them!" The rest of the boys snicker as he stammers trying to think of a rebuttal.

"Saved by the bell!" I joke as we pull up to the large stone wall surrounding an intricate garden and labyrinth of old beautiful buildings. The boys all around me start pointing out of the window and nervous chattering fills the bus. I peer around them to see what they are all excited about; through the gaps between the wall and gate, I can see movement. But between the distance and the darkness of the very early morning, I struggle to make out what exactly that movement is; however, when we de-board

the bus, we can hear what sounds like an alarm bell ringing inside the building and throughout the grounds. With the light of morning steadily growing, I can better see the movement that I couldn't identify before. It is dozens of students, girls, all running from a building helpfully labeled 'Dormitory'. Okay, this is more like it. It may look all dainty, but these girls have the same lovely morning wake up call we do.

"Lazaro! What in god's name are you doing?" Jumping at the voice, I look around and realize my group had already entered the grounds and were beginning to leave me. I quickly join them and we all continue down an expertly manicured path, leading to a large field about a mile or so from the rest of the buildings. The sun has finally shown itself over the horizon line by the time we arrive at our apparent destination. We all fall into formation, the same way we were trained to do from day one, and wait for more instructions. I take the moment of silence as my opportunity to look around. About ten feet to the right was a scary adult male who looks like a textbook Russian hitman; next to him was a group of about thirty girls in their teens. I watch in confusion for a few seconds, noticing that the whole group we have just joined are all staring out at the large running track. Then in the distance, I see a figure on the track running back towards us. Despite the fact she is sweating profusely and has some windblown frizzy hair, she is beautiful. Hello darling! *I can't help but smile as she frantically tries to tame her hair back into*

her ponytail. I try and fail to catch her eye as the Russian hitman begins addressing both of our groups.

"Right. Now that this slacker has served her morning punishment, we can begin. Ladies, these are the boys from Invictus, the brother academy to ours. There are certain ops we will coordinate with them, so Headmistress Hansen has organized some events to get you used to working with each other. So pick a partner, and behave!" He looks at the Amethyst Academy girls with annoyance when he sees the girls preening and shooting coy looks at our group of young men, who, as I glance down our lineup, appear even more excited than the girls. I look back at the runner, who freezes when I finally catch her eye. She looks caught off guard, but also intrigued. A tangible spark of attraction jumps between us and she breaks into a shy smile. I flash a confident wink at her and knew I had found my partner.

Chapter 4

Celeste

"PRU!!" I scream staring down in bewilderment at the broken shape lying bent on the concrete below me. Breathe, Celeste. This *has* to be planned. Another drill to prepare us for shock out in the real world. *I desperately try to rationalize and turn back to my own peril I am facing. I ensure that the piece of metal that had sent my roommate crashing to the ground was, in fact, still going to hold* me. *I take stock of my surroundings. There! My eyes catch on the window ledge below me about four meters to the right. I take in a deep breath, which I immediately regret, as the acrid taste of the smoke billowing out my window tries to slip its way into my lungs. The tears begin to stream out*

of my eyes, the cause a mixture between the smoke in my eyes, and the coughs racking my body trying to expel the toxic air coming from the grenade. For sure, one of Professor Chimiste's blends of poison ivy and ghost pepper smoke. That guy is just a mad scientist with a teaching job. *A rusty creak interrupts my thinking - the sign that I need to get moving.* Now. *I swing my body hard to the left. Creak. I wince as the eaves complains loudly. Using my momentum, I swing quickly back to the right and throw myself through the air, my hands flailing for purchase on the window ledge below. I wince as the majority of my fingernails are suddenly ripped free from my fingers, but that thought passes from my mind in a moment of relief. I send a silent thank you to whatever architect designed the Academy. My bruised, bleeding fingers are finally given a slight break as my toes find a gap between the two different brick patterns making the exterior of the building. I realize I had just launched myself out of a five-story building in the middle of the night with zero hesitation and my night still wasn't done.* Why couldn't the most exciting part of my night be just going to the mall or the movies, like a normal person? *Now that I am more secure, for the moment at least, I look back down at Pru and an unsettling seed of doubt is planted in my mind.* She looks actually hurt. I know they commit to drills, but this is too realistic...But they have tricked me before. Just continue. *I begin to work my way down the side of the five-story building,* using the wear in the grout like I would the cracks on the side of a mountain. Thank you rock climbing elective! *My feet hit the manicured lawn, and I spare a glance back at Pru.* It's a test. Focus. *Voices begin to get closer and I drop back into the shadows working my way through the dark of the garden. With not even the light of the moon, the darkness is impenetrable ink. I pause crouched down next to the statue of some headmaster from years before. Rapidly, I blink to give my eyes a moment to attempt to adjust to the darkness. Suddenly to my left, I hear a soft sound. If the alarms had still been sounding I never would have heard it; however, they had fallen silent only minutes ago. The quiet was now as overwhelming as the night. I struggle to regulate and calm my wild, rapid breathing. Once calmed a bit, I brace my right leg against the statue and aim. With an exhale, I target all my strength into forcing the statue to tilt over onto my unfortunate assailant of the night. I don't stick around long, but still hear the crunch of bones and the wail of the poor human who got assigned to hunt me tonight. Smiling to myself in sick triumph, I continue my way to the 'Base'.* One hundred more feet and you win again tonight. *It was as soon as I completed that thought, I saw something with lightning-fast hands loom out of the hedge shadow. There was then only pain and I crumple into the grass.*

"Oh hell!" I snap back to reality realizing that I have poured my scalding coffee way past the brim and I was now standing in a puddle of the brown bitter liquid. "Now is not the time to give into memories." I scold myself out loud and attempt to mop up the mess I had made. *I hope the spilled coffee is the only mess I make today.*

Things had been awkward last night after Naveen's quick visit and Keirion had left not long after. The hour he had stayed had been like an awkward first date; one where there wouldn't be a second. Forced small talk, not really watching what was on TV, and then just uncomfortable silence. This made me feel two very different things. First off, I was grateful to be alone. I could sit there lost in my thoughts without having to keep up a pretense that my mind was not somewhere else. Then the guilt came; I love Keirion and don't want to have to hide anything. Why was I even putting myself back into the scenario where there were secrets that had to be kept? *Oh, right...your whole life IS a lie, remember. You are doing this because you have to. No other reason.* That thought sends a stiff resolve over me, feeling like the weight of a large cement block was suddenly tied to my feet. (Which I, unfortunately, do know the feeling of.) Yanking me down, grounding me. But instead of a body of ice-cold water, this time it was reality that made me go numb. *I can handle whatever happens after I walk out that door. I walked away from this life because I wanted to. Not because I am inept or incapable.* With these thoughts bolstering me, I straighten up feeling more like the myself I had tried to forget years ago than I ever have. I turn and with my heels clicking, walk out the door to meet up with the fate I left behind. Naveen was waiting for me at the coffee shop.

I begin to lose the nerve I had amped up in my kitchen as I walk down the street filling up with people beginning their morning commute. I shuffle along with the others down the crowded sidewalk tightening my scarf against the fall chill that was a stark contrast from just a few days prior and gaze down the street. It reminds me so much of another day years ago. In my mind, I picture Naveen's face; smiling, as usual, but with a far fewer scars. I can't remember what was said, but I do remember laughing hysterically. *That was the first time that being a couple shifted from being our cover to something truly real.* I shake my head to regain my focus. *Back to the present girl.* I force myself to think of Keirion. *Remember this guy? Don't be stupid, CeeCee!* I lurch to a stop realizing I have reached the coffee shop. I earn a few mutters of complaints and irritated noises from the people behind me as I block the flow of foot traffic. I throw apologies over my shoulder turning to enter the coffee shop. I push open the door and can't help but smile and relax a little as the delicious scent of coffee beans greet me. The noise from the sidewalk traffic is immediately muted the second the heavy wooden door swings shut behind me with a thud.

This is my favorite place in this city, Only Naveen would know to pick this place. Even after years with no contact, he would know this would be my ideal "safe space". *Wow. He must have some really bad news for me.* The last time we were in a coffee shop similar to this, it was Kitties, the coffee shop next to the school where we would meet after class. As I turn to face the couches toward the back of the shop I see him. Same as he always used to be: left leg resting on top of his right, a heavy-looking book balanced on his lap. Naveen is sipping a huge mug of, I assume, a frothy caramel latte while completely absorbed in the pages in front of him. *Or so it appears.* I shake my head in amusement as I see the three twenty-something baristas all sneaking looks and whispers debating who gets to go up and talk to him. *If only they knew he was aware of everything.*

He just wants *to appear lost in the book.* Naveen knew every word the girls were saying, how much money they had in the register, how much time was left in the parking meter that the other customers had their cars parked at. And he knew I had just walked in and was staring intently at him. I know, because I remember how hard it was for me the first year to reprogram my brain to not log all those things. How to not be hyper-aware, after that is all you know, is very disconcerting. After year two I was able to actually read a book. By year three, Ridley was able to sneak up on me and scare me. Yes, I nearly killed her; but by year five I was able to react—well—less drastically. With a sigh, I walk over to Naveen who has now looked up from his pretend reading and is staring at me with his piercing dark chocolate eyes. I can tell the way I am acting is beginning to make him nervous. *I am not the girl you used to know anymore, even if your smile still makes me weak in the knees...*

"Hey V!" I say. "Good book?" Smiling at him teasingly and flop down on the couch closest to him.

"Not really," he states shutting the book with a snap. "Tolstoy isn't really in my top ten." While he sets the book and mug on the table in front of him, I get a good look at him and begin to feel nervous. *The only time I have seen him this tense is when he is on a stressful life-or-death mission.* I begin to make a mental list before I realize with a bit of a shock how quickly I can fall back into old habits. *Like riding a bike?* I ask myself, then focus back on Naveen. *Bags under his eyes, slightly wrinkled shirt, dark hair tousled; but not like on purpose. More like how he looks after an all-night stakeout. But there is something more. His nails are bitten down and it looks like his ear is slightly red.* I recall Naveen's nervous habit of tugging his left ear when he gets shaken up by something. The first few training missions failed due to this nervous habit and the unfortunate chance that our "all-clear" signal was an ear tug. Smiling at the memory, I realize he is looking at me expectantly.

"Huh?" I say, feeling like an idiot.

"Thought you were in another world there. I asked how have you been?" Naveen laughs.

"Oh." I blush. "I have been good. You know everything is normal. The things I consider *issues* would make you laugh."

"Well, that is what you wanted, right?" He asks me, laughter fading now with a serious edge to his voice.

"Yes, V. That is what I wanted." We both sit for a minute in an awkward pause, neither of us sure of what to say. "Why are you here? I mean it's good to see you, but you know the rules. And then you show up at my door and say *they are watching you*" Naveen just stares at me while I continue to word vomit, getting more passionate and louder each word comes out. "To see you at that door after all these years, just *there*. Do you know what that was like for me??" I finally stop talking, trying to catch my breath after getting worked up.

"I am so sorry, CeeCee—" Naveen says softly. "That is never what I wanted to do." He looks pained and tears start to fill my eyes. Blinking them away I reset my resolve.

"Who is watching me, V?" I ask, trying to wipe all emotion from my voice to keep myself from losing it again. "What does that even *mean*?"

"You remember how your parents infiltrated a Japanese drug ring years ago?" He says lowering his voice and glancing around.

"Are you talking about the Yoshitomi Group?" Naveen nods and continues.

"Good, you remember them then?" He picks back up his coffee and leans back in his chair.

"Not really. My parents were pretty strict about me not getting involved with or having any information on their more dangerous missions." I join him in relaxing back on the couch as the barista brings me my usual drink. The moment she is out of earshot, I continue. "Last I heard, the Oyabun was arrested, or that he was going to be? I was listening through a vent." I admit, unabashed.

"Of course you were." Naveen says, looking humored.

"Well, the plan was to capture the Oyabun, and thanks to your mom and dad they got damn close. Closer than anyone else ever has." He sighs. "I don't know quite what went wrong, but in trying to capture him he was wounded, badly. He died about fifteen hours later, despite their attempts at surgery."

"Okay. But what does this have to do with me?" Naveen leans forward, sets his coffee down on the table, and looks at me intently.

"About two years ago the Oyabun's son, Chen Feng, took over the group. He has been looking for your family, and finally found you. They know where you are." I sit frozen in shock when what he says logs in my brain.

"How? What? *How?* The Academy wiped everything when I left. I have had no contact with anyone until you showed up yesterday. I have covered all the bases!" I exclaim, adamant that Naveen must be mistaken. I stare at him wide-eyed as he shakes his head with sympathy.

"I guess they somehow attached flags or alerts if anyone searches for particular things. From there, they gain access to your computer, camera, location, everything. Then they can find whoever they are looking for, this time, you. Have you searched for anything out of the ordinary lately?"

"No. What on Earth would I have - wait..." I take in a sharp breath and Naveen looks immediately concerned and reaches out to console me, but then stops himself. "I googled the Academy the other day at work! I am so stupid!" I wail. Naveen grimaces and moves to the couch seat next to me.

"You are *not* stupid. Do you hear me, CeeCee? They pooled a *ton* of resources into finding you." He takes my hand and squeezes it, trying to reassure me. "I will help you and keep you safe in every way I possibly can."

"Thank you, V." I squeeze back, then pull my hand away. "How did you know all this and where to find me?" I ask him suspiciously. He cracks a smile and chuckles.

"I was waiting for that question. The company I work for has an informant in the group," He then blushes, looking sheepish. "And I never lost you, I have been checking up on you since you left. So I never had to find you. I just have been making sure you are safe and happy." He continues softly in a voice so faint I can barely hear it over the coffee shop music. "I couldn't live with myself if anything happened to you." I feel myself pull back at that.

"You made your choice about that, Naveen. Years ago. I appreciate the concern, but you don't need to worry about me." *Keirion. Don't forget about your amazing boyfriend who makes you happy and loves you!* "We can be friends again, V. Nothing more, okay?" A look of disappointment and hurt flashes across his face; for a such a quick second that I think I possibly imagined it.

"Well yeah, that is all I want too." He scoffs, suddenly cocky again. I feel a pang of loss, seeing him suddenly distancing himself from me again. Throwing up an invisible wall so quickly, I am sure the shock showed on my face.

"Anyway, I just came to warn you, but I'm sure your *hunky boyfriend* can protect you just fine." Naveen says, leaning back on the couch with his arms resting behind his head. He winks at the baristas behind the counter who are still staring at him. He flexes and stretches his muscles causing the girls to break into giggles.

"I am going to get more coffee." Standing up and winking back at me, I am left to absorb all the information and sludge from the past that he had just dropped on me. *What am I going to do? I thought I was prepared for the worst, but I never imagined it would be this bad.* I sigh and look over at Naveen propped up against the counter, working his charm. *And all I have to help me is my ex-boyfriend, the flirt and the years of school that I have done everything to try and forget. How am I going to go home and to work pretending everything is the same?* With a gasp, I launch off the couch. *Work!!*

"V, I gotta go!" I shout at him throwing my coat back on and snatching up my purse. He stares at me in bewilderment and walks quickly back over to me.

"Are you crazy?" He says, incredulous, grabbing my arm to try and stop me from walking away. "You aren't *really* going to work are you?"

"Um, yes V. I am." I bite back, ripping my arm from his grasp. "Did you think that I was just going to suddenly up and leave the life I have built for myself?"

"If you go back there, you are putting everyone in that building and yourself at risk. Are you willing to make that decision for all of them? To take that chance?"

"I - I don't know! What else do I do then?" I cry out, my voice cracking, drawing some looks from the other customers.

"Come work with me. I can get you a job with my company. You will have resources and backup." Naveen says in a soothing voice, trying to calm me down. "At least until we can get in touch with your parents and they can maybe help you figure this out. Okay?" I stare at him for a minute, taking deep breaths and processing this new option. After a few long seconds, I reach for my purse again and I can see the frustration cross Naveen's face. "You are still going?"

"I have to at least let them know I quit, don't I?" I say, pulling my cell phone out of the purse pocket and dialing my boss's number. I give him a half-smile with a swift kiss

on the cheek and fall back onto the couch to begin breaking
the news to my boss.

CHAPTER 5

Celeste

I watch the sleek black car driving away, staring at the tail lights for a few seconds before turning to face the grand stone and brick structure I have just been dropped off at. This is it. It is time to finally embrace my legacy! *The screeching of worn down brakes makes me cringe and turn to find the cause.* Must be another student. As mother always says, "First impressions only come around once." *I turn to greet the other girl climbing out of the cab that clearly needs to be put out of its misery. I shine one of my most dazzling smiles and step forward, excited to make my first friend here. But before I can get the greeting out, she faces me and with a look of complete loathing and condescension, she sneers.*

"Yeah, save it. I don't care who you are and where you came from, or how awesome your mommy and daddy are, OK? I am here to be the best and NOT worry about who is going to be best friends and hurting anyone's feelings. So save your energy and get over it." My jaw drops open and I sputter trying to think of anything to say, she had turned on her heel and marched in through the huge iron gate. "Ugh, what a bitch! Must be a Charity," comments the girl coming out of the same gate to meet me. If I had to choose one word to describe the girl, it would be - perfect. Perfect nails, perfect skin, perfect outfit, even perfect bouncy high ponytail.

"I'm Margo. I am the upperclassman assigned to show you the ropes. You know, how to get around and most importantly, survive."

"Wow, thank you! I am excited —" I stop suddenly when the look on Margo's face changes from the perky cheerleader to that of a sneering assassin.

"No, seriously. Welcome to jail slash hell. I will be your personal warden here to make sure you don't step a toe out of line." She moves in closer and I fight every urge not to take a step back, trying my best to hold my ground. "This is my last year," Margo continues. "The final decision on whether we graduate or fail comes down to you. Each senior is paired with a new student. You fail, we fail. No exceptions." With a flash, the cheerleader

was back. "Well, come on. Welcome to your new home!" Still reeling from the whiplash of the last five minutes of interactions, I grab my suitcase and jog to catch up to Margo, who is already passing through the giant iron entrance gate that the cranky girl had passed through shortly before.

"Don't worry Margo, I will make you proud! I have been doing training sessions with my parents for years while they were working on cases. At least, the ones that were safe enough for me to go with." Hesitant, she looks at me, but this time with a shift in her eyes. I decide to change the subject. "That other girl, you called her a 'Charity'. What does that mean?" We pass through the main gate and enter a vast, immaculately manicured garden. Only then do I begin to realize just how big this place is.

"So obviously this is the main garden; we use this mainly for the kitchens, but sometimes the botany classes will take you out here to find ingredients as well. Just don't eat anything without checking with a gardener or professor first. There are some that are deadly and management gets cranky if someone dies accidentally." I start to laugh until I realize she is not. Okay, not a joke then. Noted. *We continue toward the main building past the gardens, heading for a large stone building with huge ornate stained glass windows.*

"A Charity is the person in each class that isn't a descendent or legacy from a prior student. One girl from the outside gets chosen and the opportunity to train and become one of us." She

adds with a smirk "But they rarely make it through the year."
With that final comment on the matter, she stops outside the
building and gestures to a wooden door, slightly ajar and leaking
the noise of dozens of voices, all chattering excitedly. "Welcome
to Amethyst Academy. Don't let me down, and good luck
Celeste, um, what is your last name?" I proudly turn around and
meet her questioning gaze.

"Stone. Daughter of Beverly and Jonathan Stone." The look of
realization dawns on her face. I add, "It is not in my family's
nature to let anyone down, and I don't strive to start that bad
habit now." Before I can give into the nerves that were
threatening to boil over, I shove open the heavy wooden door and
leave Margo standing in the entrance with a genuine smile and
look of hope mingled with relief shining on her face.

I shake the memories flying around my head
and let the hot water rush over me. Trying and failing to
get some of the tension of the last twenty-four hours to
recede slightly. I step out of the shower and laugh coldly at
my naive old self. The self that used to be so proud of my
name. To think I used to be so proud of my familial history
and legacy. The family who shoved me out in the cold with

barely a glance back. Looking back now, I realize our legacy was not greatness; it was death and pain. All paid for with the blood of others. Yes, they may not have been innocent but neither was my family. We were a trail of heartless killers; thieves that followed a code filled with only what they deemed moral. During my final weeks at school, I had the full realization that it wasn't just my family. It was the world I was being inducted into. My world. *Ouch!* Yanking myself back to reality I realize that while absentmindedly brushing my hair, I had created a giant knot with my hairbrush caught in the entanglement. I sigh and glare at myself in the mirror, holding the offending brush and hair bundle still, trying to figure out how I am going to get free.

"How to free the brush..." I mutter to myself. "How to free the brush...without scissors." I dig through my drawers waiting for inspiration to hit me. *Nothing helpful. Nothing helpful.* I pause and pull out the scissors, grimacing as I set them on the counter. *Just in case. But definitely the last resort.* I continue to shuffle through my drawers looking for another comb or bobby pin to hopefully assist in my release. I pause again as I wrench open the bottom drawer and sink to my knees as I see the contents. *Keirion. What am I going to tell Keir?* I shuffle through the numerous shampoo and conditioner bottles that he had gathered for me over the year and a half we have been together. Smiling, I remember how it all started as a joke.

Keirion traveled a lot for work, and when we first started dating he returned from a long trip and I had jokingly asked him if he had brought me back a present. To my shock, he replied with a yes, very suddenly serious before pulling out a complimentary travel-sized bottle of hotel shampoo. The smile fades from my face as I return the bottle to its companions in the drawer and slide it shut again. I stand back up and see the brush I had forgotten about swinging from the side of my head. *Who says I can't be with Keirion still? I can get us both out of this!*

"Time to be a badass again, Stone," smiling back at myself in the mirror, I snatch the scissors off the counter.

CHAPTER 6

Celeste

I go rigid with anxiety when the sound of my doorbell echoes down the hallway. I slip on my "happy Celeste" mask and roll my shoulders to try and relax them a bit. I hesitate a moment, then look through the peephole of my door to make sure that it is who I think it is at the door, and not...well, a hitman. *It's Keirion.* Instead of the relief and breath of fresh air, I usually feel in his presence, all I have is a ball of nausea and unease. *Maybe this was a bad idea.*

"CeeCee? Uh, are you there?" He calls through the door. His face shows a mixture of nerves and confusion.

Through the peephole I see him glance down the street, and I can tell he is contemplating walking away. I throw open the door before he, and I, have a change of mind. A relieved smile beams from him when he sees me and greets me holding out my favorite bottle of wine. "I was beginning to think you were not home! Debating whether or not to let me in?" He jokes, kissing me and walking through the doorway. My eyes widen and I quickly turn to close the door so he can't see the embarrassment flash plainly across my face. *Awkward, but yes that was exactly what I was doing.* I reply to him in my head.

"How was work today?" I reply instead, trying to jump past that conversation. Keirion looks at me, his eyes now full of unease, and I can tell he, unfortunately, has caught on to what I was trying to do. Luckily, he either decides he doesn't want to know or at the very least not to push it. Ignoring the awkward pause, he holds up the wine bottle again and slowly wiggles it teasing me. "That good, huh?" I respond, the sarcasm in my voice thick. I walk to the cabinet and pull out two glasses and a bottle opener.

"Pretty much! I had...a lot on my mind." He opens his mouth to ask a question but then stops himself; stuck on a thought.

"How was your day?" Not as subtle as he thinks he is, I can tell he is in truth asking how my breakfast, or whatever you want to call it, with Naveen went. *If only I could tell you.* Instead, I lean in to take the glass of wine he poured for me and give him a long kiss, before taking an equally long drink.

"It would have been better with you," I respond, trying to convey the truth of this statement; while also trying to reassure him, without going into too many details.

"Well, perfect then!" Suddenly enthusiastic, Keirion grabs his phone from his pocket and starts to pull something up. "I had an idea today. We should take a mini-vacation together this weekend." He flips the screen towards me so I can see a series of beautiful pictures of a cabin covered in frost and surrounded by trees. "I found the coolest place up in the mountains we can stay at for a couple of days. Just get away and spend the whole time together, hiking...or staying in." He winks and pulls me in close and starts kissing me slowly, working his way from my lips, up to my jawline, and down my neck. I feel the want to give in and start moving with him to the couch.

"I wish I could." I force as much truth into my words that I possibly can and pray that he believes me. I feel his kisses stop and he pulls away from me. "I actually have some news!" I clear my throat and try my best to sound excited. "I got a promotion at work today!" His face changes from nervousness to relief then to excitement.

"That is great, CeeCee!" He starts to lean in to kiss me again, but then he hesitates. "Wait, but why can't you come with me this weekend?" I think back to the story that, just hours ago I had concocted with Naveen as we came up with a plan for this mess.

"It is a traveling position; that is the catch. So there are some days I will have to be away." I bite my lip and step back, turning away. I feel so uncomfortable lying to him and being so close at the same time. I take a few steps into the kitchen, pretending to dig for something in one of the drawers. "I had to take it though, you know? Gets me away from the desk and provides more options for the future!" I try to nonchalantly repeat what Naveen and I had ended up deciding would be best to say. Something to excuse my traveling and explain why I wouldn't have a cubicle anymore if Keirion decided to show up and surprise me at work; or anything similar. At that moment, I wished I was a mind-reader after a few seconds of no response.

"Keir?" I turn and see him standing there, just silently looking at me. "Enough about my day. What were you thinking for dinner?" I grab his hand and our wine and start to pull him a few steps, hoping he would follow my lead and move into the living room so that we could relax on the couch. I look at him quizzically when he continues to give no response or even any indication of his thoughts. Then with a suddenness that makes me jump, he pulls me in for a tight squeeze and smiles.

"That is amazing! I am so happy for you." He gives me another kiss. "It will make the time we have together that much more special. It might be hard for both of us to travel. But we are *worth* it." He reaches for the bottle of wine on the coffee table and tops off my already half drained glass. "It was an especially good thing I picked this up tonight then." I laugh and try to match his now upbeat attitude, curling my legs up on the couch and snuggling closer to him. He hands me back my glass and holds his up in a toast. "To CeeCee, my amazing, smart, talented, *beautiful* girlfriend. Every day I am more grateful than even before to know you and to love you. Cheers, babe!" I struggle to get down the swallow. *I am not so amazing...You wouldn't say all those wonderful things if you knew the real me.* The bitterness of the wine suddenly seems too much and I set it down without another drink. If Keirion notices my face falling at all, he does not comment on it. He continues to chatter and then insists on treating me to dinner in celebration. I just smile and nod, feeling as if I will vomit if I open my mouth at all. Whether I would vomit the truth or the glass and a half of wine I had just drunk; I will never know. I excuse myself to the bathroom while he calls in our

order at one of our favorite places. I close the door behind
me and stifle a sob with my hand. I hate having to lie and
this is a big one. Ever since leaving school and my previous
life, deceit was something my body couldn't handle, I
almost physically rejected it. I had begun to despise lies of
any kind after having everything and everyone in my life
be one. When I started my new life I promised myself,
never again. I would be the opposite. Ask anybody I know
now and they will say I am brutally honest. Nobody asks
my opinion unless they truly wanted it. No sugar coating
from me. But I preferred it that way. *Where is the line? It is
easy to say one little white lie is harmless, but that is how you get
into a habit or comfortable with all the other lies. No lie is
harmless. It can take over until it becomes your identity. A fact I
am all too familiar with,* I lean back against the bathroom
counter, letting my thoughts run through my head while
listening to Keirion's voice, faint through the door. I smile
when I hear him order my favorite. *Knowing what I want
without having to even ask...* My smile fades quickly though
and I remember Naveen's voice from earlier.

*"If you go back there, you are putting everyone in that
building and yourself at high risk. Are you willing to make that
decision for all of them? To take that chance?"* I had decided to
not go to work to keep people out of harm's way. *Am I
making that decision for* him? *Am I selfishly endangering*

Keirion by having him here tonight? With a sigh, I turn around to face the mirror and run my fingers under my eyes to make sure none of my makeup had run. After ensuring that I still look somewhat sane, I give mirror me another mental lecture. *Become* that *person to protect your life and Keir remember? Remember why you are doing this. And this is temporary! Now go out there and snuggle up to that amazing man before he changes his mind about your crazy ass.* Before I can start to crack again, I open the door and walk back out to the couch.

Finally, I allow myself to enjoy the evening with my boyfriend, while I still can.

CHAPTER 7

Naveen

"I would plan for at least a couple weeks before they would even try anything. They are going to have to mobilize some of their more experienced agents and assassins." I punch Celeste's arm playfully trying to lighten the mood. "You are qualified as a high-risk mission, babe!" She only stares back at me seriously, her wide eyes an open book. She is trying hard to push down the fear, but it threatens to overwhelm her. After deciding that it was safer to talk at a more private location, we begin to walk from the coffee shop back up the road to her house. Climbing the slight slope of the street, I notice her looking around, like a skittish animal not wanting to lead the predator back to the den.

"CeeCee, relax. This is what you have trained for, years - no - scratch that; your whole life. Your parents didn't send you out unprotected into their world. Plus you have me. And this is, you know, my *job*." She finally smiles back, even though it is only a half-smile. *I will take it.*

"It's not me I am worried about most though, V." I feel a spark of nostalgia that makes me feel like we are back to *us*, the us we used to be. But it is mixed with the irritation of what I know she is going to say next.

"I know, I know. The *boyfriend*." I can't help it, my tone shifts. She whirls around grabbing my arm with such a sudden force that I jump.

"No, Naveen. Not just *the boyfriend*." She snaps back. The look in her eyes borders on murderous, her nails digging deep into my arm. *Okay, time to backtrack before she causes permanent damage.* Wincing, I begin to ply her nails free, seeing and feeling that they had begun to draw blood. She continues, her voice colored with pure rage. "It is my friends, my family, my *life*, Naveen! Everything I tried to do to distance myself from years ago. All the pain of locking myself away from everything and everyone I have ever known...and they made it *completely pointless!*" I decide it is smarter at this point to just keep my mouth shut. "And don't even get me started on my parents; yes they prepared me, but why should I have had to have *been* prepared? Why couldn't they have made the choice to let their child have a safe, happy life." She pauses for a moment, running her shaking fingers through her hair. I wonder for a second if she is waiting for me to say something. Yet, before I can even think of anything to say she whirls around and storms up the rest of the way to her door. I trail behind her and can not help but to compare her to an animal again however, this time she was the predator. *I pity whatever animal that is being hunted by her.* I grin and follow her through her door.

I jolt awake to the sound of my phone ringing, muttering curses as my knee bounces off the steering wheel. I look around in confusion before remembering where I am. Rubbing my eyes and yawning, trying to make myself at least *sound* awake. I answer, but before I can even lift the phone to my ear I can hear my boss's voice booming through the speaker.

"Where the hell are you, Lazaro? And don't even start with the crap Belinda has been feeding me." Mr. Bently yells down the phone line, his rough British accent getting stronger with his irritation.

"Ah, right. I was going to call you today." I decide to mix the truth with a few lies to hopefully smooth everything over with one go. "I have been working on something, but I did not want to get your hopes up until I had everything nailed down." I can hear him scoff with skepticism, but his voice changes from solid irritation to a slight undertone of curiosity.

"And what is that then?"

"I have a *Stone*." I say seriously expecting a few fireworks, or at the very least excitement.

"Wha...? A stone? Like a kidney stone?" He responds, irritation starting to creep back into his voice. I have to bite my lip to stop from laughing outright.

"No, Mr. Bently. A member of the Stone family, one who is possibly interested in trying out our company." I try again, waiting for him to finally understand what I am trying to get across. When no response, aside from silence, comes through the phone line I hold the speaker away from my mouth and sigh. I rack my brain trying to think of another way to explain to him exactly who Celeste was and that he should be excited about it, without coming off like a complete asshole. But then, lucky for me, he understands with a gasp.

"*No...how...how* did you manage that?" He responds slowly, finally with a dash of the excitement I was expecting all along. "I thought they were all contracted out!" Then with an afterthought, "Or dead."

"All but this one. That is...um... part of the catch." I say, wary. I can almost hear the gears turning in his head as the puzzle pieces begin falling into place for him.

"She opted out, did she?" He asks, his voice softens and I hear the telltale squeak of his door closing in the background. I take a deep breath as some relief starts to calm me. I have worked with Bently long enough to know that if he was going to outright say no with absolutely zero consideration, he would not have made the effort to make our conversation private.

"Yes, but she has had a -" I go back over all the faux arguments I have been having with him in my head all day; trying to find a fitting explanation that would suit the situation. "- change of heart." I finish with an open-ended statement that would hopefully not lead to deeper questioning. "She was top of her class at Amethyst, and we were partnered at school. I can vouch that her work is all around impeccable, sir."

"Sir?" I hear Bently laugh aloud. "You haven't called me *sir* since the day I hired you! You either have got it bad for this girl or she is something." *Both, actually.* I think staring across the street and wish, for the millionth time that I was sitting in her warm, cozy living room rather than the cramped cold of the car for the second night in a row. I have to remind myself to focus back on the conversation that my boss has continued. "- meet her and go from there."

"Yes! Of course. I will set it up." More relief swells through me and I already begin planning the next day, figuring out how to tell Celeste to pack her bags. "I will have her there day after tomorrow."

"Fine." He responds and I hear the creak of his door opening up again and I know our conversation is done. Before I end the call, his voice comes over the line again. "And Lazaro?"

"Yes, Mr. Bently?" I respond wincing at the change in his tone of voice; now very serious.

"Don't ever take off and lie to me again. I don't care if you are having tea with Queen Elizabeth or saving my mum's life. I am your handler and I can't *handle you* if I don't know where the hell you are. Understand?"

"Yes, Mr. Bently." I agree and swallow hard as he ends the call and I pray that I am not, in fact, lying to him again that same second.

I lurch awake for the fourth time that hour during that second night in the car. Lucky for me, Beverly had extended my hotel reservation for the rest of the time I was planning on spending here; so I was able to at least sneak away for a few hours to shower and brush my teeth. With that blessing, I still was able to appear and smell like a human; however, these nights in the car were starting to get to me. I reach up and try to work out the cramp that had been plaguing me since the night before. I freeze at the sight in front of me and am out of the car within seconds, only catching a glimpse of the time on the dash. 3:19 am. The late hour makes me even more panicked and I sprint across the street pulling out my lock pick tool with a practiced hand. I reach the porch without taking my eyes off of what sent me in motion. All of Celeste's lights are turned on throughout the second floor with way too many moving shadows for the late hour of the night. Celeste had gone to bed hours ago, the house falling dark and silent shortly after the boyfriend left, about ten o'clock. *If anything happened to her and I was out here* sleeping... *I will never be able to live with myself.* I shove those thoughts to the back of my mind and take the few steps up to her door in a single leap. I try the handle first to see if it was already opened by whoever is in there to save myself a few precious seconds. *Still locked.* I palm the lock pick and have it open in a solid fourteen seconds. I am so scared for what I am going to find on the other side of the door, I don't even brag to myself about the personal record I had just broken. I push open the door slowly, despite every fiber wanting to just bust it open and get to Celeste as quickly as humanly possible. *You are only going to be able to help her if you aren't dead, idiot.* It is this thought alone that makes me revert to my training and take it all step by step. I make my way down the hallway silent as a ghost and into the living room. My eyes sweep the room with practiced movements until I finally feel sure I have cleared the first level and begin heading for the stairs coming from the second level. I hear a voice and a thumping that sounds like multiple footsteps. I make my way up the stairs and when I reach the top of them I notice a mop propped up against the wall to the right. I shrug and grab it. Anything, even a mop, can be lethal when you are trained like I was. I hear the voice again and see a flurry of movement in the crack of light underneath the closed bedroom door.

"When my last CD was out you wasn't bumping me, but now that I got this little company everybody wanna come to me like it was some disease-" *What the hell?* I shake my head in confusion, but raise my mop/weapon in one hand

and push open the door to the bedroom. "-But you won't get a crumb from me cause I'm from the streets of Compton, I told 'em all-" I feel my jaw drop at the scene I just walked into. Celeste, who is dancing wildly, turns around and sees me standing in her doorway; where I still have the mop raised, jaw open, eyes wide. With a shrill shriek as she realizes a man is standing in her door at 3 am, she steps backward, trips and flails, ass over end with a heavy thunk to the floor. I lower the mop and begin laughing more than I have in all eight years combined when she releases a steady flow of curses that would have made the nuns of the world cry. She pulls the headphones off of her ears and sits up rubbing her now bruised tailbone. "WHAT IN THE FUCK ARE YOU DOING??" She yells, but I only continue to laugh. My muscles are unable to keep me standing while exerting all their energy into laughter, so I join her on the floor. I gasp in what breath I can, trying to regain my self-control. She just glares at me, breathing heavily from her own scare. She reaches for a pillow off the bed and begins hitting me over the head with it. "WHAT THE HELL DO YOU THINK YOU ARE DOING, V?"

"I saw your light on and thought you were in trouble." I manage to gasp out between gulps of breath. "What the hell were *you* doing?? You know, besides throwing down some *hot beats.*"

"I couldn't sleep, so I started cleaning," she grabs the mop and gestures wildly with it. "Hence the cleaning supplies, you dork! And only people with no soul can help but sing along when *Forgot About Dre* comes on. It's just one of those jams. *Freebird, Thriller, Sweet Caroline;* all in that category and you know it." She just glares at me throwing down the mop and continuing to rub her back while moving to prop herself up against her bed. Even through the glare, I can tell she is struggling not to laugh along with me and she finally gives into a smile. I smile back at her and we both sit quietly on the floor for a few moments. "Wait." Her gaze narrows and the smile transforms to a scowl, and I gulp suddenly nervous at the change. "What do you mean you saw my light on?" I stare at her stupidly and my mouth opens, but nothing comes out. My 'reply" is enough. Her eyes flicker and she is on her feet, marching to the window. *Aw crap.* She spots my car parked across the street; lights on, and the door still wide open in my haste to get over here. Celeste whirls back towards me, her face part shock, part still the scowl. "Have you been watching me?" Incredulity thick in her voice and I can tell she is pissed.

"I... I... um," I say. *Wow, eloquently put, Lazaro. That should smooth everything over.* I grimace and hold my hands up in surrender. "I just wanted to make sure you were safe. It wasn't to be creepy or anything, I swear." I close my eyes and brace for another whack of the pillow. I wait a few seconds and when no hit comes I slowly open one eye to peek. She stares back at me her eyes filled with an unidentifiable emotion, anger, or thankfulness, I can't tell. I lower my hands when she throws the pillow back on the bed and crosses her arms.

"Well if you wanted to do that, you might as well do it properly." She says as passing me and walks to the room opposite hers with the door standing open. I stare at her, confusion clear on my face. "I do have a guest room, you know." She flicks on the light and turns around to smile at me and gestures at the neatly made bed. "Freshly cleaned too." She winks at me and I shake my head.

"You are crazy, CeeCee. You really think *the boyfriend* would be okay with me staying here?" She grimaces but replies, her voice calm and sure.

"Let me worry about *Keirion*." She gestures at the room again. "Well, bodyguard? I am only going to offer this once."

"That bed does look a lot more comfortable than the car..." I rub the knot still tight in my neck. "If you are sure, I will go grab my things and lock up again."

"At least you didn't break my door with your heroism,"

she comments. I just laugh in reply as I reach the bottom of the stairs and head out to the chilly night. When I return, I make sure the door is sturdy and locked up behind me. Passing by the kitchen I see a light on so I step in to find Celeste putting her late-night cleaning supplies back away. I gesture with my bag. " Well, I am going to go to bed before you change your mind." She smiles, nodding in return.

"Now don't you expect breakfast in the morning. I am not *that* nice." She turns back to the supply closet and I start up the stairs.

"Hey, CeeCee." I call out, turning back to face her. She looks back up at me with her piercing eyes and I have to bite my tongue from saying what I truly want. *Please forgive me for being a stupid kid and not choosing you all those years ago. I regret it, every day.* But instead, I just say, "Did you cut your hair?" She beams back at me.

"You noticed??" She shakes her head at herself. "Of course you did. I figured it might be nice to switch it up a bit."

"Looks great! And thanks. For, you know, not being attacked. And then not freaking out when *I* almost attacked you." She barks out a laugh.

"Any time, V. Thanks for being here. If I was being attacked though, I would much rather you across the hall and well-rested. I will try to be quiet and not keep you up." She closes the door and moves to the refrigerator to pour herself a drink. I can't help it, I climb the stairs and start to rap loud enough that she can still hear me. "Nowadays everybody wanna talk like they got something to say, but nothing comes out when they move their lips. Just a bunch of gibberish and motherfuckers act like they forgot about Dre." All I get in return before closing the bedroom door, my grin still wide, is the sound of her choking on her drink.

Then I laugh again, for what feels like the millionth time that night, and through the door, I hear, "GOODNIGHT, ASSHOLE."

CHAPTER 8

Naveen

I wake the next morning, disoriented. After a second of looking around, my confusion clears and I remember all of last night's crazy events. I lay in bed content and comfortable, enjoying the sunshine streaming through the large windows. *Much better than the car.* Only when I hear a door shut downstairs do I finally venture out from the extremely comfortable, though floral, cotton sheets. I quickly shower and throw on some clothes. But by the time I open the door and leave the sunny bedroom, I can tell my host was already up and gone. There is a fluttering behind me as I pull the door shut and I see a note waving on the wall.

> *Morning Stalker,*
>
> *Went for a run. Be back later. Help yourself to anything in the cabinets.*
>
> *CeeCee*
>
> *P.S. Except my Oreos. Don't you even think about touching my Oreos.*

I laugh, crumpling the note and walk slowly down the stairs. Last night in my haste I didn't notice the photos that lined the walls. I stop to examine them. Some from her college years, looking almost the same as she did from our academy years. Many of these featured Celeste and a girl with various shades of brightly colored hair coupled with crazy outfits and a wild look in her eye. Not surprising in some graduation photos that same girl now sported a numerous amount of piercings. Mixed in with those were more current ones; one that looked like maybe a work retreat. A bunch of people all wearing matching t-shirts with the *ST&T* logo. *There she is.* I finally spot her in the background of the photo smiling and laughing with some guy. They both are holding what looks like knives, pretending to slash at each other. While another, more aged, a gentleman looks on, certainly not very pleased with the two. A sudden lance of jealous pain pierces through me when I spot the photo at the bottom of the stairs, the largest picture of them all. Begrudgingly, I have to admit it is a great picture. Celeste and *the boyfriend- Keirion -* I correct myself, stare lovingly into each other's eyes in the middle of a snowstorm under mistletoe and the glow of Christmas lights. *Alright, I have had enough of that.* I continue into the kitchen and begin investigating the cupboards, already trying to plot how that picture will get *accidentally,* permanently damaged. I am finishing my delicious scrambled eggs when Celeste returns from her run. Breathing heavy, cheeks red, and bits of her hair frizzed out from her ponytail. I stare at her, frozen. My fork raised partway to my mouth. We make eye contact and I know we are both thinking of the same memory. I feel like I am ten years in the past, seeing her for the first time. I shake myself back to reality and she just smiles and reaches into the fridge, thankfully choosing to ignore the awkward silence.

"I put your Gatorade in the freezer so it would be icy when you got home." Scraping the plate for the last of my breakfast, I look up to see surprise flash across her face.

"Thanks, V!" She rips off the lid and sighs as she enjoys the first frosty swallow.

"So what is on the agenda today?" She shrugs while

taking a few gulps. Sliding into the chair across from me she laughs and says with a wicked tone.

"I have a twelve pack of beer and half of a bottle of tequila!"

"I can't tell if you are joking or not..." I respond, matching her grin. She just shrugs again and drains the rest of her Gatorade. She eyes my empty plate and bats her eyes at me.

"What are the chances of you making me a plate of those while I hop in the shower quick?" I clutch my chest and pretend to struggle a moment.

"I am powerless to your charms! I shall concede..." I say, dramatically.

"Thank yoooooou!" She sings while climbing the stairs. "I shall release you from my servitude when I have had my breakfast." She shouts before closing her door behind her. After another second, it opens again and she adds with another shout. "So long as I find it satisfactory!" Then the door shuts again with a final bang. I rise from the chair shaking my head and laughing from Celeste's antics and the realization that maybe the girl I knew is not totally gone. I start preparing another batch of scrambled eggs for her and finish the rest of my coffee. I yawn and begin looking through her cupboards again for the coffee beans I know I spotted on my earlier investigation. Then I spot the beloved Oreos. Thanks to my never-ending curiosity, I decide to see if she truly would know if I ate just one. I hear the shower above me shut off and I shove the dangerous cookie in my mouth. In a rush, I shove the container back onto the shelf. *What was that?* I hear a weird crackle and pause. I pull the container back out and reach for the corner of a paper that had been hidden behind the cookies. No, not a paper. My heart seizes in my chest. *A photo.* That day stands out in my memories clearer than any others in my life. I hear the door upstairs open; quick as I can, replacing the photo and the cookies I return to the stove. I try and slow my heart rate and force myself to think about the photo later when I can try and puzzle out what it meant.

"Smells delicious!" Celeste comments, exaggerating sniffs in the air, trying to elicit another laugh from me. I concede and turn to reply. The second she sees my face, her eyes narrow into a glare. *Shit! Did she see me somehow? She looks pissed.*

"Umm, CeeCee? You okay-?" She raises her hand up to cut me off. Standing she slowly begins walking toward me. All I can do is stare at her, wide-eyed.

"Did you eat my Oreos?" She asks in a monotone, razor-thin voice.

"Wha-? Noooo!" *Oh, thank god. This is just about the*

freaking cookies?? I smile innocently but she reaches a finger up and touches it gently to my chin.

"I know you are an *elite warrior* or whatever bullshit the Invictus Academy tries to sell that you guys are. But you have crumbs on your face, *oh, elite warrior.*" Celeste raises her eyebrow and gives a cocky crooked grin as she turns her finger around to show the smallest crumble that has given me away.I stare at her, incredulous, and mock a bow to her.

"You win, Miss Stone. I concede." I turn back to the stove and scape the finished breakfast onto her plate. "That took you only about fifteen seconds! I am impressed. Could have fooled me that you have been out of the game all this ti-." I cut off suddenly as I go to hand her the plate and see her face suddenly as pale as it was during the semester we spent in Northern Russia completing our survival training. That was the longest winter ever and neither of us saw the sun for weeks during the stronger blizzards. I move to set the plate back onto the counter but end up half throwing it there when she begins to sway. I grab for her and feel her shaking. Without a second of hesitation, I scoop her up and take her to her couch. Celeste begins to insist I put her down, and that she is fine; but with such weakness in her voice, I decide to just ignore her. I set her gently onto the fluffy, sunflower-colored couch.

She just looks at me and sticks out her tongue. "What was that about?" I finally ask after the color began to come back to her cheeks, from the chair I pulled up next to her. She sits up and pulls her knees to her chest. We both just sit quietly for a few more minutes, and I only keep my mouth shut because I can tell she is fighting back tears. When she first speaks it is so soft, I can't understand a word of what she said, so I just stare at her, patient, yet confused.

She clears her throat and repeats, "That was the first time in over eight years I have heard my real name." Celeste pauses again, thinking. "I guess it shook me more than I thought it would."

"*CeeCee*," I say, swallowing the lump of emotion that was threatening to choke me. "I just- I didn't- I just didn't think."

"Did you know I have heard nothing from my parents?" She laughs, her tone darkening while trying to hide her true hurt. "I know the rules, everyone does." She shrugs and leans her head down on the top of her knees, curling in on herself and hugging her legs even tighter to her chest. "But I don't know a single parent that did not at least keep some contact with their child." I open my mouth, then snap it shut again. Not sure even what to say, I try to quiet the anger beginning to peak in my thoughts and threaten to take over.

"What does" *the boyfriend,* "Keirion think about your parents?" I ask, cautious not to upset her further.

"I told Keir that they died years ago. I figured it was the easiest explanation, the easiest cover." She stretches her legs out and wiggles her toes, trying to distract her thoughts from caving in on her. *Screw it.* I stand and walk out of the room. Returning to the living room, I rip the caps off of the two bottles that I grabbed from the fridge and juggle her plate of eggs. She tilts her head, watching me with curiosity and then humor when she sees what I am carrying. Celeste laughs and holds out her hands.

"Now you have ten beers and a half bottle of tequila." I clink my beer against hers and take a big gulp of the ice-cold liquid. I frown at the label and then shake my head in bewilderment. *Peanut Butter Porter.* CeeCee just laughs at my expression again and takes a drink of her own. Grabbing the remote, she queues up Netflix and relaxes back into the couch with her plate of food, I swing my chair to face the TV. Out of the corner of my eye, I allow myself to watch her; focusing on picking a movie to watch. Again I reflect back on my choice I made years ago. I wonder if I would be with her in the photo in the hall, or curled up on the couch, her head in my lap. If I had made a different decision would this have been our life, together? I wince at the pain these thoughts cause and flashback to the photo I found in the kitchen. *Maybe it isn't too late to make the right choice...* The voice in my head betrays me and even as I shove that down, I smile and take another sip. *After all, there is peanut butter beer in the world. Anything can be possible.*

Chapter 9

Celeste

I wake to the long shadows and the last sunlight of the day streaming through the curtains. I stretch and groan at the stiffness in my neck. I palpate the knot and sit up, looking around for Keirion, before snatching up my phone that had fallen to the floor during my restless tossing.

"Keir?" My voice croaks out, I clear my throat to wake up my vocal cords. I try again. "Keir?" Silence. I move to stand up and stop with momentary confusion as my legs catch on something. My heart melts as I recognize the blanket from the spare room that Keirion must have draped over me as I slept. I stand and the last bit of sleepiness falls away. *Not Keirion. Naveen.* Unlocking my phone, I wince as I see multiple missed messages from Keirion.

9:02am *Hey babe. Hope your day is going well.*

11:56am *Thinking about you. Still on for dinner tonight?*

1:20pm *Everything okay?*

4:38pm *I am still okay to come for dinner, right?*

5:47pm *Getting worried. I am going to swing by and make sure you are okay when I get off work at 6...*

Looking at the time display on the oven I mutter, "Shit." *6:07.* I quickly pull up the closest restaurant's number and order some food for us to eat. I then type out a response to Keirion.

SO SORRY!! I accidentally fell asleep on the couch and just woke up... must have been more tired than I thought I was. Dinner is for sure still on! Come on over.

I move to press send as the doorbell rings. Glancing out the kitchen window, I can see that Keirion has just arrived and is bouncing on his toes, clearly nervous. I set the phone down on the counter and stride hastily to the door. I throw it open just as he lifts his fist to knock. A look of relief washes across his face. Then annoyance. Then shame.

"I was just texting you back. Come on in!" I wave him in and he still has a clear look of abashment.

He opens his mouth to speak, then hesitates. Trying again, he says, "I pulled a psycho boyfriend move, didn't I?" He shakes his head and laughs without humor. "I don't know what has gotten into me, I'm sorry, CeeCee. You didn't respond and..." His voice fades and he shoves his hands in his pockets, clearly not knowing what to say next. I watch him with surprise. Never having seen Keirion look like this before I am as at a loss for words as he is. I decide to just smile and give him a kiss.

"I appreciate you caring that much, Keir. That means more than anything." A ghost of a smile starts to crack through his embarrassment.

"I should have assumed you would be busy all day with the job and new duties." He reaches out and pulls me closer, giving me another slow kiss, trying to transmit his apologies through our lips. He lets me go when the doorbell rings, looking confused.

"Food," I explain. "Go pour us some wine?" Laughing when the word has a magic effect on him. Washing away the last bit of doubt remaining in his mind, he realizes I did want him there for dinner. I open the door again and sign for the food. Joining Keirion in the kitchen, I feel my stomach clench seeing my phone sitting on the counter, the message I never sent still pulled up on the screen. I pause in puzzlement for a moment, trying to figure out what caused the sudden subconscious panic and what could be wrong. Then it hits me and I clench my fist to fight the human instinct that pummels through me. *Do not drop the bag. Do not let Keir see the screen.* I also send up a quick thanks to whoever or whatever intervened on my idiotic lapse in mental function. *It is a workday. He doesn't know that you quit. And yet you were going to tell him you were NAPPING? Ugh. Maybe V was wrong and you aren't cut out to rejoin his world - even temporarily.* The next thought that hits me with even greater alarm that I can't prevent my reaction this time. Both my brain and my body goes numb and before I realize it, the food bag has slid through my fingers and slammed to the floor.

Where is Naveen?!

My brain restarts with such a surge of thoughts and

energy, I picture a reaction akin to a defibrillator restarting a heart. I scramble to the floor, vaguely hearing Keirion's exclamation. I take the blessing of having to clean up the spillage on the floor and hide my face, trying to think through the complication of my life of the last 24 hours. I don't realize tears have started to slip out until I feel gentle hands join mine. One stopping the scattering chaotic movements of my hands, trying to shove the still edible parts of the entrees back into some semblance in the foam containers. The other lifts to my face and raises my chin level to his. I stare back into his piercing, loving, blue eyes as he wipes the betraying tear that had trickled out away with his thumb. I tilt my face and kiss the palm of his hand softly caressing my cheek as all he says, with more understanding than I have ever heard, "Bad day?"

I open my mouth to attempt and explain everything he deserves to know. "I..." But that is all I can get out before the front door swings open, and Naveen walks in.

"Oh, honey! I'm home!" Naveen calls out. Oblivious that both Keirion and I are now kneeling frozen in the kitchen, dumbstruck and at a loss for words. He continues, throwing my keys on the entry table. *He must have grabbed them while I was sleeping.* I think distantly, my brain focusing on the only thing I can comprehend. I continue to gawk, unable to shut my mouth when Keirion turns to look back at me. Naveen continues, not realizing the disaster that was unfolding only a room away. "I ran out while you were sleeping and picked up some more eggs. I noticed this morning during breakfast, you were almost... out." His voice drops in volume and tone as he turns the corner holding a paper sack and sees the two of us, still petrified kneeling on the floor, with stray french fries and foam take-out boxes scattered in between.

I watch as Keirion's eyes shift from love and care to confusion, then betrayal. *Say something, you idiot!* My inner voice screams desperately at me. "Keirion..." is all I manage to squeak out. Grasping desperately at his sleeve as he stands up, pulling away from me.

"Is there anything you need to tell me?" He says breaking the silence after what feels like an eternity. I cringe at the steel tone. It is one I have never heard from him before. *What else would you expect from him? No. Anyone?? If he was anyone else, he would be out that door and I would never hear from him again. This looks really, really bad.* I glance at Naveen and see he is looking at me with mortification, from the pain in his eyes he has nothing but regret for everything that had happened since he walked through that door not three minutes ago.

I clear my throat. "Keir... Baby... this is *not* what I am sure you are thinking it is. I can explain everything, if-" My

voice cracks with emotion, but I force myself to continue. "-
if you give me the chance to." I slowly stand, every
movement careful; like I was approaching a skittish
animal. When he doesn't respond or move, I take a deep
breath and turn to Naveen. "V, can you please wait
outside." But he is already gone. *One distraught male at a
time.* I turn back to Keirion and find he has moved across
the room from me to pick up his glass of wine he had
poured before the whole evening had been annihilated. I
walk to the counter opposite the one he is leaning against
and turn around to find him holding the other glass out to
me. Despite the look of betrayal and anger that is still thick
in his face, I can tell I haven't lost him completely. *Yet.*

I take the peace offering from him and offer a cautious
smile of thanks. The corner of his cheek twitches, but does
not return the smile. I swirl the dark burgundy liquid
around and try to think of what to say first, how to say it,
and how much to say. Keirion waits patiently, only
watching me with no comment. I become suddenly aware
of how deranged I surely look. My hair still mussed from
my nap on the couch, dried tear tracks on my flushed
cheeks, and my bottom lip chapped and raw from my
anxious chewing. I release a long sigh, wet my mouth with
a sip of the wine, and begin talking.

CHAPTER 10

<u>Celeste</u>

I decide to start from where Keirion and I had last talked about Naveen. "As you know yesterday we met for coffee to catch up on each others' stories from the last few years." At this, I made up my mind. Give the partial truth. *Partial lies*, my inner voice chimes in helpfully with a sinister, hissing whisper. But I keep going, the story I just came up with flowing out of me like a steadily flowing river of artful deception. "After we met for coffee I didn't see him again like I told you. We parted ways and that was that... until last night." I pause, trying to plan my next words with care. "Last night, I was thinking about work and couldn't sleep and decided to stress- clean. It was late but I ran out of my favorite cleaning wipes, you know, the lavender ones?" Keirion doesn't respond other than a slight nod, enough to acknowledge that he was still partially listening to me. *Truth, truth, truth...* I continue "Anyway, I was still nowhere near tired so I ran to the only 24-hour store on this side of town that sells them." *Lie...* "I was driving past the park across from the store when I saw someone familiar. He was sleeping in his car, Keir. When I saw that... I... I couldn't in good conscience let him do that, not when I could maybe help." These new details finally broke through the icy mask he was wearing. The glimmer of hope created from the offering of wine was fanned into a small flame at the look of slight understanding. Yet a part of him was still unsure whether or not he believed me. After a few seconds of pause, despite internally continuing to fight the disgust at myself and the web of lies I was weaving so beautifully well, I force myself to continue. "He was so embarrassed after I found him like that, and he didn't want to put me... us... in this hard position. But I insisted."

Keirion opens his mouth to interject, undoubtedly in anger from what was flared in his eyes, his clenched jaw muscle jumping. I hold up my hand in a placating gesture. "I know. Okay, I know." I cut him off before he can get a word out. "I meant to talk to you and explain all this before it got, well," I gesture to the room and ourselves, "to this. And if you let me finish, I will do so now." He slams his mouth shut again with a snap and only responds with a sharp nod. I take another big breath. "It is only for two more days, then he already has a job lined up in a different city. He just didn't have the money to cover a room somewhere after paying for the plane ticket." *Lie, lie, lie, lie, LIE.* "He slept in the other room and I was in mine. He made me breakfast as a thank you, and that is it." *Truth.* I breathe with some relief at the fact I could at least end this torrential downpour of utter bullshit with a final truth. *The one that really matters.* I try and reassure myself. "V is the closest thing I have to family left, Keir. Please don't hate me for trying to protect that last remaining part." I add with a whisper, not having to fake the subtle crack in my voice.

We stand there in silence. Unsure of what to do, I look down at my feet and without thinking begin tracing the pattern painted on the vintage tile of the kitchen. I retreat deep into my thoughts and try to shove the shame that is burning my throat like bad heartburn. I dare not look up at Keirion, for two reasons. 1. I don't want to see the emotion that is sure to be evident on his face, because from the potent, heavy silence, I am assuming the worst. 2. This is the closest I am going to get to privacy without leaving the kitchen. And that would *for sure* be the wrong thing to do, the final nail in the coffin. *Walking out after a big fight? Not great for relationship longevity.* So I wait and wish. We both break out of our silent stillness at the soft *thud, thud, thud* of footsteps on the stairs. Looking up, I see Naveen stomping down the last few steps, exaggerating his normally silent gait, graciously giving us enough of a heads up to try to avoid any awkwardness.Well, *more* awkwardness. In response to this, Keirion and I just stare at him. *Yeah... not comfortable.* Naveen clears his throat and shrugs, adjusting his duffel-bag looped over his shoulder.

"I am just gonna go..." He motions with his thumb, feigning nonchalance. "Super sorry for this... um... thing." Turning to the door, he only makes it about three steps before sighing and spinning back around. Staring down Keirion with an austere look, he begins to talk with a voice I have only heard a handful of times- the voice he only uses when he is being *truly* sincere. "Listen, dude. This is your crossroads. Learn from my mistake. This girl," he gestures at me, "is one in a million. One you will regret every second from the one you let her walk away, as I did. I..." At that, he clenches his fists at his side and turns out of sight down the hall to the front door. He adds, "Good luck at the new job, CeeCee." Then with a final bang, the door closes behind him.

Three seconds is all it takes before Keirion follows him, striding quick and determined across the kitchen and through the entryway. I still am propped up against the counter, slack-jawed and completely confused. *Wow. That has to be a new record for the number of attractive males that just stormed out of my door in sixty seconds.* I shake myself out of my surprised trance and begin to run after him. *Which him?* I think for the even smallest second; at that, I mentally scold myself again. *Keirion. Of course, I am going after Keirion.* I don't make it past that thought though. I reach the door and through the glass, I see the two of them standing in front of my house on the sidewalk, thankfully, just talking. I pause in my pursuit and press back into the corner of the wall and the door, giving myself enough room to see them, yet not allowing them to see me watching. I strain my ears, but can not hear more than faint, jumbled words; their conversation muted through the glass. Not more than a minute later, both of their body languages had changed dramatically. Naveen had dropped his bag off his shoulder onto the sidewalk, and Keirion had relaxed the tension that had been set in his muscles since the beginning of the whole exchange. I nearly gasp out loud as relief and shock flood my body when they break out into a smile joined with laughter and even a cordial handshake. Seeing this, I feel my shoulders start to release their own tension and I slip back down the hall to find sanctuary from this crazy day in my favorite spot on the couch. I settle into the cluster of pillows and sigh. *I never should have gotten up out of this spot.* Spotting my blanket still strewn atop the couch from my nap, I pull it over my legs and tuck them up into the couch; fully giving in to the familiar embrace. Five minutes pass, then ten... Frowning in unease I stand up, tossing the blanket off of me again, and peek around the corner to see what they could be doing. *There is no one there.* I blink then, shake my head to clear that thought, not wanting to believe what I was seeing. I exhale and take another two steps, centering myself in the entryway. I let the image sink in this time, my brain processing all of this in slow motion. *Why is my brain not working properly anymore??* I shove open the door in a rush and do not get a respite, only a surge of panic as my eyes spot no one even on my street. No Keirion, and no Naveen. Feeling my breath start to increase its pace, I try to rationalize the situation and not immediately jump to the worst-case scenario. *Okay, yes. Keirion was mad, obviously. Naveen, well, I don't think he is, and with his whole* 'good luck at the new job' *comment, he is not going to leave me high and dry. But maybe he is still pretending with Keir? So worst case is, whoever the Yoshitomi sent decided to take them... But with my front door open that doesn't seem like something they would pass up, taking them instead of me. Plus, they would have to get past Naveen and unless they were expecting a one-manned war machine, it seems highly unlikely they would get that far. No. I think they are safe.* My breath finally calms to a regular pace, but I cringe at my new thinking. *So I guess the best, worst-case scenario is the winner. Keir left... Naveen with him.* I sink, most ungracefully, to the front step and choke back a sob. *Fuck. I messed up.* Hearing soft voices coming up the street. I debate for a moment with myself whether it is worth the effort of giving up and going inside to save what little dignity I seemed to have left. Then I decide that I don't actually care about being the mess I probably appear to be. *My life is in tatters. Who cares if some stranger sees me, puffy-eyed and pathetic.* So I stay there, head resting on my arms, stomach grumbling, and feeling very disconsolate, wallowing in self-pity. I look up with a jolt at the sound of a rustling plastic sack coming from right in front of me. I stare dumbly at the two men standing a few steps away, both of whom have huge smirks on their faces. Not knowing what to say, I just decide to wait for them to break the silence.

CHAPTER 11

Naveen

After pacing in my temporary room, trying to figure out what to do for about five minutes, I decide to make the obvious choice. The same one that was going to be easiest for Celeste. I quickly pack what little of my belongings that had escaped the bag in my one night stay at *Hotel Stone* and then realize that I probably should be listening to whatever Celeste had decided to say, to explain why her ex-boyfriend A) Had a key to her house and B) Why he had spent the night when her current boyfriend had not. I cringe inwardly at the situation I had put her in. *Stupid! You gave in to her offer too easily. You knew this was a bad idea from the beginning.* I choose to disregard these thoughts and to focus now on getting us both out of the mess I caused. Silently, I ease the door open and slip out to the stair landing. Her voice echoes perfectly from the kitchen up to where I stand, lurking on the top stair. I can't help but be impressed at the way Celeste is weaving her story in such a way that no one could help but forgive her, *because she was only trying to help.*

Masterful. I hear the kitchen fall into a heavy silence. *That is my queue.* I take a deep breath and then make my footsteps as heavy as I can, without making it over the top obvious, I thud loudly down the stairs; pausing at the bottom when I see them both looking in my direction. Celeste's eyes drift to the bag strap thrown over my shoulder. I feel a momentary pause in the decision I had made only a minute ago. *What if she thinks I am truly leaving her?* I scramble internally for a way I can hint to her that I am not abandoning her; just trying to do what I can to help her get out of this, without losing everything she cares about. *You did ditch out on her before. What is going to make her think that you won't again?* It is at that point that I realize that I am still standing awkwardly just staring at them. Knowing that they are waiting for me to say something, I just blurt out whatever sounds good until I can get my thoughts in working order again. Luckily this was something that one had to get used to when in my line of work. Staying cool and collected, despite the fact my mind is racing through about a dozen things at once. All while appearing as if I was not, in fact, scrambling for the end solution to whatever problem I was dealing with that hour. I hear my brain create and spit out human sentences, but don't fully compute what they are. Almost as if my brain was buffering and the rainbow wheel was spinning. That is until I see Celeste's jaw drop and I hear my subconscious deciding to join in on the fun and decide to shove myself under the bus; successfully making this even more uncomfortable. *Nice job. You aced that little sabotage, you rotten bastard.* I am moving in slow motion, and feel myself gesture at Celeste and hear the words continue to flow out of my big mouth.

"This girl is one in a million." I hear myself say. *"One you will regret every second, as I did, from the second I let her walk away."* Finally, my self-preservation kicks in, and I choke down the words that continue threatening to surface. Luckily, only one more word slips out before I regain control. *"I..."* I make myself focus on what had driven my mental train down this broken track and bite out one last sentence before I bolt out of the door. "Good luck with the new job, CeeCee." With that, all I can do is hope that it is enough for her to understand that our deal and plan was

still on and I *would not* leave her to fight off the monsters that were coming for her. I make it down the stairs and debate on what to do next. *I could go to the hotel room that Belinda had still booked for me. But I still don't want to leave CeeCee with no one here in the awful chance that something happens. Yet I also don't want to make things worse by hanging out here and waiting for the other guy to come out and leave; risking starting this whole ordeal over again, and probably disintegrating any hope that CeeCee had of keeping someone that was clearly important to her.* I am still hesitating, trying to decide the rest of my night when the sound of a screen door slamming shut, echoes down the street in the soft twilight. Realizing which door it is, I turn around more than half expecting to see a fist swinging at me; and more than willing to take the hit. *You know you deserve* at least *that*. Instead, to my complete shock, he is holding his hands up in a placating truce.

"I just want to talk man." Keirion begins. I nod and let my bag slide down my shoulder and drop to the ground.

"Fair enough." That is all I respond, mainly because there is nothing really that I can say at this moment that wouldn't make it even more tense; seeing as I usually revert to my sarcastic asshole self in tense situations. *Plus, I am genuinely curious to hear what exactly he has to say.* Keirion did not look angry, per se, just not pleased. Which was shocking, seeing as if I was in his shoes, I would have already narrowed down which of the 264 ways to make a body disappear with no trace, in all of which I was trained. What does come out of his mouth shocks me.

"Look, I am not going to run you out of the house." He smirks when I only gape in response. "CeeCee is her own woman and I have no right to tell her who to open her life to." I begin to speak but halt as he continues. "I trust her. Plain and simple. Was I... um... surprised? Hell yes. But that is not what this is about." He watches me with such intensity that I can tell he is choosing his next words carefully. "She has earned my trust." He gestures back at the house. "You have not."

Ah. Here we go. I decide to just wait, patient, for him to continue.

"You make a move. You put her in any danger. You try and weasel your way in. I *will* kick your ass. Agreed?"

I can't help but feel a grudging respect for the guy and his level of maturity. Yet, also wish I had the opportunity to at least get one punch in. But hey, this way we all win. Sort of. I grin and reach to return his handshake. I grasp the outstretched hand when a thin line of unease hits me. Unable to place the origin, I disregard it for the time being and but still mentally log it for further perusal. *Right next to the photo hidden in the Oreos on my dissection shelf.* We both pause hesitating, neither of us sure of what to do next. I clear my throat and begin to break the silence, but Keirion does so first.

"Well, I think our dinner is on the floor. We probably should go grab something else. CeeCee can get very hangry and there is a place she likes right around the corner." Even more befuddled than before, all I can do is nod and follow him leading the way. Turning north up the sidewalk, he began to ask questions about myself. Where I was from, how long I knew Celeste, what the new job was. The usual get to know you conversation material. *Why can't you just* like *the guy?* I ask myself when we return to Celeste's street. The devil on my shoulder chimes in. *Because he is with your girl, you dumb ass. It would be easier to get along with him if he was an asshole, because then* maybe *you would get another chance with CeeCee when* he *messes up. Now she has a winner and you have missed out.*

Okay. As much as I hate to admit it. Keirion is a pretty cool guy. Damn it. Walking back up the sidewalk to Celeste's house, I take advantage of the silence to reanalyze the events of the last thirty minutes. Unable to listen to my thoughts any more, I pick up the questioning now, unsuccessfully trying to find a flaw that I could work with. As we approach the house, both of our steps falter slightly when we see a crouched figure on the front landing. I am torn between wanting to laugh at the sight of Celeste crouched over, looking like a little child who has been sent to time out, or pulling her in for a hug.

"I guess we were gone longer than I thought. She is definitely pouting." Keirion whispers conspiratorially over his shoulder, I fall back and let him pass through the gap in the bushes first. I can't help but return with a smile and chuckle, then the look of confusion that passes between us as Celeste makes no notice of us. When I look again at Keirion, he winks and mouths, *Watch this.* I wait, intrigued as to what he is up to and watch on when he lifts his other hand and the one holding the bag out to meet in front of his chest. With a slight movement, he expertly makes the plastic bag and its contents rustle loudly. That is all it takes. With a snap Celeste raises her head from where it was previously cradled, on top of her arms resting on her knees. What is initially a look of panic transforms into relief, then irritation when she catches sight of the grins wide on our faces. Knowing CeeCee, she is stubborn enough to sit here for the next ten years, unless given an explanation to our sudden apparent friendship. But I also know that it is not my place, nor my desire to break this silence.

CHAPTER 12

Celeste

Keirion decides to give in first. *Good. Because I sure was not planning on it.* For some reason, despite my initial relief that they were both back, a bit of irritation still flickers inside me. *I have been sitting here distraught for who knows how long while they are out being all buddy-buddy??* I attempt to shove that feeling away and focus on the good feeling. *Keirion doesn't* look *like he is about to dump me at least.* I shoot a look at Naveen to see if he will give me any hints as to what the hell has happened tonight. *Nothing. Just a stone wall with a smirk.* I grit my teeth to keep a snarl from coming out. Dragging my attention back to my boyfriend, I see him holding a carryout bag, the culprit of the noise that jolted me from my reverie.

"We went to grab some fresh dinner." He shrugs, feigning ease, but I can see through it clearly when he locks his sharp blue eyes with mine. He tries to convey everything through that look. *I'm sorry about leaving without telling you. I'm sorry for causing you to doubt that I would come back. And I'm sorry that the night turned out this way.* I don't even bother to respond with my eyes. I simply give in to what my heart was screaming at me. Leaping up off the stairs, ignoring the look Naveen is giving us, I throw my arms around Keirion. He passes the bag to Naveen and then I am enveloped. Both of us whispering our apologies and quiet I love you's. I am not surprised when I hear my screen door shut with a slam, for yet another time that evening. Naveen had graciously left our little circle to us and gave us some privacy. Even as I burrow into the safety of Keirion's embrace, I can not help but feel some sadness when the brief flash of Naveen's face that I caught appears in my mind's eye. The look of utter sorrow and longing makes my breath hitch and, for just a moment, I contemplate racing after him and wrapping my arms around him instead, like I used to. Appalled at myself for even the thought, I shove it deep, deep down. *Something to contemplate... well... never, if you know what is good for you.*

Keirion and I finally pull away from each other, smiling, and return to the house. We make our way to the living room where the smell of breakfast is wafting. I feel my mouth start to water, it only just now occurring to me that I was starving. Fresh pancakes, bacon, eggs, and hashbrowns all in their different plastic containers are spread out on my coffee table. Naveen is sitting on the floor, surprisingly patient.

"Come *on!* I am starving and this smells phenomenal." He says, trying to hurry us along. *Maybe not so patient after all.* I examine his face, but no remains of the early look shows on his face, only hunger. I look at Keirion, and when he just shakes his head and laughs, I decide not to question it, at least not now. Not while there were grins on our faces and delicious food on my table. So I plop down on the floor, opposite Naveen with my back to the couch, and begin to fill my plate. Keirion joins the two of us, sitting next to me and planting a quick peck on my cheek before digging in. Content silence fills the room as we all stuff our faces with amazing food.

"How had I never eaten at this place before??" Naveen groans and falls over, hand on his stomach. "I am so full, but I just couldn't stop. What the heck was that place called again?"

Keirion wipes his hands clean and leans back into the

support of the couch, hand also on his stomach. "Penelope's. Best breakfast joint in the world in my professional opinion." Keirion issues a grunt as he gives a push and rolls up onto the couch, beginning to lapse into a food coma. I try to just relax there, enjoying the happy, quiet moment, but of course, I have to know what the hell happened that caused such a sudden switch. *How do I approach this without causing a disagreement?* A loud, insistent banging comes from my front door, interrupting my thoughts. BANG. BANG. BANG. Naveen and I launch to our feet in a single breath. My heart accelerates and I am sure I am seconds away from throwing up all the food I just ate. All grogginess from the meal vanishes in the blink of an eye. Keirion looks at both of us with astonishment, but we ignore it.

Naveen motions for me to get down, "I take it you were not expecting anyone else tonight?" He asks in a soft voice, filled with urgency. I just shake my head no.

Keirion sits up and asks in a normal volume, but now one that is infinitely too loud. "What the hell is going-" I leap at him and cover his mouth to smother the rest of his question. Naveen and I both scramble for an explanation. Unable to come up with anything, we just brush off the question. Keirion remains quiet, but I can tell the easy mood he had fallen back into was rapidly changing to anger again. I slowly remove my hands when I can trust that he understands, if nothing else, that he needs to remain silent. I open my mouth to try and come up with anything that might explain this. Nothing comes to me. BANG. BANG. BANG. Sounds once more from the door and I jump again, my nerves taking over any rational thought. Naveen silently approaches me, mouthing and signaling his report of what he gathered from his view at the window. I flashback to our earlier years of training together with a mixture of elation and sadness. *Not now CeeCee. Don't lose focus.* For a few seconds, I think over Naveen's report. *Black clothes, no face view, two people, no visible weapons.* I ponder this and signal back to Naveen. *Does not add up.* I decide that unless they have seriously amazing hearing there is no way they can hear my whisper. *If they can, then I have some serious apologies to make to my neighbors for whenever Keirion spends the night.*

"V, that doesn't make sense." I glance sideways at Keirion and hesitate on how much to say. "Would they really - um - try to take on three of us with no weapons and after knocking and letting us know they were here??"

"I don't know what the *shit* is going on, but even *I* know that is not logical at all." Keirion joins our conversation and steps between us, whispering as well. Naveen glances at me to see how I want to proceed.

"There has been a bunch of break in's in the neighborhood lately..." I spit out as a flimsy explanation. Before turning back to Naveen with a sharp nod.

"Okay, CeeCee you-" Naveen starts, but is interrupted as the blaring tone of my phone ringing shatters the delicate quiet of my living room. All three of us jump this time and I lunge to quiet the betraying device. I click the decline button on accident trying to shut it up.

"Oh *hell no*. That bitch just ignored my call!!" Keirion, Naveen, and I all gape at each other when we hear a voice exclaim loudly outside. I glance down at my screen to where my iPhone shows a missed call from Ridley. I moan out of irritated relief and start toward the front door. Naveen reaches to stop me, but I pass him too quickly and throw open the door.

"What the shit, Rid?" I yell at the disrupters standing at my door.

"Why the hell are you all dressed in black, you psycho?" I continue yelling.

Ridley responds with a flip of her newly dyed electric blue hair, yelling in turn. "Why the hell did you send me to voicemail, you asshole?"

"Because there where two people banging on my door late at night dressed in all black!"

"That is because we just came from our dress rehearsal! Remember the off-broadway I am doing in two days?" Rid, in typical Ridley manner, continuing with her extreme volume. "This is Charlie, by the way."

"Nice to meet you, Charlie! Oh." I realize I am also still shouting, now at this guy, but he is taking it in stride. *He has to be if he likes Rid because weird little quips like this are her style.* But I reduce my volume noticing both of the boys are now standing behind me. Naveen is looking at me like I have lost my mind but Keirion, used to this, just waves at Ridley. She flashes her megawatt smile and grabbing Charlie's hand, pulls him past me and into my house. I sigh out of exhaustion from the night so far and linger at the door for a few seconds longer of peace, then finally give in and rejoin the group, all of whom had meandered back into my living room where introductions for Naveen are being held. I shoot a thankful smile at Keirion who is clearing the coffee table of the discarded remains of our dinner. Ridley pours herself onto the couch and reminds me of a cat as she stretches and snuggles her lanky body onto the place designated as *her spot.*

"So, how was everybody's day?" Ridley chimes out,

casually, completely unaware of how much of a can of worms that question was, the three of us just look at each other awkwardly and respond in unison.

"Fine."

I cringe when she sits up with the spark of mischief lighting in her eyes. Like a bloodhound, she picks up the tone of that single betraying word. I clear my throat and catch her attention. Signaling with my eyes, I convey, *Don't do it. I will fill you in later. But don't you dare poke holes right now.* She understands, for once, and falls back into the embrace of the couch, disappointment dousing the spark only to replace it with satisfaction, at least for the moment. I change the subject.

"So how is the play going?" That one question is just what was needed. Like a windup toy, Ridley starts off, giving us conversation for the rest of the night.

"So that is how the play ends! I am super excited for you to see it because my description does not do it justice, you know?" Ridley finally concludes her one-woman conversation that had been carrying on for the last two hours. All of us jolt out of our dazed stupor we had fallen into at the sound of silence, the first moment since I had asked that single question. *Man, did that work.* I fail to hide a yawn that I cannot keep down.

"Yeah, Rid. I can't wait! It is next Saturday at nine, right?"

"Yes! And I already got your tickets at will call." She beams back at me. Glancing at the clock, she unfurls from the couch and jumps up, motioning at Charlie to join her. "We have a party we have to get to. Gotta go!" She reaches me and pecks me twice on each cheek with a loud *Muah!* But before she pulls away, she whispers in my right ear. "Details. Tomorrow. I will call you." Then pulls away and flashes a wink and a smile before she is out the door and back to blending in with the dark, moon-free night.

For about two minutes we sit there in silence together, then one by one, we all begin to laugh at the spectacle that this whole night had become. When the laughter finally dies down, we all are clutching our sides and huffing for air. Now calmed down enough to talk, Naveen stands and begins to move for his bag when Keirion stops him. Looking at me he simply states. "It is your choice, CeeCee." Then as if reading my mind, he adds, "And no, this is not a test." I take a deep breath and force myself to make up my mind.

Turning to Naveen I say, "The guest bedroom is still

yours if you want it," Before he can respond, however, I then turn to Keirion and say, "and my bed is open for you if you would like to stay as well." At that, Keirion breaks into a smile and I know he has accepted. I turn back to Naveen to see his answer. I am aware that by allowing Naveen to stay, even though Keirion said it wasn't a test, it still would cause a shift in our relationship. But by also requesting Keirion to stay gave us a buffer, along with drawing a line. One that was between Naveen and me; saying this is your *temporary* place and mine is with Keirion. If this line of thinking occurred to Naveen or affected him even at all, it did not show in the least.

With a roguish grin spread wide, his only reply, "Good thing I have my earplugs."

I groan as Keirion laughs and retorts, "So long as you know the house shaking is not an earthquake, and don't panic."

I bury my face in the pillow laying next to me so they can't see the bright blush I know is blooming on my cheeks. *It is better these guys are friends now... isn't it?*

CHAPTER 13

I crouch, hidden, watching the lights and shadows moving from the house. From what I can tell there are at least three people in the house. Something happened earlier with them and I was almost able to get my target. *She was just sitting there, totally helpless. Until that meddlesome agent came back into her life, she was mine. Only the boyfriend standing in my way, which is a problem easily remedied. Especially in the dating world today. Such a convenient term,* ghosting. *Such an easy excuse for what I do to people. But then again people can't handle the truth, so they come up with easy excuses.* I laugh at the dark thoughts, momentarily sidetracked. *How many boys have suddenly vanished, and the first thing the shunned girls do is make it about them. Poor little dead men. Technically, everything they do is ghosting now.* I refocus back on my current assignment. *Two fully trained agents, one meaningless citizen. I have to find out how much she knows. I like a challenge, so this should be fun. But now I have to call in for assistance. How irritating.*

CHAPTER 14

Celeste

"*Naveen, you will give the signal when Celeste is clear to retrieve the package,*" *instructs the strong voice of Ivanov over both of our earpieces. I flick my eyes to the ice cream shop that Naveen is posted across the street, about sixty feet from the park bench I am currently sitting.*

"*I am signing off. This is on you two now. Complete your mission. Don't get caught. Good luck.*" *With the sound of a click, I know that it is just us two on the comm unit.*

"*You have got this, V! We have practiced to perfection. You could pull this off on* me *if you wanted to.*" *I continue my pep talk to silence. "Just don't forget the right signal this time, and* leave your ear alone!" *I continue teasing to try and relax Naveen. The earbud spouts out a weird noise. "Um, V?" I nervously glance up to where he is sitting.*

"Jesus, Celeste. You just made me spit my coffee! I am sitting alone, laughing and spitting out coffee. Do you know how much of a nutter you just made me look?" He scolds, terse, but still with humor in his voice. I can tell he is still trying to hide his laughter and I smile, holding back my own. "Not as crazy as we both would look if we were in the time before Bluetooth. Thank god for technology advancement!" I laugh, pulling my jacket closer to myself against the autumn wind cutting through the light material. Silence. I look back over at the shop and see our target taking his seat. Here we go. *I take a deep breath and set my focus back on the task at hand.*

Thirty minutes later, we rush down the street laughing and celebrating. Naveen's giddiness at our success is so contagious I ignore the stares of the other people walking down the sidewalk.

"We did it! That was so smooth, even Professor Carpenter could not have done better." Naveen boasts. "And you!" He exclaims, picking me up and twirling me around. "You were

perfect. You are *perfect! Who knew I would pick the best partner three years ago!* The late girl. *Haha! That is what they called you. If only they knew.* I *knew you were special."* He laughs and his breath catches as he sets me down, suddenly serious. "I knew *you were special."* He says again, a whisper this time. It was *then I noticed how close we were and how good he smelled.*

After all these years, should we give in to the spark that was between us since day one? *I feel my heartbeat accelerate and my breath starts to come faster looking into his beautiful brown eyes and I see that yes, he is thinking the same thing.* Is our friendship worth the risk? *Before I can answer that question to myself, he has pulled me in and his lips are on mine. As the crisp autumn wind blew, picking up dry leaves and scattering them across the pavement; I realize I was completely in love with my best friend, my partner, my Naveen.* There couldn't be a risk with this. Right?

I wake from my dream with tears streaming down my face. Quickly wiping them away as Keirion quietly opens the door and crawls back into bed with me. I debate for a moment, then decide it is not worth the effort to pretend that I am still asleep. So I fix my expression and sit up, bunching the cozy sheets around me to hold in my cocoon of heat against the fall morning's crisp chill. I feel my heart ache with love when I see his smiling face, tousled bed-head, and still sleepy eyes. Reaching for the coffee cup he extended out to me, I pull it in and let the steam curl over my face, letting the smell of the delicious brew envelop me. I try to sort out what my dream meant, and if I even needed to give it any stock. *Maybe it was a bad idea to continue to let him stay here.* I think for one moment before the reality of my situation dawns on my still waking brain. *You need his help and protection. That is the* only *reason.* I continue to lie even to my self, but my annoying subconscious points at the facts I am choosing to ignore in the only way it can: through my dreams. It isn't the fact that I don't remember all of the amazing years with Naveen, it is simply the fact that everything that happened between us has overshadowed those moments. I rub my eyes and croak out a sleepy thank you.

"I have to go and get ready for work, but I wanted to at least have some coffee with you before I left." He gives me a long, deep kiss before pulling away with a sigh, getting up to leave.

"Will you come over for dinner tonight again?" I ask, taking a sip of my coffee. He turns back to me at the door and shakes his head.

"I told someone I would stay late at work tonight and help them with some of the paperwork they got behind on."

"Ah, Pete still taking his daily desk nap?" I reference the usual culprit with a laugh.

"No, actually! But ironically, Pete's replacement. He just stopped showing up last week, so they hired a new girl to take over. Ann something. But now she has to catch up on all of his stuff, on top of her own."

I just nod sympathetically and, thanks to the coffee, fully emerge from the bundle of sheets. "I will text you, okay?" I add, remembering Naveen and my story. "I probably will be working late too, so it all works out actually." I walk Keirion to the front door and give him a final kiss goodbye.

Shutting the door behind me, I look up to see Naveen standing at the top of the stairs, fully dressed. He greets me with a devious grin.

"Morning sunshine. Let's get to work."

I stare at the form in the mirror and the sense of familiarity floors me. *I look like my mother...* My long, shimmery blonde hair is wrapped up tight into a low bun.

I am dressed casual enough to the naked eye, but everything about my attire is purposeful. Skinny jeans, tucked into leather boots is close enough to my usual attire that I barely register them. Discarded on the bed are my favorite t-shirt and khaki jacket; replaced now by a tight long-sleeved black shirt and my old red leather jacket. Nothing loose, or comfortable. Nothing able to be caught, ripped, or grabbed. I think back to the Academy where I first chose my jacket at the school tailor. All the other girls went with the classic sleek black. But when I saw the red material hidden in the cart, I had to have it. I see myself smirk in the mirror remembering my response when questioned about my choice. *Red is easier to hide blood.*

I look up from running my fingers along the edge of my jacket to see Naveen standing in the doorway, watching me. If the word to describe how I was feeling was unsettled, that was the look, times ten, showing on Naveen's face. I smirk, content to see him pale at the sight of me in my old look. "Weird, huh?" I smile, he just nods in return. Then with a shake of his head, he was back to business.

"You all set?" He asks after looking me over again, this time with a professional eye, mostly. "Do you need to borrow any weapons? I can set up a meeting with the Armory so you can refill your arsenal." Already he has pulled out his phone and is typing away. I clear my throat to get his attention, then with a smooth, subtle motion I flick my wrist and a set of sleek onyx lightning spikes slide out of my sheath concealed on my right wrist and into my palm with a slick, oiled click. At the same time, I tap the toe of my right boot and a thick Karambit is expelled out the back of my heel. All while with my left hand, I pull a razored hairpin out of my bun and display these all to Naveen.

Then with a single rhythmic motion, I thunk my heel to the floor, press the return trigger, and slip my pin back into my flawless bun; returning all the exposed weapons into concealment. I turn back to inspect myself one last time. Mentally reviewing that the weapons that I had not exposed were also attached and accessible. When I turn to exit the room, I make momentary eye contact with Naveen. With his returning look, I can see that he understands my message perfectly. *Yes, I left the game, but I have never forgotten how to play.*

Chapter 15

Celeste

We pull up in front of the Pueblo address that Naveen gave me hours before. I shoot him a quizzical look as he gets out of the passenger seat and stretches. Groaning, I join him, feeling the immediate relief of being able to stretch out my stiff muscles. I look up at the seemingly abandoned brick warehouse on my right and feel slightly amused.

"Wow. They are seriously going with the whole *abandoned building* cliche here, huh?" Naveen follows my gaze and squints at me, first in confusion, then understanding followed by humor spreads wide across his clean-cut face. After a few days of seeing him relaxed and lounging around my place, even letting the shadow of his stubble grow, it is a bit disorienting to see him back to his sleek suave self. He just shakes his head and with a nod gestures toward the building across the street. *Sentinel Security Co.* is painted in bold, black lettering on the front glass door. I pause for a moment then huff out a partial laugh.

"I guess they decided against the whole subtle approach?" He begins to walk across the nearly abandoned street and I jog to catch up.

"Mr. Bently does not even give the word subtle the time of day. He was tired of having to explain why a bunch of big burly, usually bloody, men kept going into a flower shop for hours at a time. So he gave up on the facade and decided to just give in to what everyone already suspected, the only exception he made was to leave out all the gloriously gory details." He looks over his shoulder with a knowing look and his question plain in his eyes.

I nod and straighten up, rolling my shoulders. "I am ready." *Liar.* With that, he pulls open the door and I step out of the fall wind. I gape at the calm, clean interior that did not match the rundown exterior. A beautiful brunette receptionist greets us from behind a large black and white marble desk.

"Hello, Mr. Lazaro! We have missed you." She says with a sensuous look in her eyes and a matching tone. A look that quickly dimmed the second she saw me, who was clearly familiar and at ease with him. However, her sense of superiority returns as Naveen leans into her, one hand on the desktop, clearly focusing on her and disregarding me entirely. I snort to myself and decide to look around while he is otherwise occupied. It appeared to be the lobby, similar to any New York City high rise office building; just copy and pasted into a small Colorado town. I walk around slowly, running my hands along the black leather couch and letting my gaze drift to the centerpiece of the waiting room. Across the lobby, opposite the waiting room, to the left of the desk was a large water fountain. In the center of the large pool was an intricate nine-foot-tall sculpture. I look at it for a few minutes, distracted from everything else due to the complexity of the design before continuing to walk around examining the luxury they had poured into such an un-seeming space.

"CeeCee, ready?" Naveen calls out, returning his attention to me now that the receptionist had been distracted by a ringing phone. He waves me over to an elevator and we step in the glass-enclosed box. With a futuristic *whoosh*, the elevator shoots us down deep below the pavement. *Like a reverse skyscraper?* I can't help but think. For some reason, this humors me, and the corner of my mouth quirks up. Even though it was the slightest of movement, Naveen catches sight of it in the glass reflection and I can tell he wants to know what I am thinking. But before I can explain, our reflections and the dark walls of the shaft are replaced suddenly by bright factory lights hanging in a gigantic, well-lit cement room; reminiscent of an abandoned airport hangar. Then just as quickly, and before I can even fathom the huge space, it returns to the dark cement walls. For a few minutes, we stand in silence, and the view in the glass flickers back and forth between the two scenes. More matching rooms fly by as Naveen and I continue to hurtle downwards. Even though the helpful number panel keeps us informed of what floor we have just passed, I can't help but wonder if this is all a trick and maybe they were all the *same* room.

"A lot has changed since you have been out of the game. Technology has given us... the opportunity to grow," Naveen finally says in an attempt to explain.

The luxurious woman's voice over the speaker announces, "Thirteenth Floor."

Then the doors slide open at last to another large space. It looks like the same as all of the other levels we had passed on our way down, except this one was full. Full of people, weapons, training mats, and equipment. Some of the people we pass spare us a glance, but most just ignore us. I follow Naveen on a metal walkway suspended from the high ceilings. One or two grant me a double-take when they recognize me, a mixture of prior classmates or old friends of the family. I can't help but feel self-satisfied at their shock at seeing me again. *Thanks for all turning your backs on me. Bitches.* For a second, I feel my gut twist and hesitate at the thought of what I am about to do, at what world I am about to rejoin. *It is only temporary,* I reassure myself yet again, before pulling my focus back to Naveen as he raises his fist to knock on a heavy steel door at the opposite end of the hanger from the elevator. It opens with a creak and we walk into a large lavish office, one extravagant as the lobby upstairs. *I am going to get whiplash from all the atmosphere changes.* Naveen looks back at me and cracks a laugh. For a second, I think I must have accidentally said this out loud.

"You might want to get your facial expressions under control, CeeCee. Your thoughts are plain as day and Mr. Bently is *very* proud of his office."

"And what is there not to be proud of, *Mr. Lazaro?*" Comes a gruff British voice from the door to the left of the ornate oak desk, a shorter balding gentleman saunters in and sits behind the desk with an offended air. Naveen is not fazed, settling into a vibrant red egg chair; kicking off his shoes, resting his feet on the desktop. The man I assume is Mr. Bently gestures for me to sit, annoyed, but not as much as I would assume he would be. *He is either used to V's attitude or just has a great sense of humor.*

"Besides the fact that this room has more plaid than the entirety of Scotland? That realization would cause most people to rethink their decor, but you have seemed to embrace it!" The answer to my question is quickly solved as both when he only issues a hearty guffaw to Naveen's response. Mr. Bently then turns his attention to me.

"Welcome, Miss Stone." He pauses and glances between the two of us before continuing. "I see why Mr. Lazaro was so... distracted the last few days." I shift uncomfortably in my chair but am spared responding by a young male assistant entering the room with a tray full of drinks for each of us. The assistant passes us our coffees, and I try to think of how to explain my predicament. Naveen had warned me on our way to the office to not let him know everything. If he decided that my joining his company was too much of a risk, then I was majorly screwed. As if he can tell what is running through my mind, Mr. Bently suddenly shifts and becomes the total opposite of the jovial, aging man he was only seconds before. His eyes, so intense and seemingly all-knowing, focus on me. I freeze like a mouse caught in the gaze of a hungry cat.

"Convince me." He only utters these two words, but I now feel the pressure to impress him. This is not a man to take lightly and now, I need something from him. His dark brown eyes, almost black, bore into me. *You are* not *a mouse,* I remind myself. I let my old pride in my history rise up and open my mouth to begin a story. A story of a person that I had not let myself be in a very long time.

CHAPTER 16

Naveen

I force myself to act nonchalant, but in reality, I am rocked. Although Celeste and I had known each other for years and I, oh so humbly, thought I was pretty *in the know*. There were things she was saying that *I* had never even had any idea about. Jobs her parents had included her on, training at her school, and her extensive list of credentials and accomplishments. I take all of this in while quietly reclining in the chair, arms behind my head, feet still kicked up on Bently's desk, and eyes closed. This is the only way I get away with not revealing my shock and giving away the fact that I had not in fact "recruited" her for selfish reasons, which of course was the actual case. The number of things I *didn't* know wasn't that unusual in our line of work. The less you knew, the less you could spill. No need to give anyone extra reasons to go after your friends and loved ones; especially if one of those loved ones could and would fight back. I fight the urge to tense up when Celeste starts to approach the current time's events and hear her, so eloquently, describe her *desire to return to our business* and *how mundane average lives are,* and my personal favorite, *how Naveen came sweeping back into her life, convincing her that the only place for her was Sentinel Securities.* I knew Old Bently would snatch that up like the coiled snake that he was. I vaguely wonder if Celeste can see him for what he is, too. Or if she is blinded by the unimpressive shell he tried to maintain. I know I was duped for the first few months I had been here. Then after a shocking turn of events, one day I saw him pluck a traitor's eyes out with only his thumbs and a gruesome smile and I knew that facade would never fool me again. The room falls silent as Celeste ends her impressive, albeit lengthy, monologue, and I open my eyes again. Mr. Bently, is still sitting in his extraordinarily high backed leather chair, resting his finger between his upper lip and his well-manicured mustache. At first, he doesn't speak. The only indication that anything was happening in either his brain or body were the wheels turning behind his solid black eyes. With a suddenness that causes both Celeste and me to jump, he slaps his thighs and stands abruptly.

"Well, I can't think of a reason why you wouldn't be qualified enough to work here. And with your history and, of course, the excellent recommendation from our own Mr. Lazaro, I do believe we can find a spot for you here. I have been looking for a new secretary for a while and you would be able to handle that I think." The room falls back into silence, this time an uncomfortable one. But before either of us can even think of a polite way to reply something along the lines of *go to hell*, he lets out a loud "Ha!!" Celeste catches on first and laughs along. "Of course I am joking!" He plops back down again, causing the chair to emit a groan. I contemplate for a brief second that if the chair were to give in to his weight, if I would jump forward to try and catch him, or if I would let him fall on his big fat ass.

"Naveen." He waves his hand between Celeste and me. "Get her set up with the usual equipment, give her the tour, and just set her up in Annette's old office." Then, to Celeste, he says, with his classic morbid humor, "She won't mind." Then mimes with his hands a knife being drawn across his throat, complete with a gruesome smile in place. Much to Celeste's credit, she doesn't even shudder. She just extends her hand, shaking it and thanking Mr. Bently for the opportunity. With a final smile and wave, we exit the room. Only as we wait for the elevator to take us further down below to the offices does she finally break face. Her only reaction was a full body shake and emitting a *yuuuuuuuuugh.*

Under her breath, she mutters to me "Something is definitely wrong with that guy..." We step into the elevator and it starts its descent, taking us even further underground. "That was your boss??"

We quickly reach the floor I selected, but before we step out, I turn and say with an evil grin. "Oh no, honey. That is *our* boss."

The next few days flew in a whirlwind of activity. After taking Celeste to get set up with her gear, or should I say *more* gear... turns out she was hiding even more weapons than what she had revealed to me earlier; a fact I could tell she was slightly embarrassed about as the Weapons Director accidentally discovered the stiletto knife she had tucked up underneath her shirt. Next, I lead her to my office; and directly across the hall she discovered her own.

She didn't reveal much that day, or since, about how this transition has been. I did however discover her more than once lost in thought, lights out, absentmindedly spinning a travel-sized shampoo bottle on the cold, wooden desktop. I reflect on all this riding the elevator the many floors down until I reach my office floor. I run my fingers through my hair and grip the file grasped in my right hand tight. Unwittingly hard enough that I concave the manilla folder. I reach the open door of Celeste's office and rap a quick knock on the frame. She looks up from whatever she had pulled up on the computer screen and beams a smile at me. I swear my heart stops in my chest and I have to gather myself a moment before I trust myself to speak.

"Good morning CeeCee! You are here bright and early today." The sentence is plain enough, but there is an open question in my gaze. Her smile dims briefly before responding.

"I'm just scanning for any word of my parents, or if any chatter has been out there about them." She looks worried for a second, but she waves off my look of concern and swivels her chair straight to the desk, giving me her full attention, and her eyes catch the contents of my hand. "What's up?"

I hold it up and say, "Here is your golden ticket. Ready

to get out of the dungeon?" I toss the folder on her desk and it slides a bit on the polished surface before she pins it in place with a smack of her hand. She chews her lip adorably and hesitates to open it.

"CeeCee..." I say and lean up against the door frame, crossing my arms. "I know it's tough, but this is the only way right now. Pull some jobs, get in good with Bently, then tell him what is happening with the Yoshitomi. Then you will get all the resources you need to back you up. That is the whole reason why anyone gets in a Company. Same concept as a wolf pack. We are stronger when we are together." Before I even finish my little speech, she is already nodding along and rolling her eyes.

"I know, I know. That's why I'm here. The only reason." She replies. With a deep breath, she flips open the file cover and starts to absorb all the information. I can tell she is already lost in the folder and done with our conversation for now.

"Have fun!" I say with a wave and exit the room. When I turn to look back she in deep concentration and despite the fact I know all that I said was true; this is her best shot, I still regret having to subject her back into this life after she sacrificed so much to leave. I shut my door behind me and prepare to fall into the contents of my own assignment but I can't help but return to one thought. *I hope that she doesn't have to sacrifice anything more.*

.

CHAPTER 17

Celeste

"Other than work, that is pretty much all I have been up to. I have been having to work a little later this week, still trying to catch Ann up." Keirion's laugh trickles down the phone line, crackling a little from the distance. I join in, but not as hearty. "But what about you? I feel like I haven't seen you in forever CeeCee..."

"Yeah... I know! This new job... It's harder than I thought." I pause for a second, trying to compose myself, but the emotion finally wells up as I stare at the wallpapered wall of the latest hotel room that I was sleeping in that night. "I miss you, Keir."

"Love, I miss you more."

"Impossible!" I say weakly, but a smile finally flickers on my face again.

"I promise you. This weekend it will be you and me okay? We can have a movie marathon! Your choice. And I will make you homemade popcorn, deal?" I issue a real laugh now.

"So long as you throw some of those peanut M&Ms in the mix, you have yourself a deal." I sigh and flick my wrist to straighten my watch.

Our routine of talking on the phone has become predictable when Keirion hears this and mumbles, "Gotta go I'm guessing?"

"Yes, unfortunately, I do." I sigh again, just to make my irritation extremely evident. "Germany waits for no man."

"Or woman, apparently." There is a long pause and the miles spread between us now seem as tangible as the hideous orange and green comforter spread over the bed that I lay sprawled across.

"I love you, Keir."

"I love you, CeeCee. I will see you soon okay?"

"Okay." I can't even hide the crack in my voice, the tears welling up and a single tear spills out. I hang up quickly before I can turn into a sobbing mess. *You are a strong independent woman. You can handle a few weeks away from your boyfriend.*

I force myself to sit up and check my watch yet again. I really should be getting ready. While I was honestly in Germany, like I had told Keirion, I was not there however to try and break ST&T into the Berlin selling market. I was there for a certain Dutch ambassador that had a certain proclivity and distinct fondness for an exclusive night club in downtown Berlin. I drift my gaze over to the outfit hanging in the closet and eye it warily. I roll over and reach for my laptop to scan my notes one more time. The last three weeks had been a combination of familiarizing my face with the locals along with acquaintances of the ambassador, flirting with a very buff, blonde bouncer at the coffee shop I found out that he went to regularly, all while also monitoring the day to day routine of my target. I close my computer down and shove it in my bag, then force myself to get up and with an ominous feeling, I grab the hanger and start to get ready for my night out on the town.

I throw a wad of euros at the cab driver and step out onto the bustling sidewalk. I look both ways and for a moment I am in awe of the unexpected beauty of the night coming alive around me. Women in heels tiptoe together in packs, their makeup and hair done to perfection. The men are just as well-groomed and well dressed, already eying the women lining up to get into the various clubs and venues. *This is a little different then the Colorado and Nebraska bars I am used to.* I straighten up and channel my training. This is not my first mission since I have been 'back' but it is the first one that I am completely and totally out of my element. Yet in order to pull this off, I can not act like it. I pull out my phone and pretend to answer and appear very distracted. I stumble up to a door and do a double-take at the sign. I talk loud enough over the clamor of voices, growing louder by the second as more people spill out to enjoy the beautiful night.

"This guy totally just hit on me! I know right? Wait... Esprit is where you are right? Girl! I am right outside! I... shut up! I am going to come find you!" I continue my fake conversation loud enough that I draw the eyes of the bouncer standing out front. *Oh look, it's my new coffee buddy. Perfect.* "Hey! How long is the... wait, Peter?? That you?? Oh my god, what are the odds?" I can tell he recognizes me and even though I am seriously annoying myself, it works and a look of excitement sparks in his eyes.

"Damn girl, you look a little different tonight!" He

responds with his thick, but still, understandable accent, gesturing me over closer.

"I know... this is my PM wear not my AM." I cringe internally and send a silent apology to Keirion, turning on my charm.

"Do you work here?" I ask. *Like I don't know.* When he nods I bat my eyes and reach out and grab his arm. "My friend is actually in there. Is it cool if I just run in and find her quick?" He glances at the long line of people watching our exchange.

"I don't know..."

"Just really quick? Coffee on me tomorrow!" I wink at him and I know that it's a done deal.

"It's a date." With that, the whole sidewalk erupts with angry protestations. He ignores them all and opens the door for me to enter into the dark hallway beyond.

The steady thrum of the beat reverberates through the walls as I walk down the neon and blacklight hallway. I step between scattered groups lingering in space, gathering to make last phone calls, and meeting up with other members of their group. Finally, I step into the large room, the main dance floor area, and absorb the atmosphere. I can't help but pause and grin at the energy bouncing around the place. The song changes and I drag myself back to a semi- hidden corner to assess the area and try to catch a look at my target. I decide that a spot closer to the bar is my best bet for rooting through the tangle of people whose number continues to grow. *He will have to get a drink at some point. Unless he sends someone to get it for him, then I will have to revisit that plan.* After deciding that this still is my best route, I order a drink and melt into another one of the far corners. While I sit, I let my thoughts drift for a bit to my parents. They had met on a case that they accidentally both were assigned too, to make contact with a target in a club; not one even remotely similar to this one. That was the 70's in London. Not exactly the same scene as Berlin in the 2000s. Suddenly a face that looks familiar catches my eye briefly but then is lost in the crowd. Without being too obvious I stand and scan the crowd with quick eyes; no success. *Was that my guy?* I didn't get a great look, just something in my brain flared when I thought I saw something familiar. I sit back down when my search yields nothing. *Okay, plan B...* I look again over the room that I had been meticulously noting during my wait. *Maybe he is upstairs?* I pull out my phone and queue up my notes on the club. *Bingo.* The club had a private VIP lounge on the second floor.

CHAPTER 18

Celeste

I blend into the boisterous crowd gathering around the bar and swipe my hair up into a messy ponytail. I spot a discarded apron and snatch that up, adding it to my disguise. I send a glance downward and deem my outfit as passible for a waitress, albeit one who decided to wear a really tight dress to work. Shrugging this off after deeming it a detail no one else would notice, I slip behind the counter. *If you believe that you belong, then so will they.* I hear Naveen's voice echo through my thoughts. So I delve into the chaos of shouted orders and begin taking the extended hands filled with cash and making the drinks.

Once or twice, the other bartenders and staff eye me with confusion, but after about twenty minutes they accept me as one of their own and we all begin moving together in sync. Nobody had time to question the girl they have never seen before, and if she is pitching in who the hell cares.

Another fifteen minutes pass and I spot my opportunity. A ticket comes in from upstairs and I snatch it up. Grabbing a tray, I load it full of the ice bucket, glasses and dig through the ice chest for the extremely expensive bottle of champagne ordered. It takes everything in me not to gape at the number of digits added to the tab for this single bottle. I shove the bottle into the waiting bucket, trying to forget the total of what will be balanced on my hand. I smoothly hoist the tray into the air above my head. I hold my breath briefly when it tips a bit, but then relax when it evens out and remains steady.

I shout at the other staff members around me, "Be right back!" One of the male bartenders - Kurt according to what some of the already tipsy female club attendees had been shouting - smiles back at me in response.

"Don't trip."

I respond playfully with my tongue stuck out and then, like I do this every day, I make my way through the packed floor. Making sure my confidence is radiating, I reach the door that leads to the upstairs, only to find my way blocked by a huge security guard who stops me with a look. I halt and bite my lip trying to stifle my unease as the tray wobbles again from my sudden pace change. I hold up the ticket.

"This order came in from upstairs and everyone else was too busy." I flash him a hundred-watt smile and the man at last waves me past. Complete disinterest washes over his face when a group of scantily clad women sashay up to him and start commenting on his muscles. I breathe a sigh of relief and make my way up the stairs. The atmosphere between the two floors is dramatically different. While music is playing on both floors, on this level it is softer and more contemporary rather than the techno dance beats that thump below. I bustle past seven tables of suited businessmen and women all muttering in different dialects.

Finally, I spot the man I have been looking for, which coincidentally happened to also be the table that ordered the champagne I was carrying. I mutter a greeting to them and set down the ice bucket and glasses. After popping the cork and filling the first glass, I move to place it in front of one of the men and freeze. I take in the face, realizing this was who I had seen downstairs, and fight to keep my cool. I continue to distribute the rest of the champagne and turn to leave. I take a few steps and melt back into the shadow of a nearby empty alcove until I hear the familiar voice excuse himself from the table. I wait until he steps into view and reach out to yank him into the dark alcove to join me. Naveen's smirk is barely visible in the trickle of light reaching into the corner.

"What the hell, V?" I growl.

"I thought you would be happier to see me!" He feigns a pout. I only respond with an angry glare and crossed arms. Despite the fact that he startled me, I *was* glad he was here. While I was doing perfectly fine on my own, I at least felt like I wasn't completely alone anymore.

Able to read my thoughts, he breaks his pout and says, "Okay so what's the plan, Bond?" I think for a moment, mentally reorganizing a few things, now that I had my partner back.

I whisper the new plan to him, quick and quiet, filling him in with what I now need him to do. Our discussion is broken suddenly when Naveen's eyes suddenly flare open wide before I can react or question anything. He reaches out, cupping my face, and pulls it closer to his own. His lips meet mine and my mind goes completely blank. I gasp into his mouth and my knees threaten to give out. Grasping his back in an attempt to remain on my feet, my fingers wrinkling into his shirt. Seconds later, my brain catches up and at the same time I move to pull away in indignation, the beam of a flashlight shines into the secluded pocket we were in. Both of us jump apart wincing, and raise our hands to shield our eyes from the sudden light. When the possessor of the flashlight sees us, obviously in the middle of something, the twenty-something waiter only rolls his eyes. Redirecting the light back to the ground, the intruder grabs a box of napkin refills and leaves us in peace without a word. Reality swells back over me as Naveen immediately pulls away and straightens his shirt.

"Sorry. I uh... heard someone coming and figured any other way of finding us would lead them to ask questions on why we were hiding."

I clear my throat and reply, "Right, totally." We stand in uncomfortable silence for a minute.

Finally, Naveen says, "So I will see you back out at the table and we can finish your assignment." He ducks and weaves his head, moving it around until I finally made eye contact with him. "Cool?"

I just nod and force myself to smile. With a returning smile he leaves me and I hear him returning to the table. In the back of my head, though dazed, I can't help but think *I need to remember how he got* invited *to join them. This could have been so much easier!*

Adapting to the change of plans we had made, I discard the apron I had borrowed and release my hair from its ponytail, returning to my original guise of *girl out on the town.*

I had gambled the new plan for the rest of this night on the thinking that no one besides Naveen had paid any attention to the random girl who had brought them their drinks only a little while earlier. I toss my hair a bit to loosen the curls and pause briefly to lift my fingers to brush my still tingling lips. But I shove away the betraying thoughts and exit the shadows. This time I approach the table as pure party girl, channeling deep for my inner Ridley.

I stumble up to one of the other tables full of younger, yet obviously extremely rich gentlemen. Of course, they immediately want to befriend the girl showing up in a small dress, and what appeared to be an even smaller alcohol tolerance. So I slide into the leather-covered booth and snuggle up to the one closest to me. They predictably begin peppering me with friendly questions.

"What is your name?"

"What would you like to drink?"

"Where are you from?"

All that is suddenly cut off when an angry voice from across the walkway cuts in.

"That is my *girlfriend* you are snuggled up to." I look up with my drunken smile and see Naveen standing tall and indignant with his hand outstretched to me. "Wrong table there, love."

"Baby!" I squeak and jump out of the booth and the other man's arms, throwing my own around Naveen's neck. I feel him stiffen in brief surprise, but he adapts like the true professional he is and puts on the show of irritated, yet still in love boyfriend. After some coercion and "dragging" me over to join the table of his new buddies, we finally sit back down. Fortunately for me, I squeeze in next to the one and only, Ambassador Mertin Brann. He side-eyes me, looking irritated at being forced to sit next to the drunk girl so I decide to tone it down and fall into Naveen's shoulder, not having to feign my exhaustion. While slumped against him with my eyes shut, I draw up my mental whiteboard and envision my objectives that I had to have done to complete my assignment.

0 implant chip on phone

0 obtain a useable blood sample

0 gain access to his apartment where he has his encrypted laptop

0 download the plans for their nuclear material recently

found

Easy peasy.

CHAPTER 19

Celeste

Naveen orders me a plate full of food and some water, continuing to play the good boyfriend. Grateful, I help myself to the delicious plates spread across the tabletop. I know I should have eaten before arriving at the club tonight, but I was so nervous about my evening that I couldn't make myself. Now that I had Naveen there with me, I let myself soak in the comforting feeling of his presence. I feel him watching me and fight the urge to let my eyes drift to his. To think of what happened in the alcove was to linger on the past and on the fact I had just kissed a man that was not my loving, handsome, wonderful boyfriend. *Nope, I kissed the sarcastic, unreliable, ex-fling from school. How cliche of you, CeeCee.* I stop eating as the wad of guilt tightens into a hard knot deep in the pit of my stomach. *Just focus on your task and you can berate yourself later.* I reach for a swig of my water and curse loudly as the glass clips the edge of a platter, wrenching it out of my hand dumping its ice-cold contents directly onto the laps of Mertin and the girl he had been flirting shamelessly with. I snatch up all the cloth napkins in reach and begin patting him down before anyone else realizes what has happened. Seeing me get up close and personal with his chest and hips, he shoots Naveen a nervous yet satisfied glance. *Ugh. Perve.* I continue to wipe down the sopping man and apologize profusely, looking up at him with wide eyes. Naveen pulls me back to him and then takes the napkin away to dry the water coating my own front and legs. Still groveling loudly, with nimble near-invisible fingers, I slip the phone I had smuggled from Mertin's suit pocket during my watery mishap, into Naveen's pant pocket. With an exasperated sigh, he throws down the now useless cloth into a pile with the other soaked napkins.

"I am going to find someone who knows where there are dry towels." With a scolding look, he turns to me. "Don't touch anything." I dress myself in a look of shame while he is gone, but can't help the elation that floods through my system as soon as he calmly returns to our table with a stack of fresh napkins. *Chip in the phone. Check.* Naveen reaches over me, handing Mertin's date some of the cloths to continue mopping up the still wet Ambassador. When suddenly the pale shade of his hands are smeared with dark red. Spitting out a loud curse, he sucks his index finger as blood pours from a fresh slice. The poor girl gapes, looking like a fish, staring in confusion. Naveen reaches back out for the cloth and appears to investigate only for a second. Triumphant, he pulls out a silver pin stuck in the cloth.

"Ah geez, sorry, mate! The girl said it was fresh laundry, I guess it was too fresh." He tosses the pin in a nearby trash bin as the attending waitress, concerned at all the uproar, rushes over and begins apologizing profusely. This accomplishes nothing except to add to the chaos unfolding at our table and drawing the eyes of the other unfortunate patrons that evening.

I feel pressure in my right hand as Naveen palms the newly bugged phone to me and out of the corner of my eye see him slip the bloodied cloth in his pocket. *Now to put the phone back.* I look up to where Mertin is still standing, sucking on his finger and pouting like an upset two-year-old. *Can't slip this back in his pocket while he is standing... A* wave of panic starts to peak when he begins patting his suit, clearly looking for the phone that is not going to be there. I glance around the table and try to come up with a solution. Unless he is one of those people who lose their phone all the time, we were about to have a problem. Unfortunately, due to the fact people were going to so much trouble to get information from the phone, I highly doubted that he was usually careless with the device. So I toss the phone back into the booth seat and nonchalantly pat it down into one of the crevices between the seat padding. At that same moment, he erupts.

"Where the bloody hell is my phone? I am not dealing with this bullshit tonight." He whips to where I am sitting, leaning into Naveen while casually playing with his hair.

I look up into his eyes, nearly flaming with anger. "Maybe you lost it." I giggle and turn my attention back to Naveen. He casually strokes his thumb back and forth, his hand resting on my knee. I know he can feel my heartbeat racing and his hand continues to draw reassuring circles. *Wait. No, not circles. Letters.* Mertin begins accusing everyone at the table and is so angry now he is the shade of a ripe tomato. *C A L L. I T.* 44 20 7234 3456 I flick my eyes up to him, but he is focused on the show Mertin is putting on, growing more purple than red by the second. I roll my eyes and wonder why no one is stopping him or even why no one is speaking up. Pulling out my phone, I dial his number unseen underneath the table. The whole group freezes when the first chime of the phone is heard. Then the second, still silence. I look at Naveen, conveying with my eyes, *What the hell?* As the third chime sounds, I clear my throat and reach over to where Mertin had been sitting, wiggling the phone out from the crevice in full view of everyone. Mertin, still standing with his finger raised mid-shout begins to rapidly look more pink than red. Without a word, he takes the phone from me and sits back down, his remaining color now due to his embarrassment. I decide to break the silence.

"Well, now that that whole thing is solved, I think its time for us to depart." I shoo Naveen out the end of the booth and we quickly leave the still silent table. Neither of us can help the grins threatening to spread as we make our way back downstairs. But we both feel the pressure of waiting until we are outside, to avoid any chance of being seen and questioned at our excitement when word of the events from upstairs had traveled. I pass a waitress on the stairs and request two bottles of something containing alcohol sent to the table we had just vacated, slipping her a few hundred dollar bills for her trouble. Naveen looks at me, multiple questions fill his eyes. Trying to appear humble, yet still high off the elation of pulling this job off, I shrug seeming nonchalant.

"Should keep them occupied for an hour or so, wouldn't you say?"

Naveen continues to pepper me with questions as we slide into a cab outside the club. Finally, when I am certain it is safe I request the driver to turn up the music.

"We have the sample," I say gesturing with my eyes to the bloody napkin Naveen had stashed away, "the phone is taken care of, and now I have the key to his place so we can check out the laptop." A look of understanding lights in Naveen's eyes.

"Hence the bottles of booze you just sent to occupy them for a while." He laughs with appreciation. "Genius! You truly were meant for this line of work!" His laughter fades to silence at the look of my face after that comment. "That-that was meant to be a compliment. I... CeeCee?" I don't respond. Taking the opportunity to simply look at him, and my breath quickens when I realize how close we were, shoved together in the back seat of this cab. Tears well up in my eyes as I bite my lip, trying to compose myself from all the thoughts rushing through my head. I shake my head and turn away, facing the window and the dark street, empty on these slower streets at this time of night. I feel a soft touch brush my cheek, wiping away a betraying drop that had escaped down my face. He pulls my face gently towards his own again, and my breath catches at the look of pure longing on his face.

"V?" I whisper as his thumb drifts down and traces my lips with the barest of caresses, only the sound of our mingled breaths fill the cab. Naveen leans in even closer and my hands tangle in the front of his shirt, his fingers get lost in the tangle of my hair. With our lips only centimeters apart he whispers my name when suddenly a flash of Keirion's face appears in my head. I jerk back in horror. Naveen's face mirrors my own shattered heart and I retreat as far away from him as I can. In the sudden cold of the cab, I shudder and run my hands up and down my arms trying to create some body heat in my not so warm dress. Without a word, Naveen shrugs off his suit jacket and passes it to me. I turn away stubbornly until I hear his exasperated sigh and he throws the jacket over my turned back anyway.

"Thank you" I mutter, grateful for his obstinacy. At that, the backseat falls silent until we pull up in front of a huge house. I quickly compare the address we had given the driver and after confirming that he took us to the right palace, we pay the fare and step out onto the abandoned street. "I didn't expect it to be so... elegant?" I comment, but Naveen doesn't respond. He only stalks off to the northern corner of the wrought iron fence that surrounds the house that could only be described as a manor. The plaque on the front gate read something in German that, due to age, I couldn't make out along with a year, 1816. I turn just in time to see Naveen clambering over the top of the gate and I watch open-mouthed as he lands with unexpected grace. Unable to resist, I can't help but remark, "Have you been taking ballet lessons? The V I used to know would have not been able to stick that landing!"

He turns his dark eyes to mine and only replies, "You don't know me anymore then." At that, he turns his back towards me and vanishes into the dark shadows of the surrounding gardens.

CHAPTER 20

Naveen

Once I had been hidden in the darkness of the landscaping leading to the house, I lose focus and trip catching myself on the nearest tree trunk. I rest my head on the back of my hand pressed against the cool, rough bark trying to reorganizing my thoughts. *What just happened?* I mentally kick myself for what had gone through my head and what I had nearly let happen in the back of that car. *She still despises you.* The voice in my head interjects, full of malice. *She is just using you for what protection you provide. Once this is all done, she will vanish again and she will go back to her happily ever after with that guy.* I flip around and lean my back against the tree, gazing unfocused at the well-kept lawn. *This is what I chose. This is what I decided when she asked me to choose eight years ago.* I shove off the tree and continue onto a footpath and turn down it hoping to find a gate to let Celeste in. But I pause as a soft clang sounds, followed by gentle footsteps in the grass.

"V?" A whisper sounds through the darkness. *Pull it together, man.* I growl to myself.

"Over here, CeeCee. I was coming to let you in, but I see you managed." She eyes me warily, understandable after what I had said to her last.

"So... I was thinking the third window on the second floor looks a little loose. Doesn't even have a screen from what I can tell." I glance up at the window she was talking about and start to walk in that direction. She reaches out and stops me before I can take two steps, however and I shoot her a confused look. "Or we can just use this that I snagged from his pocket." I feel a surprising smile spread across my face as she dramatically pulls a bundle of keys out from her breasts and jangles them with a devious look. I feel my eyes widen and force myself to not let them drift downwards.

"Where the hell did you hide those?" I can't help but ask. Celeste only responds with a soft laugh and strides confidently to the front door, letting herself in before spinning back towards me and the front gate. With a calculated look and a gentle toss, the keys land with a loud clang on the edge of the walking path.

"Oops, guess who dropped their keys on the way out tonight." She spins back around and vanishes through the doorway. I huff a chuckle and cast a quick look around, then follow her into the silent house.

"V?" Celeste's sleepy voice calls out from above.

"Yeah?"

"How did you know I was going to try to make contact with my target tonight? At that very club?"

I roll over in my makeshift bed on the floor of Celeste's hotel room to see her face peeking out at me amidst the pillows and comforter pulled tight around her. I chuckle at the sight, she looks so much the same as when we met it makes my heart pulse faster.

"Because I know you, CeeCee, and it is what I would do." She doesn't reply so I keep talking to fill the silence. "We trained together and had to know each other's thoughts and actions so we could work well together remember? I guess that just kind of stuck with me." I laugh quietly. "Like a WWCD." Her eyes glaze over, clearly trying to make out what that means. "What would CeeCee do?" I explain and a look of humored comprehension hits her.

"Wow, you make it seem like I meant something to you." Celeste replies with a sudden a bite in her tone. I blink with shock at that comment and sit up, so our eyes are level. She just looks at the bedsheets and pulls at a loose thread, refusing now to look at my face.

"What the hell does that mean?" I ask, not bothering to hide my anger. She just rolls over, facing away from me.

"Nothing. Forget I said anything. Goodnight." I stare at her back with shock and lay back down, only to sit straight back up, my blood boiling.

"No. You don't get to say something like that and then just shut me down." I stand up and walk to the opposite side of the bed, where Celeste is facing. I can see her faintly in the streetlights gleaming through a gap in the window curtains. She flips back over to her other side, and I shake my head and stalk back around the bed again. This time she sits up with a huff and tucks her knees to her chest. She mumbles something in reply that I don't understand.

"What??" This time she enunciates her response, drawing out each word and sharpening it with malice and pain.

"Yeah, you made it clear how much you cared about me when I asked you to leave this," she gestures wildly, "and have a life with me." Then as she looks me dead in the eye she says even louder and more clearly. "Then you informed me how I was one of *many* girls and that in no way you were going to give up your life of *excitement* for *little old me*. So I could do what I wanted, but *count you out*." Silence fills the room and I struggle to find a response. I knew this would come up someday but I had hoped, like a fool, that it would not. I sink onto the edge of the bed, suddenly exhausted.

"CeeCee... " I say reaching my hand out for hers, but she bats me away and I shatter inside when I see her brush away tears filling up her eyes and start to trickle down her cheeks, pale in the soft light.

"I was- *am*- an idiot." I whisper. "I was a stupid kid and I freaked when you asked me to make that monumental decision." She doesn't move her head from where it rests on top of her knees, but I know from her sniffling that she is, at least, still listening. I move in a little closer on the bed and reach for her again. She doesn't stop me this time and I pull one of her arms free, taking her hand in mine. *I will take that as she is not going to kill me. Yet.* "The second you walked out that door, I realized how majorly I messed up, but like I said I am an idiot and was too proud to chase after you. I thought, like a teenage boy, that you weren't serious and you would come back to me and everything would be okay." I look down at our hands now entwined and feel my own eyes start to well up. I cough and blink, doing everything to hold them back and continue.

"I knew a love," my voice catches on the word, but I continue anyway, unable to stop now that I have started to spill my thoughts. "I *thought* a love like ours wouldn't be able to be conquered. By anything. If I had realized sooner, or if I had realized that you were serious... Everything would have been different." Celeste finally raises her eyes and looks at me, her beautiful green eyes shimmering as she asks the one question that we would never know the true answer of.

"If you could go back, would you leave with me?" My mind flashes back to the picture of us together that I had found hidden in her cupboard and I wonder how long that question had been on her mind.

But all I can respond is with an honest, "I don't know." And silence fills the room again.

CHAPTER 21

<u>Celeste</u>

It was two days later and I still didn't know what to think about the conversation that Naveen and I had in the hotel room. He had not brought it up since and I certainly was not going to break the silence. I watch him standing next to the luggage carousel waiting for his checked bag to appear. *You should be thinking about seeing your boyfriend after weeks, not staring at the man who abandoned you years ago.* Sighing, I turn to look at the airport exit where lines were growing longer by the second for a taxi. Turning to find Naveen again in the crowd, I instead spot a man with a large, colorful bouquet of flowers and a smile spread wide on a face I know and love so well. A face that I was not expecting.

"Keirion??" Before I know it, I am running towards him and have thrown myself into his arms. Crushed into his chest, I don't catch Naveen's look before he disappears behind us, melting into the crowd.

I fall back onto the bed with my arms spread wide with Keirion standing in the doorway laughing at me.

"You have no idea how good it feels to be back!" I take a deep breath, inhaling the ever comforting scent of home sweet home. Setting my suitcase down Keirion comes toward me and joins me on the bed, giving me a deep kiss. I feel my arms tingle and start to warm as he moves his hand down my sides, his strong fingers catch on my belt. My mouth goes dry as he trails kisses across my abdomen, pushing up my shirt. The look in his eyes goes predatory as I make quick work of unbuttoning his shirt, ripping it off to reveal his toned chest. I rake my fingernails just hard enough to get a response; he delivers by releasing a groan and with the next second my shirt joins his on the floor. As his hands trail down to my hips, our lips tangle together. Then my doorbell echos through my house. We both freeze, looking at each other. Deciding to ignore it, Keirion leans in giving me a deep delicious kiss and I tremble with the need for more. But another chime rings, so he breaks away, nearly growling with irritation. I laugh and shove him off of me. Throwing my shirt back on, I run my fingers through my hair so it didn't look so... *rumpled* and thunder down the stairs to answer the door; just as it rings for the third time. The concern I was starting to feel at the person's need for me to answer my door is doused the second I throw open the door to Naveen.

"V??" I hiss and pull the door closed behind me, stepping out to join him on my porch. "What the actual hell are you doing here?" I put my ear to the door to see if Keirion had come downstairs yet. One look at Naveen and I could tell the ease in our friendship that had been rediscovered the last few days had vanished.

"Well, you ditched me at the airport and I figured you would want this back." He practically shoves my accessory bag at me and turns to leave. But before he can even make it down the steps, the front door opens to a perplexed Keirion.

"Naveen? What are you doing here?" He spots the bag in my arms and looks at me with utter confusion. "Were you dropping that off? How- how did you get that?" Naveen and I share an *oh shit* look and both begin to give some explanation. But before either of us can get a word out, he cuts us off. Raising his hand and shaking his head, we stop our stammered reasonings mid-breath.

"Forget it. I saw that look. How is it that you knew she was home when she *just got home.*" He moves in between us, protectively placing me behind him.

Something must have made more sense to Naveen than it did to me because the look of a lightbulb going off in his head suddenly beams on his face. He doesn't respond, only lets Keirion continue.

"You had your chance and now you need to move on and leave her alone. If you keep up your stalking, we *will* go to the police and let them handle it."

Naveen just looks at me, clearly waiting to see if I was going to intervene. I bite my lip, trying to figure out what to do, and knowing that whatever happened in the next five minutes was going to determine which man walked off my porch. I take a deep breath and decide to take the plunge. Grabbing Keirion's arm, I pull him around to face me.

"Keir, there is something you should know." A mixture of surprise and wariness show on both of their faces, but I don't give myself I second to doubt my choice. "V and I are working together now. That is why he has my bag and how he knew that I was now home. He- he is not a stalker. He was with me on the trip I was on."

This time I don't stop him when he walks away. I only let my hand fall limply to my side when he pushes away from me. He reaches the end of the sidewalk and gets into his car. Driving away, he doesn't look back.

Not once.

I watch Keirion drive away and wonder if I should be worried at the nothing I was feeling. Completely numb, I turn my back on Naveen and open my door to go back inside. Gawking openly at me, he just murmurs my name and I turn back to him.

"Why?" He asks simply.

"I couldn't keep lying to him. He didn't deserve it." I shrug again, it seems to be the only motion I can make at the moment. My brain moves at the speed of molasses and

I feel like I am watching everything in slow motion and from a distance.

"CeeCee..." Naveen says again and this time, I wince at the pity that is thick in his voice. I turn to respond, but a sharp pinch and heavy pressure suddenly flares on the side of my neck, so hard that I stumble back. I trip on my doormat and unable to catch myself collapse in a slump on the ground.

Everything blurs and I can hear Naveen screaming my name as the world flurries with white and grey specks. I try to talk, but can't get anything out besides a choking noise and some unintelligible gurgles. Confusion floods me, and my brain can't understand why Naveen is so upset, I just am suddenly so *tired*. He pulls me in and cradles me on his lap, pulling me back into my slightly more protected entryway. I see him kick the door shut and pull out his phone, tears stream down his face and he peppers my forehead with wet, cold kisses while pushing my hair back from my face and gently rocking me back and forth. *He shouldn't be sad. I don't want him to be sad.*

I hear him saying, again and again, to stay awake, but I don't know why he wants me to. *I am so tired. He should understand I just want some sleep.*

"I love you.... Please.... CeeCee.... I love you..."

I try so hard to tell him I love him too, but it's too hard. *I am so tired. I will tell him in the morning.* And so I finally give in to the lull of being rocked in Naveen's arms.

CHAPTER 22

———————

       I laugh at the spectacle the man makes as he sees her drop to the ground and quickly fade before his eyes. *So much for all your training. It did you* so *much good.* I should have taken the man out first, but I saw her moving inside and didn't want to miss out on the opportunity of her standing, so stupidly, out in the open and unprotected. I look through my scope one more time to watch him shuffle both of them inside the house, clearly in a panic. *Too late buddy. Far too late.* I pull out my second dart and handle it cautiously as I replace it into its special protective case. *Don't want* that *to shatter.* I shudder to think of enduring the special toxin, twin to the one I just shot into Celeste Stone. I could have done the same job with a simple bullet, but this client was very particular on the details. He wanted a long drawn out death, painful to be exact. I look back for the last time through the scope to make sure the toxin was working appropriately and grin at the sight. *Three to five minutes for simulated death. Heart rate fades to almost nothing, then the real fun begins. The brain wakes back up but the entire body is paralyzed. Then the rot begins in the extremities and works its way inwards, hitting the brain last. But that is only if it lasts that long.* I snap a picture of the scene and then begin to disassemble my gun and exit the rooftop I had been sitting on all day waiting for Little Miss Sunshine to come home. *I wonder if she will make it long enough for the medical examiner to cut her open. Now that is a way to go. My client should be satisfied.* With a few quick clicks, I send the picture to them and wait for my payment.

Chapter 23

<u>Naveen</u>

I can hardly breathe as I feel Celeste's pulse beat more and more slowly, until it finally stops. I pull her closer and can't believe that I was *right there*. I should have done *something...* Now the woman I have loved for the last twelve years has died in my arms. Everything I sacrificed, all I said, and all I did to protect her came down to... this.... I push the hair back from her pale, but still beautiful face. Feeling my heart burn full of hate and anger, I want to run and hunt whoever took Celeste from this world, to make them pay. But I can't bring myself to leave her, not alone like this. I tense when I feel someone push on the door, trying to get in. I kick it closed again and begin to lay Celeste gently on the ground. I pray that it is her killer, come to ensure their success. But I am only disappointed when a voice shouts that they are there to help. I only remember then that I had called Belinda to send for anyone, everyone. She always fixed my problems, but this is one she can't fix. Not this time. I edge open the door and see a face I had seen once or twice at different times in our office. He pushes past me and throws a bag on the floor next to Celeste before he kneels on the ground next to her, then begins checking pulse, breath, and her neck wound.

"She is gone." I hear myself say, but the man just ignores me and before I can stop him, he has pulled a large needle and syringe out of his bag full of supplies and has jammed it into her neck. I freeze in shock to see it filled with the thick red liquid that I hate to think is Celeste's blood. I know I should be more put together. In my line of work, death is not only frequent but, more often than not, it is expected. But frankly, I don't give a damn anymore. *Focus, V.* My brain and body catch up to reality and I shove the man back into the wall and land a punch on his cheek and stomach before another agent arrives just in time to yank me off of him. The first man, totally unfazed, hurries back to Celeste and taking the syringe full of blood in one hand, pulls a machine out of the bag, and inserts the blood into it.

I stop fighting the man restraining me to watch, my curiosity starting to peak just barely above the grief. After proving that I wasn't going to assault him any more my restrainer releases me.

"I am Bruner and this is Grove." He explains softly. "After you called, Belinda sent out the alarm that two of ours were attacked. We are the only ones in Denver, so we both came running." He nods his head at Grove who was still clicking away at a series of buttons on the machine. "Correct me if I am wrong," he continues, "but you look okay." He looks me up and down quickly. I nod that he was right and try to catch my breath and explain.

"She was the target. Something her parents got caught up in; we thought we were aware of the danger and she was safe for the moment." My voice breaks and I try to cough it away. "I guess we- I- was wrong." I look down at Celeste laying silent on the floor and I can't look longer than a second without feeling the urge to vomit. I lean up against the wall and brace my hands on my knees. Bruner doesn't respond, just pats me on my back. *There is nothing to say.*

The machine begins emitting an alerting beep and all three of us look at it in surprise. Grove blinks and looks at Bruner with shock, then back down to the machine screen; double-checking whatever it was telling him.

"What??" I ask as seconds go by with no further comment.

"It's..." He gulps and shoots a terrified look at Celeste then begins packing up his equipment, hurriedly throwing it back in the bag. His haste is so intense Bruner and I look at each other and then back at him and start demanding answers. "We have to get her help. *Now.*"

I feel as if my throat is closing up at that. My mouth goes dry and I spit out the only question I can focus on. "She is alive?!"

All packed up, Grove throws his bag over his shoulder and motions for us to help him. I push him aside and with a heavy breath lift Celeste up, cradling her in my arms again and pulling her close into my body. I try not to let the hope of her still being alive die when I feel her lifeless body, already growing cold. I inhale her scent and try not to give in to the dark thoughts that are echoing through my brain.

"Where are we going?" Grove eyes Bruner and says with such reservation that I struggle not to rush over and shake him to explain everything, and fast.

"It is Revenant."

Bruner utters a gasp and whips out his phone and, rushing out the front door, I can hear him chattering on the phone, but decide to focus my attention on the one who will hopefully give me answers, so I don't pummel him again in return.

"It's an extremely rare and deadly toxin. Near impossible to detect and even harder to cure. There is a short window of opportunity for recovery and an even slimmer chance of survival." I try to interject to wring some more information from him, but he cuts me off, so serious, I take in every word he says. "Listen to me." I shut my mouth with a snap. "You have fifteen to twenty minutes to find someone who has an antidote. Maximum. And that is even rarer than the actual toxin itself."

At that moment, Bruner rushes back in with a grim look on his face. "I have the car running and I found someone who has an antidote that we can maybe get to in time. But you might have to make a deal with the devil to get it." He shares a somber look with Grove. "What is this worth to you?" I know he asks this with zero judgment and is honest about the cost, but looking down at the girl in my arms I already know what I am going to say, without having to think about it.

"Take me. Now."

CHAPTER 24

<u>Naveen</u>

Bruner and Grove exchange a worried look in the front seat, but I don't care. Refusing to let anyone even touch her, I still have Celeste cradled in my arms as I sit in the back seat of the speeding car. Unable to lift my eyes from inspecting every inch that I silently pray for even the slightest movement. Anything to keep my hope alive that Grove is correct and there is a chance she is still in there. I finally tear my eyes away to look at my watch, continuing my silent count down of how much time she has left. I know they are doing everything they can but I can't help it.

"Hurry!" I shout again, not bothering to keep my

pleading out of my voice. I see Bruner look up in the rearview mirror, his mouth pulled tight with concern, then press down on the gas pedal even more, now going fifty miles per hour over the speed limit. I send him a silent thanks with a terse nod and then resume my vigil of Celeste. Once or twice I jolt when I think I see movement, only to realize it was the bump of the car. After the longest ten minutes I have ever experienced we speed up into a parking lot of a large brick building. We all tumble out of the car and take off running, Bruner leading the way. He fills me in with directions as we run-up to the building and he throws open a door that leads to an old filthy stairwell.

"Third floor, second door on the right. Usually has some curtains or crap dangling in front of it. Knock four times and say you need help from the goddess." I do a double-take, and he nods. "Yes, you heard that right. Now *move!* You have four, maybe five minutes left. If you are lucky." With those words echoing in my head, I run up the stairwell full bore. My shoulders and legs burn from the extra dead weight of Celeste in my arms and I begin talking to her again, trying to pretend that everything was okay and I wasn't about to lose my mind.

"You always did like me hot and sweaty. And I am big enough to admit you were right, I really should train on stairs more. Never know when you have to run up a bunch of them." Finally, I throw open the door to the third floor, beginning to pray as I can almost tangibly feel the seconds of her life slipping from my grasp. I look down the hall and look for the identifying door of my savior. "Please baby. CeeCee, stay with me." Unable to knock, I kick the door four times as directed and yell, urgency pouring into my voice. "Please, I need help from the goddess!!"

No answer.

I try again. Nearly kicking down the door this time as I wail on the wooden barrier four more times. "Please, goddess! She is hurt!" The door is suddenly thrown open and I shove into the dark, candlelit room.

"It is Revenant toxin. She has seconds at least, a minute at most." I reach a relatively clean surface, a high top rectangular table, and shoving items aside, rest Celeste on the top. I turn to see the figure still standing at the door watching me.

"Please!" I plead, but the woman does not move other than to close the door and step into the faded light of the numerous candles balanced precariously throughout the room. I try not to flinch as her visage becomes clear; painted with tattoos, chains, and piercings her appearance, when unexpected, is a shock. "Help her! Please..."

She only tilts her head in response and says with a soft Greek accent, "Are you willing to pay the price?"

"Wha-? Yes! Just help me!" I yell, anger taking over.

She only shakes her head and asks again, "Are you willing to pay the price? Hecate's magic is not worth any cheap coin."

"Hecate...?" I stop distracted for a moment, then I remember what Grove said about a deal with the devil. I know I should ask more about what that means, but I can't bring myself to care. I square my shoulders, suddenly calm. "Yes. Anything. She is the love of my life. I will do anything."

At that, she nods in reply and moves quickly to a table full of tinctures and tins of dried leaves. In a flurry of movement, she throws a bunch of different things in a pot on the stove that immediately begins to reek of burnt rubber. I cough, choking for a moment on the smoke, but quickly the smell turns into a refreshing soap and peppermint scent. I turn back to Celeste and push the hair back from her face again and kiss her forehead. Weak I beg, "Hurry..." But she is already crossing the room towards us and before I can stop her, she raises her hands above her head and with a deep exhale shoves a giant needle straight into Celeste's heart. I roar with fury and move to shove the strange woman off of Celeste, but she yells before I can.

"If you move me *at all* you will doom your love for

good!" I freeze and can only watch helplessly as she begins inching the plunger down. Bit by bit, injecting whatever antidote she had just made directly into Celeste's heart. I grasp Celeste's hand and alternate whispering her name and placing kisses on the pulse-free palm. Minutes pass until the woman, at last, removes the needle and steps back, watching and waiting. I stare at Celeste, barely even allowing myself to blink. I feel tears begin to well up in my eyes again as ten minutes, then twenty, finally thirty minutes pass with no change.

"I was too late..." I croak and look at the woman still unmoving, staring unblinking at Celeste too.

"No, you weren't." She finally says and looks up at me smiling. "You got her to Hecate just in time." She points down and I follow her direction with confusion, then ecstasy floods me. The blush had started to fill back into Celeste's complection. She was still extremely pale, but life was beginning to shine out of her again. I inhale softly to try and slow my rapid heartbeat and call her name again.

"CeeCee? Baby? Can you hear me?" I say, moving up even closer and tucking her hand into my chest. I nearly jump out of my body when I feel a finger twitch against my own and I hold my breath in wait for another.

"You couldn't find a more comfortable bed?" A quiet groan comes from the table. My head cracks up from where I am watching her hands, so hard, I wouldn't be surprised if I gave myself whiplash. But I gasp in shock and cry out in exhilaration at hearing a voice I never thought I would hear again. I leap up and begin kissing every part of her face, until Hecate shoves me off and begins checking Celeste's vital signs, making sure everything is waking up appropriately. I stand back, but can not stop my exhausted grinning in pure relief. She looks back at me in awe until her blinking begins to take longer and longer.

"V, I am so tired. I am going to close my eyes, just for a little bit." She murmurs after a few minutes of being poked and prodded. I smile and lean over her, trailing gentle caresses across her face. I glance up to Hecate.

"Do you have somewhere she can lie down, other than this table?" She nods and gestures to a small room off the living area with a bed. I scoop Celeste into my arms again and gentle as I can, carry her over to the bed. I feel her rest her head on my shoulder and from her breathing, I know she is already fast asleep. Cradling her like an infant, I lay her down on the blanket- covered bed and tuck her in, all the while praying not to wake her. I move to leave the room and turn back for one more glance of her sleeping form. I pull the door shut and with a heavy sigh turn to Hecate who was standing, waiting in the middle of the room.

"Now what exactly is it that I agreed as payment?"

CHAPTER 25

Celeste

I regain consciousness, and know immediately I am somewhere that is not my own bed. I listen to my instincts and training; resisting the urge to move or make any sound. I hear people rustling around and muttering something indiscernible. From the tone that whatever they were saying, it was not well received. I hear two different sets of footsteps getting closer and at last, I can discern what they are saying now, so I focus on keeping my breathing steady.

"How could you have let this happen? We trust our girls with you and now mere weeks before graduation-" Another voice interrupts.

"This is the risk we all take. Unfortunately, it seems she was not cut out for this life and nature *eliminated her. She will be missed, but we all must move on. It is not in our nature to grieve." I recognize Headmistress Hansen's voice and unease sets deep in my gut. She continues, each word she utters makes me feel increasingly nauseous. "I let our contact at the media know to spread the story of a car accident and someone will contact her family, so on and so forth. Luckily she was only a* Charity student, *so it will all blow over and will be out of our hair by tomorrow."*

"Good." I now recognize the voice of my mother, nonchalant but deadly serious. "So long as you realize this will be the last risk you will take with a student's life. Or it will not be nature who eliminates you.*"*

Headmistress Hansen must understand the message perfectly because her next words are filled with tension. But she knows exactly who she is talking to and doesn't dare respond with anything other than a cordial, "Yes, of course, Mrs. Stone." Then with a clip of her heels, she leaves my mother in the room alone with me, the only sign of her true irritation is the slam of a door behind her.

With a sigh, my mother begins talking again. "Alright, you can open your eyes now." Busted.

I sit up slowly, only wincing a little when the pain spikes through my head; a welt standing out. Damn it. That is going to be a nasty bruise. *All my thoughts screech to a halt at the look on my mother's face. Face lined and grey, my mind returns to the conversation I had just overheard, and the smile slides from my face. My heart starts to pound faster when she slides onto the hospital bed that I have been laid out on, looking more maternal than she had since I.... well, ever actually....*

I bite my lip and ask, "What was that about?"

She smacks my hand before responding. "Quit biting your lip." She sighs, heavy with exhaustion. "There was an accident, and since you were present, Headmistress wanted your father and me here to tell you." I look around for my father, but she waves me off before I can ask.

"He is in Hong Kong at the moment and couldn't be here." I try not to let the disappointment show. Growing up, I had always had a better relationship with my dad. "Anyway," she continues, "good news is, you will have your whole room to yourself now until graduation." She rambles on like she was telling me what she had for breakfast that morning, but I don't hear anything more, my ears begin ringing and I go numb with realization.

I interrupt her, for the first time, ignoring the look of irritation that flashes on her face. "Pru... that was real?? *I thought that was part of the-" I cut off fully realizing now that thought had been ridiculous. My mother reaches out and grasps my hands in her tight, ice-cold grip; anything but reassuring.*

She hisses, looking around, appearing embarrassed, despite the fact we are alone. "Pull yourself together, Celeste." I tug my hands out of hers and feel the sting of her sharp nails slicing the back of my already bruised hands. "You didn't even like her, and besides, it is better that this happened now before she got out on her own for the first time then was killed viciously. The weak have no place in our world, Celeste. You know this."

My memories drift back to the nights shared with Pru; both of us curled on our beds, studying late into the night. The rare nights that we would attempt to act like regular teenagers, sneaking in sweets, and binge-watching episodes of Veronica Mars. I remember how excited she would get when she would ace each of her finals. "You didn't know her. How could you even be so flippant? That could have been me."

My mother doesn't answer right away, only sits in quiet thought. I stare at her, angry yet hopeful. Maybe some maternal instinct will kick in for the first time in my life, maybe she will apologize and give me some sort of comfort. *But I should have known better; when her next response comes, my heart breaks.*

"If it had been you, I would have had the same response." I gape at her, unable to even respond to that. She doesn't say another word, just stands and strides from the room. Not even a door slam. *That is as long as I can hold myself together. I collapse on the floor, hidden in the corner; sobbing for Pru, for*

myself, and for the lives we both could have, and should have had.

CHAPTER 26

Celeste

I jolt awake in a room I have never seen before, my head throbbing with each beat of my heart. I groan and reach up to feel the sensitive welt on my neck. It is that thought that propels me up from where I lay, onto my feet, but have to sit right back down on the bed as my head swirls and I nearly lose consciousness once again. Out of the corner of my eyes, I spot a woman with flowing skirts and a *ton* of body jewelry. I lunge up again and grab for a large stick of some kind leaning against the wall. But the woman, faster than me, grabs my wrist and holds it in an extremely tight grasp.

"Do not move so fast. Your body is still recovering." She says in a reassuring tone, and despite the initial shocking appearance, I listen to her and sink back into the comfort of the bed. "I am Hecate. Your lover had to step out but will be back shortly. He was beginning to smell after so many days without a cleaning." The woman, Hecate, moves with a haunting grace through the room lighting incense sticks and various candles. I should correct her about her assumption of Naveen, but that sounds too confusing to try and explain, even to myself. I start to ask her why exactly I was here, but she is out of the room before I can. I take the solitude as my chance to look around. It was a smaller room, but clean and cozy, even though it was crammed full of different knickknacks. Russian tea dolls, large iridescent seashells, silk oriental fans, and teacups decorate the walls, all interspersed with a hundred or more candles of various shapes and sizes. Hecate soon returns with a tray balancing a bowl of soup, a cup of tea, and a small fresh loaf of bread. Only then do I realize how hungry I am and I begin devouring it the second she sets it down in front of me. As she moves around the room, I try to find out where I am.

"So... your accent? It is Greek, right?" I ask between mouthfuls of the soup while she grabs some neatly pressed clothes from a dresser covered in paint splatters of green and white.

"Yes, I got chased out of my country about nine years ago and ended up here." She replies, smiling wide and showing all of her extremely white teeth. I swallow hard, gulping down a chunk of the bread, a whole new slew of questions race through my brain. But all of that ceases to matter when I hear a knock come from what I assume is the front door. Quick as a flash, she bolts to the door and I carefully rise to my feet and pad silent as a panther to the bedroom door and peek around, nerves rising the second I see her pull a small pistol from a pocket hidden in the folds of her skirt. She looks through the peephole and must feel reassured as she flips the deadbolt and stashes the gun back into her hidden pocket before opening the door. My relief is immediate when I see it is Naveen coming through the door and it takes everything in me not to run to him. I bite my lip and run my fingers through my disaster of hair. I decide this woman is my new best friend when I hear her tell him that I was changing and would be out soon. I glance back to the bed, only now remembering the clothes she had pulled out of the drawer. Jeans and a normal t-shirt. *Thank god.* Not was what I was expecting from her attire, but I wasn't going to complain about it. I notice on the farthest wall is a little washtub with a faded and slightly cracked mirror. I hurry over and rinse my face, wincing a bit at how pale I look, but then I have to shrug it off when I think about how much worse it could be. I run my fingers once more through my hair and come to the conclusion it is as good as it is going to get without a shower. With careful steps, I make my way out to join the other two in the main room. Naveen's gaze shifts immediately to me and the blood drains from his face. *Well, I guess I look worse than I thought....* I tug self consciously on the hem of the shirt but when I look up again, I am startled at the sight of tears filling his eyes. Without a word, Hecate looks between us and then quickly exits the room. We hear a door shut down the hall and Naveen cracks a smile, but the tears stay brimmed on his eyes. He sets down a steaming mug and just walks over to me, his eyes wide, as if he blinked I would vanish.

"Hey, V." He reaches me, hesitating only briefly before reaching out and cupping my face, just staring at me. Before I can ask him what is wrong, he pulls me in for a nearly bone- crushing hug.

"CeeCee... you have no idea." His voice breaks with emotion and he tries to cough it away.

"Can we sit and talk?" I ask, muffled from being smothered in his chest. Nodding, he leads me to the couch and we sit down to face each other. He doesn't let go of my hand but sits a little ways apart from me. I don't know what to ask first so I look at him, expectant for his explanation.

"Someone got you." He starts the story, fury filling his voice. "One second we were standing on your porch and next, you had a toxin dart stuck in your neck..." He shakes his head, still clearly distraught at the memory. "I thought you were gone. You had no heartbeat, no breath, nothing."

"Oh my god... but then how?" I gesture slowly at myself. "How am I here... alive?"

"Well I didn't know what else to do, so I called the Company, well I called Belinda, and she alerted everyone else. Two other agents live here in Denver and they came rushing to help. Thank god it turns out one of them is a medic for us and he brought this special machine. With it, he was able to test your blood and that told us that it was just a trick of the poison. You were actually alive! But we had only *minutes* to get you help and the antidote is extremely rare." He looks around at the living room of Hecate's apartment, decorated with the same style as the bedroom I had been occupying. We both fall into heavy silence, created by the realization of how close to death I truly came. "Thank god I got you here when I did. According to him, the toxin that you were shot with is literally living hell. He clenches his fist until his knuckles turn bone white. I reach out and pat it, attempting to calm both him and myself.

"Hey, I am alive. You saved me. Against *all odds*. There is no way I can ever repay you." I say and take a deep breath, absorbing all the information into my pounding head.

He eyes me, "You need to get some rest; I can tell." I begin to disagree, but he just shakes his head. "I insist. We can talk more when you can look at me and not wince every few seconds." I almost wilt with gratitude and he helps me off the couch. I pause before I head for the bed to fall into what I hope is a heavy sleep; I turn to look up into his dark eyes. I run my thumb   tenderly across his cheekbone, and before I can doubt myself, rise up on my tiptoes and plant a kiss on his sultry waiting mouth. I see the surprise shoot across his face and turn before I pad back to the comfortable room. In another moment of impulse, I swivel back around to face him and beckon to him. He is so stunned that he doesn't question or even reply when I shove him into the twin bed. Without another word between the two of us, I curl up next to him and within seconds fade into sleep.

CHAPTER 27

Celeste

       I blink awake to the bright rays of sunset streaming into the room. I look up to where Naveen sleeps soundly still, an educated guess telling me that this is the first proper sleep in days. Not wanting to wake him, I ease myself up off his chest from where I had been curled sleeping *and drooling.... Oops... sorry V.* I quickly wipe my chin off and yawn as I stand and stretch, pausing my steps when one of the old floorboards creak. I make it to the door without waking him and pull the door shut behind me as I exit the room. Making my way to the kitchen, I sniff like a wild animal, and my stomach rumbles at the delicious scent wafting from the big pot of stew that I find Hecate standing over.

"Smells wonderful!" I say, walking over for a closer look. She answers with a smile and grabs two bowls from a nearby cabinet. After filling them both with what appeared to be a steak and vegetable stew, we sit down on the worn sofa and contented silence falls over the room as we both devour every morsel of our meal. After we had consumed our fill, I decide to see what more I can find out about my generous host.

"So you said you were from Greece? That place is so beautiful."

She nods in reply, then with her melodic voice, "And you are from England, no?" I return her nod.

"How did you learn so much about medicine? You... you are so young!"

"You grew up learning about your craft, how to hunt and gather information. I just learned how to hunt and gather herbs. From there I just... adapted and learned more and more toxins and antidotes." She responds. "My mother and grandmother taught me everything I know. It is how she met my father." She gestures with her spoon to the door leading to where Naveen still soundly slept. "He was like your Naveen." I blush, thankfully she ignores this and just continues talking. "He got hurt and had to go to my mother to help. He must not have been too badly hurt, because much to my grandmother's dismay, nine months later they had me." She stands and returns to the kitchen, putting a kettle on and bustling around checking a variety of other pots simmering on the stovetop. When she rejoins me in the living room, she now carries two mugs of sweet-smelling tea, I pull it in close to my chest, absorbing the comforting warmth and letting the steam curl over my face.

"So do you know Naveen then, or how did he convince you to save me?" She looks uneasy and thinks for a moment before responding but she is cut off as a sleep-filled voice interrupts her.

"We go way back. I had to work with her on another job a while ago." Hecate doesn't respond or even look at me, only rises to her feet again and returns to the kitchen once more, this time filling up another bowl for Naveen. I eye them both immediately suspicious. Their story didn't exactly make any sense with Hecate's reaction. *But why lie about it? And to me?* I wave the doubt away and figure it is just one of her quirks. After all, it is kind of hard to tell her expression with all the jewelry dangling from her face. I look up at Naveen when he slides in next to me, rubbing at a pillow crease indenting the side of his face.

"Good nap?"

"Oh yeah. Slept like a baby! Until you started snoring that is." He accepted the bowl handed to him from Hecate and immediately begins slurping it up.

"When did you eat last??" I ask as he returns it to her, now emptied only seconds later. Hecate rolls her eyes, but floats back to the stove and fills it again. The two of us girls watch with silent awe as this is repeated two more times. Finally full, he wipes his mouth and moans.

"It was when we ate at the airport on our layover in Chicago." He counts out the days. "So three days ago."

Hecate chimes in. "So one for every bowl!" I laugh and an unusual look mixes with her smile but vanishes at some thought that hits her.

"I need to run to the market for some fresh supplies. I will be back in a few hours." Without another word, or even stopping to grab anything else, she stalks from the room, locking the front door behind her.

Naveen and I just look at each other in wonder, until Naveen is the first to say, "Well isn't she an unusual one..." We both break down in laughter for a moment and then it begins to fade; Naveen looks at me, laser-focused again.

"How are you feeling? You seem... normal?"

"Wow, *thanks!* I like to think I am relatively normal." He doesn't join in my laughter this time and I frown at the look on his face.

"No, seriously. Are you feeling back to yourself?"

"I mean, I am a little sore, especially my neck, but all in all," I stretch my arms out and wiggle around slightly to show everything working perfectly. "I feel basically like just a slight hangover." He nods, but looks away from me, attempting to hide the shadow that crosses his face. I grab his arm and try to turn him back to me.

"Woah... why? Do I not look okay?" He forces a smile that doesn't shine through the rest of his face.

"You don't understand, CeeCee. You were *gone*. You didn't have a heartbeat and weren't breathing." He shakes his head trying to make the memories vanish. Running his fingers through his hair, already sticking everywhere from his nap, he releases a heavy sigh. I don't know how to even respond to that and just continue to sit there in silence, trying to process it all, just like earlier.

"What was it?" I ask. As he explains about the Revenant toxin and everything it was supposed to have done to me, I begin to feel dizzy and nauseous. I must have turned an attractive shade of green because alarm suddenly flashes on his face and he stammers into silence. The damage is already done however and I run, covering my mouth and praying to make it to the bathroom. I doubt Hecate would be as welcoming if I disgorged the contents of my recently filled stomach all over her apartment. Luckily, I make it in enough time to even slam the door behind me to try and save some face in front of Naveen. After splashing my face and making sure I was settled enough to not have to go round two with the toilet, I finally open the door and rejoin Naveen on the couch. He eyes me with concern but thankfully doesn't comment.

"Who did this, V?" I ask, hoarse and whispering, once I trust myself to speak again. He sighs again and pulls out his phone, checking the screen.

"I don't know. Everyone at the Company is pouring everything into finding out. But so far, nothing." I chew on my lip trying to remember anything about that day. Suddenly I gasp as a thought dawns on me.

"Keirion! What does he know?" I swear a look of anger shutters in his eyes but in the next second, it is gone.

"To the world, CeeCee, you are dead..."

I gape at him when what he just says hits me. I can't even bring myself to argue with him though. It makes the most sense. If everyone thinks I am dead, no one is going to be looking for me. But it still doesn't stop me from feeling a bit upset at being dead. I get up and start pacing the room as I think about it more and more and the complications start piling up. *My boyfriend, well maybe ex-boyfriend, not so sure about how we left things. Either way, Keir thinks I am dead! And Ridley, man... and my house.... If someone steals my adorable little house from me I am going to be* pissed. But once I put these issues aside, the logical reasonings begin to outweigh them. *I don't have to worry about someone killing me, at least for a while. It might draw my parents out.* And finally, *It will give me time to figure out what to do, at least, hopefully, it will.* I take a deep breath and stop my circling. Only then do I realize Naveen has been watching me gingerly.

"So are you going to kick my ass now? Or have you decided not to kill me, at least right at this moment? I roll my eyes and shoot a punch into his arm.

"I am still deciding." I retort, but he visibly relaxes anyway. I pull one of the fluffy tribal pattern pillows close to me and squeeze it, trying to comfort myself. *But this isn't my pillow, and this isn't my couch....* I lean my head back, hoping that gravity will help the tears from spilling out. After several deep breaths and reminding myself that I am lucky to just still be alive; a few pillows and a piece of furniture are collateral damage I can handle. Once he is sure I am not going to puke again, he continues with more information from the few days I have been out.

"The police have questioned...." He stops abruptly at the name I know he is trying to avoid.

"Keirion? It's okay, V. I need to know what is going on." He tentatively continues.

"Yeah, they have questioned him, but it was determined that you were killed in a random robbery attempt from a local notorious gang member." He rolls his eyes, "The cleanup crew from work had a little too much fun setting the scene." I wince at the thought. "Of course the local police didn't take too long or too much convincing, since the guy has caused so much trouble in the past. Before now they hadn't been able to pin any of his other... indiscretions... against him. So they didn't look too closely." I stammer with anger.

"An innocent man is not going to be sitting in jail for my murder, when I am clearly *not* murdered!" I move to grab the nearby phone to solve this injustice when Naveen stops me with a laugh.

"If you do that, nobody wins." I pause, my confusion getting the best of me. Seeing my face, Naveen continues explaining.

"This isn't the first time the Company has had to fix a situation like this. They know what they are doing." He sighs. "The man is being *compensated* and he may or may not be getting out in the next few days, courtesy of one of our lawyers who will conveniently find a piece of mishandled evidence that will get him out with time served for all of his prior run ins with the law." I settle back into my couch, feeling better but still not comfortable with the situation.

"Other than that, only you, me, and Hecate know you are still alive and well." His phone buzzes and he glances at it again. "One of the tech guys found some footage from a business a bit up from your street and maybe it has your real shooter on it. They are going to send it if they spot anything useful." I nod feeling hopeful and start picking at one of the beads dangling from the pillow in my arms.

"How soon can I get into my house?" I blurt out. He grimaces and I can tell he was hoping I wouldn't ask that.

"Someone already bought it..."

"What??" I explode. "How is that *possible?*"

"After they said it was no longer a crime scene, some rich bitch showed up and offered to buy it. Cash offer. She already has a construction crew showing up tomorrow to start on repairs." I can't even think of a coherent sentence to begin to explain how pissed off I was. *In the span of only a few days, I lost my boyfriend, had my house and all my possessions sold out from under me, oh and I am dead.*

"Is it possible-?" I start, but Naveen cuts me off, finishing my thought.

"-that she is the shooter? I wondered and so did the police, but our check came through clean, and the story she gave the police during questioning made sense..." He hesitates.

"What now? What could be worse that you don't want to tell me?"

"She knew about the house because she works with Keirion. She had gone there to check on it with him on one of their late work nights when you were out of town." He spits all of this out with rapid succession like he thought that if he says it fast, I wouldn't catch it or would reduce the sting of what it all implied.

"Interesting." I eventually force out. But before I could launch into how *I didn't care,* Hecate busts back in through the door and with a flourish pulls a box of hair dye out of a woven bag.

"Time for a makeover!" She calls over to me.

I groan and catch the box as she tosses it at me. Yet, find myself unable to not smile at the unexpected look of pleasure alight in her eyes.

Let your plans be dark and impenetrable as night, and when you move, fall like a thunderbolt.

-Sun Tzu

CHAPTER 28

<u>Celeste</u>

I stare at the woman in the mirror and, with apprehensive fingers, caress my new dark locks. I meet the eyes of Hecate, who stands behind me hands clasped in anticipation at my reaction of her unveiling. She had stubbornly not allowed even a peek as she worked her magic.

"For the love of god... hurry up. Need I remind you, there is only one bathroom here?" I hear Naveen calling through the door for the millionth time, obviously growing more impatient by the second.

"Well?" Hecate asks, her eyes bright with an excitement

I hadn't seen before today but was growing more familiar with.

"I love it!" I almost whisper, not even having to lie; my breath was taken away by her hours of dedicated work. Through our last few hours in front of the mirror, I had begun to feel closer and closer with the woman who had saved my life. Beneath the quiet and hesitant exterior was a badass. While she worked, more of her story had begun to be revealed to me and I couldn't help but feel our connection and friendship grow even by the second. I turn towards her and pull her into a tight squeeze. At first, she stiffens with awkward hesitation, but soon she relaxes into it and even laughs when I pull away and tell her with complete seriousness. "You are my new hairdresser. One hundred percent." She blushes but doesn't reply. After one last, now confident, glance in the mirror I nod at her and she throws open the door. An unexpected man yell greets us; Naveen who had his back leaning on the door tumbles into the already tight bathroom. A pause of shocked silence is shattered as all three of us erupt into laughter. Finally getting to his feet, he lets out a whistle and tugs a strand of my hair.

"You know I loved you as a blonde, but you know, this works too!" I shoot him a playful glare and spin, my fresh, gently curled hair bouncing with the movement. Hours had passed as Hecate painstakingly filled my thick, long hair with a perfect ensemble of mixed strands of dark chocolate, caramel, and shiny honey gold. My stomach rumbles at those thoughts of food and the realization of how long it had been since I last ate. I turn to find the other two still watching me.

"What do you think?" I put my hands on my hips, posing for them. "Think anyone would recognize me?" When they both agree that unless someone looked very closely, that it was likely I would never be identified as Celeste again, I seize my opportunity.

"Perfect! That was the answer I was looking for. Can we *please* do a jailbreak and go grab some food now?" They eye each other, seeming to have a mental conversation. I get a wave of a sudden impression of a mom and dad uniting in telling a child no. But something must have been decided because Hecate sighs, but then agrees.

"I have no desire to cook right now anyway. Let's try out the new.... Bonnie?" She asks, looking for approval at the name she had suggested earlier.

"She always was my favorite character off Vampire Diaries!" At that response, Naveen rolls his eyes and reaches for his coat.

"What is open at 2 am?" He asks the two of us; Hecate shrugs but I know already what I want.

"Follow me, my friends!" I say grabbing my coat and handing the other to Hecate. With an exaggerated and faux sigh, they follow me out the door.

I wake the next morning with a start, curled up on the couch next to Hecate. Sitting up, the blanket that had been draped over me slides to the floor, where I spot Naveen sprawled out alongside a few pillows. Scattered across the tables were dozens of take out containers. Last night we ended up hitting a variety of late-night food trucks and by the time we had returned with stacks of styrofoam, we were all laughing and the worries from the last couple days had melted away.... if only temporarily. Hecate was slowly being pulled out of her shell and I hoped a lifelong friendship was blossoming. I tiptoe around the room stepping over various limbs, tinfoil, and styrofoam. Silent as a snake I snatch my jacket from where it hangs on a hook near the door and grab my boots. I ease the door open and shut as quiet as I can and slip through. Now out in the hallway, I release my bated breath and joyous smile. I had escaped my babysitters, at least for a little bit. I slide on my boots and jacket, finally making it out into the crisp fresh morning air. I inhale it in deeply. Then sigh when I hear footsteps behind me. I turn to find Naveen, sleep still lingering on his face, but his eyes are bright and smiling.

"Where do you think you are going?" he asks.

I look up at the sunny blue sky and the fog from my breath trails up and reaches for the clouds. "I just needed to see the sky today." I pause for a moment to gather my thoughts into a coherent sentence while Naveen continues to wait patiently.

"To think I was that close to death." I look down at the ground and pull my jacket in closer as the wind blows down the desolate sidewalk. "It made me think about some things." I stammer out. I turn to face the mountains and the direction that my old house is located. "I have to find my parents, V. Even if it is just to get my life back. They got me into this, and they need to help get me out."

Naveen clears his throat, and then asks, trying to not sound condescending, but failing. "And how do you plan on doing that, CeeCee? Everybody thinks you are dead... remember? You can't just go about yelling who you are and who you are looking for. *Especially* since we haven't narrowed down who shot you."

I shoot him an irritated look, then start walking back in the direction of the nearest coffee shop. "I have a couple of ideas." Then over my shoulder, I call back, "Tell Hecate I will be back for tea." He stands there, watching me go with his hands in his pockets and shoulders braced against the cold. I want to stop and turn around and say.... I don't even know. But I don't let myself. I can't make any decisions or promises to anyone until I get my life back in my own hands once again. I reach up to my bare throat and think of the ornament that used to hang there. *The key to my survival, and the last gift from my mother.* I pull out the phone I had slipped from Naveen and call for a cab while I stop at a coffee shop on the next street. By the time it finally pulls up outside, I had drained the delicious drink that had warmed me from the inside out. At last, I pull up in front of my familiar two-story, adorable, *safe* home. *Not anymore. Not any of those things.* The cab drives off behind me and I glance around at the surrounding buildings. The paranoia of the last time I was here is starting to affect me, I take a deep breath and collect myself, reviewing what I had come up with to get the new girl, *Ann,* to let me into my house. *I am Bonnie, the cousin of the girl who used to live here and I was curious to see if you had anything of hers still that I could maybe have.*

I climb the stairs ignoring all the patched bullet holes and boarded windows. After a moment's hesitation, I knock at the door, trying to ignore the weirdness of knocking at my own house. I hear footsteps on the other side, but as the door opens, I realized that everything I had known was a lie.

My stomach drops and I stumble back a few steps, nearly falling backward down the stairs. A smirking face looks back at me, just watching my reaction with pleasure. That is quickly wiped off her face as my fist connects with a crack and now it is her turn to stumble.

"Welcome back to the living, sunshine." Her reply comes coupled with the irritating quip in her tone that I remember so well.

"Same to you, *Pru.*"

CHAPTER 29

Celeste

After I had gotten over my initial shock, I storm past Pru, fighting the urge to punch the self-satisfied smirk off her face again. She follows me into the living room and I flop into my spot, for a moment, at last feeling like everything was back to normal. I want to curl up and fall back asleep, suddenly exhausted from my brain working overtime trying to comprehend the girl that I had thought to be long dead, now standing in front of me. *Then again, who am I to talk?* I take a deep breath and try to gather myself and my thoughts. I stare down Pru.

"Explain." I start. But she only shakes her head.

"You first, Stone." I debate arguing, but figure it is not worth it and is a waste of time to even try. So I give a quick explanation of Naveen and Hecate, but she takes it all in without much reaction. Nothing other than an eye roll when I mention Naveen and a brief look of shock when I mention Hecate, but I chose to analyze that later. When I finally get caught up to the present, she sits in silence thinking over all that I just had told her. Then with a sigh, she begins her own tale.

"There is a lot I am going to throw at you, but just hang in there until the end." She says this with such intensity that I can only agree. I can't help but be in awe of the contrast of the girl that I used to know compared to the collected woman sitting before me, despite the same attitude problem and irritating smirk.

"The day before my *accident*, I was contacted by a mysterious client with a job offer. The catch was I would have to die, and I could not know who I was working for until I was extracted and my prior life over." She shifts in her chair, looking for the first time upset. "So that night, we both went out of the window. But the fall, for me, was planned... and I was given an extremely powerful sedative that made me have the complete appearance of death. Similar to what you got shot with, only with the antidote built into it, so it just wears off after a certain amount of time." She falls quiet for a bit and I continue to wait eagerly for the truth at last. She opens her mouth to continue with her tale but then closes it with a snap. "I need some wine. You?" I laugh, unbelievably not forced.

"Oh god, yes."

She returns a minute later with two large glasses filled to the brim with white wine and takes a few large swigs before returning to her seat and continuing.

"Okay so this is where it gets.... well you will see.... The next thing I am aware of is waking up in a sort of castle or mansion. It had this amazing driveway lined with trees and a little lake to the south, with a giant hedge all around the property. Everything was decorated with a family crest and it was like stepping back in time." She looks at me, partially expectant and the other part hesitant. My blood goes ice cold and a tingle of uncertainty trickles up my spine, causing goosebumps to break out all over my arms. Her description had been uncanny, and too similar for a coincidence. *Nonsense. There are hundreds of old places that could be described the same way.* But I can't stop the feeling of dread mixed with disbelief from starting to churn in the pit of my stomach. I swallow hard and listen to the rest of what she has to say, trying to remain stoic.

"I have only spoken to my employers in person a grand total of four times. This day would be the first time that it was revealed who I had, in a word, *sold* my life to." She takes another long drink from her glass and I do the same.

"I tell you all this so you know that one hundred percent, I had no clue or even an inkling of who I was working with." She shakes her head, anger flashing briefly on her face - anger at herself. "I should have asked more questions. But I was young and wanted to prove my worth. I know what I was to those people. *The Charity.*" Her anger is now replaced with pride. "The first Charity in thirty-two years to make all the way to graduation." She takes another gulp. "Anyway, I walked into the dining room of the place, and I knew exactly why they had been so secretive in their identity. Even in our line of work, incredibly secretive." She stares down at some focal point on the floor and then as if she were bracing herself, she practically spits out, "It was your parents, Celeste. I was hired by the Stones."

As if this day could not throw me for any other loops, my whole world shifts yet again. I nearly drop the wine glass I had cradled in my hand. Pru eyes me, concerned.

"I- I don't even know what to say to that..." I say, honest.

"Yeah, been there.... Unfortunately, that is just the tip of the iceberg. I told you, there is a lot you are going to learn today." I look down at the glass, thankfully, still in my hand and without a second thought, drain the glass completely. I then nod at Pru, and she proceeds.

"They had the usual welcome we were told to expect: these are the accommodations, pay, how we will contact you, etc. But for me, they had a special mission. They said, yes I may get called away from time to time to assist on other assignments, but my number one priority is and will always be *you*." My head darts up and I catch her dead in the eyes.

"Me? What does that *mean*?"

"This was the plan." She gestures her hand at our surroundings. "Your mom was the mastermind behind it, I gathered, but your dad supported it fully."

"I still don't understand."

She sighs, impatience bubbling over. "They wanted you out. And they were going to do anything to make that happen. They orchestrated, pushed, and made things happen to cause you to doubt it all and want something different. All of it."

I stare at her, completely dumbfounded.

"I don't know exactly who all has been in on it, but I know for sure I was not the only chess piece in motion.

Everything, even down to the conversations your parents had with you, all was to plant the idea that you wanted a normal, *safe* life." She falls into a revere to let me process all of this overwhelming information.

I think back to everything that had lead to my decision, but decided to hold off until I knew the whole story, because from the look on Pru's face, she was not done.

"So to sum up, I have always been two steps behind you, watching for threats, monitoring you, and letting your parents know you are okay. They don't actually know where you are. That is why they brought me into the fold in the first place. They don't want to know anything that could put you in danger and draw you back in."

I open my mouth to interrupt, but she shoots me a visible *shut up* and I decide to wait.

"Then one day, I catch word that Chen Feng had taken an *extremely* large hit out on you. I was shocked how that had gotten past me and right away contacted your parents as instructed. But I received no reply. Now obviously, I couldn't just come striding up to your door for something I perceived as what could be a minor threat. I had no information if this was even a valid threat who had your location and information or just someone who was angry and wanted to throw your name and some money around." She sounds exasperated now. "So I did the only thing I could think of.... I sent a little trickle of information to an agent at Sentinel Security Co. where I knew the ex of yours currently worked. I was hoping that when he caught wind of that he would do - well not exactly what he did - but the general idea of it." Pru rolls her eyes and glares at me. "I never could have dreamed that he would pull you back into the very thing so many people have tried to keep you from for years and *years*. But that you would be *stupid* enough to just dive back in??" Releasing a groan she stands and starts pacing around the room. "I was dreading the fact I was going to have to go back to your mom and say, oh yeah sorry I fucked up and now your daughter is back and working for Creepy Old Bently. Sorry!" She takes a heavy breath and collapses back into the chair. "So I tried to run damage control. I conveniently caused one of your boyfriend's coworkers to come into a generous amount of money from a 'distant relative' and the lazy man snatched it right up and quit his job." She releases a loud laugh at her genius. That is when a lightbulb goes off in my overloaded brain.

"Ann.... Prusilla Ann..." I gasp. "That is you!"

"Um duh. Try to keep up here please." I can't help but smile at the conversation that makes me feel back in the Academy again. "I then got all friendly with your *gorgeous* boyfriend to keep a close eye on you as you are flying all over the world." She shoots me a patronizing look. "Then you go and get yourself shot!" She throws up her hands with exasperation.

"In my defense," I butt in, pointing the blame back at her. "That was completely unintentional and not exactly my fault." She concedes that point with the nod of her head but continues to glare at me.

"Intentional or not, it was stupid and I thought you had been killed." She waves away the thought. "It gets only worse. I tried to contact your parents again after the attack... still no response." She looks hard at me, clearly trying to figure out how to say what she wants to. "They are missing. Both of them."

Out of everything she had just told me, this was what was harder to believe. *My parents are missing? That is impossible. No one would mess with the Stone family. We are not exactly fluffy bunnies. Hell, our family motto comes down from our ancestor Caligula. Oderint dum metuant. Literally translated to 'Let them hate so long as they fear. Not exactly welcoming when it is inscribed on every heirloom and wall of the Stone estate.* I realize all of a sudden, reemerging from my thoughts, Pru is watching me with concern.

"I just can't believe that they would be in danger or even anyone would threaten them. Stone justice is swift but harsh. The only reason that they would even come after me at all was because I left the protection behind when I was exiled from the family."

Pru looks unsure, but not as wholly freaked as she was a moment before, slightly reassured.

"Well, we have to find them. They are my key to figuring this all out. My guess is that they all went underground."

Pru looks skeptical. "And how are you planning on doing that, sunshine? I have tried everything to find them, but they are just gone."

Now it is my turn to smirk. "Come on, give me some credit." I look around at the living room, distraught at the sight of my wall, punctured with the bullet holes created by the cover-up crew from *Sentinel Securities*. "That is the reason why I came here today, I needed to grab something that can help me hopefully find them." I then ask her something that had been bothering me. "Why did you buy my house? Just to spite me or something?"

She laughs, "No, I am not that petty! I just figured your parents would probably want some piece of you, so I bought it just in case." She laughs again, this time maliciously. "Your boyfriend was *pissed*, by the way, when he found out I did." Pru looks at me and raises her eyebrows, mischievousness shining out of her eyes. "You do know he has been a *wreck* since you, well died. Didn't even jump at the chance when I made a pass at him yesterday."

I jump to my feet and take a step forward, preparing to jump on her, but she holds out her hands, looking a little afraid; an unusual look for her. *I could learn to like that expression on her* .

"Hey, hey! I was joking!" She insists, then under her breath mutters, "I only *thought* about it."

I decide to just ignore her; starting up the stairs and glancing behind me to ensure she wasn't following me, at last, I let myself into my bedroom. I close the door behind me for privacy with a click. I take in my small yet bright bedroom, my sight lingering on my bed, but shake off the urge to sink underneath the sheets and ignore the world. Instead, I slide my boots off and, the bed creaking, and climb up onto it. With an expert twist, I pop out the whole light fixture and reach into the newly visible opening into the ceiling. After prodding around with my fingers, I finally locate the small box I was looking for and drag it out before snapping the fixture back into place. Reclining back down on the mattress, I open the box, a strange feeling of nostalgia passes through me as I recall the moment I was given this particular heirloom. The ancient, engraved locket inscribed with the family motto had been passed down generation to generation. The silver circle gleams in the light streaming from the windows as I clip it around my neck. I inspect it and remember my mother's words, fuzzy after the night of heartbreak and disbelief. I was gifted this treasure the night I had told them I was leaving school, without signing with a company and was planning on having a normal civilian life.

Only now that I knew the truth behind my parent's actions leading up to my decision, did their actions after my news begin to make any sort of sense. Their response to my decision had been hours of debate and finally, with the judgment from the patriarch, my grandfather, it was final. I was exiled from the family as of that very moment. I then had to walk in shame past the stony faces of my aunts and uncles who had been called into the deliberation and had given me zero support, aside from my favorite uncle, Joseph Stone. He had at least given me a sympathetic smile and, without the awareness of the rest of the family, pulled some strings to get me a full scholarship and into a great college, despite the fact, I had zero references or anything viable to add to a college application. I undo the clasp and stare at the words that every Stone was taught as soon as you were able to form a thought. Against all of my better judgment, my thoughts are drawn back to the last memory I have of my mother.

After departing the house, I fight against the tears threatening to stream out, turning only at the sound of my name. Chasing me down the path to where a car was waiting to take me away, was my mother. Uncharacteristically, she looks distraught, the only reason I don't let her know all the betrayed thoughts that were sloshing around my head.

She presses an ice-cold disk into my hands and says, "Never forget the power you have inside you. If you ever need safety or need somewhere to go, when you have nowhere else to turn, this is the key." I start to question her, but she cuts me off.

"Just listen! If you have an heirloom, you get admitted into any Stone estate. No questions asked. This is your back up plan. Only use it in dire need. They will take it from you when they discover you have been exiled." She pauses and for the first time in my life, I see tears shining in her eyes. She cups my cheek with her coarse, action torn hands and smiles sadly at me. "I wish I could have done more.... Be happy, my Celeste." With that, she closes my hand over the disk and pulls away. Not looking back, she returns to the house. I watch her go, hoping that she would turn back. She never did.

As the heavy door slams shut behind her, I look down at the object she had pressed into my hand and see the shining of the locket.

CHAPTER 30

Celeste

I rejoin Pru who has now migrated into the kitchen. When I walk in, she ends a conversation and hangs up her phone.

"Got what you came for?" She asks, with a curious gaze. I ignore her questions and ask one myself.

"Who was that you were talking to?" I know I sound paranoid, but after everything that I had been through lately, we both know that I have every reason to be. Lucky for me, she doesn't avoid it.

"I heard back from another contact of your parents. Still no word." She looks out the cracked and taped up window, concerned and distracted now; lost in her thoughts. I try not to let myself dwell on that issue, drawing my attention to one problem at a time. I feel a buzz from my back pocket and pull out Naveen's cell phone. I wince at the multiple messages that pull up on the screen, all from an unknown number that I would guess was Hecate's.

12:02pm You stole my phone?? You could have just asked you know....

12:05pm What happened with the Ann chick?

While reading the waiting messages, a new one pops up on the screen and I try to hide my smile from Pru, but she looks over my shoulder suspicious before I can stop her.

12:06pm Need help hiding the body? :)

"Nice." Is all she comments, issuing a snort of laughter. I dial the number and Naveen quickly picks up.

"Is that a yes? I will bring a shovel."

"V.... no!" I pause, trying to think of what all to say over the phone. I end up deciding to say nothing, despite the knowledge that his phone is more than likely secure; in the wake of all that I have just learned, I don't want to take any risks right now. "Just get over here okay? We need to figure some stuff out."

"Okay...? Blink twice if there is a gun to your head." He says, dripping with sarcasm.

"Haha."

I hang up, muttering under my breath, and the familiar tone of my doorbell chimes through the house before I can return the phone to my pocket. Pru and I both freeze, wide-eyed, staring at each other. She motions at me to hide, and she moves to the front door to open it. I can't see anything around the corner from where I stand, silent and motionless. Yet, I relax when I hear a familiar voice spout out a stream of curses. Naveen steps into the house, the shock still plain on his face.

"What in the land of hell is going on! Does Satan know you snuck out?" Needless to say, Pru and Naveen had never gotten along very well, about as well as Pru and I did. When he finally sees me and discards his coat on the hook, he stares me down, daring me to explain.

"How did you get here so fast?" Incredulous at his sudden appearance, I don't even try to hide my surprise.

"I have been standing outside for about twenty minutes. Couldn't have warned me, huh?" He asks and holds out his palm out between us. I shoot him an apologetic look and slip the phone back out of the pocket and into his hand. Before I can pull my hand back, however, his fingers close over my own ever so gently. Stunned for a moment, my eyes meet his own and I tilt my head, questioning at the look in his eyes. But as quick as it happened, he had released my hand and was moving into the living room as if nothing had happened at all. I look up from where I am standing, at the edge of the kitchen, and see the large frame filled with the picture of Keirion and me. *That was such a different day.* But I don't let my thoughts trail any further than that. *There is no use dwelling on it until there is something I can do about it.* I take in a heavy breath and return to my spot on the couch. I can tell from the expression on Naveen's face that Pru was filling him in on the craziness that I had just been privy to that day. Finishing her tale for the second time that day, Pru falls into a contemplative silence. This time when Naveen meets my eyes, they are filled with sympathy.

"Are you okay?" He asks and I want nothing more, to be honest, then to collapse into tears while he pulls me close and helps me understand everything. Instead, I straighten up and force my internal strength into my facade. I know he can tell it is an act, but graciously he doesn't push it right now. Like a sixth sense is letting him know just how fragile I truly was at that second. He turns back to Pru and thankfully starts to take charge.

"When was the last time you or anyone else had contact with the Stone's?"

"From those who have been willing to give me that information, thirty-six days since last contact. After that," She shrugs, "nothing from either of them."

I watch as if from a distance as they both fall into habits from years of training. After a while of information exchange like this, and both of them trying to come up with the next step, I clear my throat and their attention snaps back to me. I stand and unclasp the chain to pull the locket out from where it hangs hidden underneath my shirt. I let it dangle midair and they watch it swing back and forth, confusion plain on their faces.

"This is our next step. Stone's have our own resources and with this I will have all the access we need. If anyone knows where they are or what happened to them, it will be at the main estate in Wales."

"It's pretty, CeeCee. But I don't understand how a piece of jewelry will help us." Naveen says. Pru helpfully cuts in. "You wouldn't, numbskull. That is the beauty of it. It's a key, isn't it?" She turns to me for that last statement and reaches out to take the locket. I tug it back from her out of impulse and slip it back around my neck. She retracts her hand, but I see a glimpse of hurt from the lack of trust between us.

"I'm sorry. I just can't let anyone take it. It is the last piece I have from my family."

"I understand." She says, and I believe her. We all fall silent now, lost in our thoughts. After a short time passes and I realize how hungry I am, I hold out my palm to Naveen and he looks strangely at me. I laugh at the unusual face for him.

"I promise to give it back! I just want to order some food." I put on my expert puppy dog pout and, with an exaggerated sigh, he returns the phone to me. I order an unusual amount of food for three people, but I am ravenous and can't decide what I want. I hang up and take in the humored faces on the other two.

"I'm hungry!" Is all I provide in response, and with raised eyebrows they shake their heads in unison. A thought dawns on me and smacking my forehead, request the phone back.

"What now?" Naveen asks, exasperated.

"I forgot to tell Hecate to meet us here."At that name, Pru lurches up straight and glares at Naveen. I stare in consternation at that reaction. "What??"

But she only directs her attention to Naveen. "Yeah. Meant to yell at you about that earlier, but got distracted. What the HELL were you doing taking her to Hecate?? What deal did you make with the devil? What was the cost?"

My disbelief changes to outrage. "Hey. Don't talk about her like that? She didn't even ask for anything! Tell her V." I spin around, only to see him avoid all eye contact. At that non-response, I sink slowly into the couch.

"V?"

"I took on the cost. There is nothing that you have to worry about." Still avoiding both of our gazes, he stands and walks from the room. "Excuse me." I watch him leave, completely thrown.

I turn to Pru who was watching the two of us, arms crossed and smug. "I don't understand. Hecate is so nice. We were.... I thought we were friends... or something." I let my head drop into my hands, trying to relive the last few days spent, the three of us. "What did I miss?" I ask, looking up at Pru again. This time her face is colored with pity.

"I learn more and more that I actually know nothing at all about anyone..." At that, I stand, and following Naveen's example, I exit the room. Instead of leaving, however, I return to my well-known place of comfort and peace. Shutting my bedroom door behind me, I hear the chime of the doorbell. Despite the lull of my empty stomach and the smell of delicious food trailing up the stair; I ignore it and kick off my boots once again. This time I give into my urge and slip underneath the familiar cotton of my sheets. Two breaths later, I fall fast asleep.

CHAPTER 31

<u>Naveen</u>

After a quick walk around the block, I return to Celeste's house. Locking the door behind me. I find the house is quiet and only find Pru, making tea in the kitchen. I lean up against the wall and cross my arms. She doesn't acknowledge me, other than to grab for another mug and fill it with a tea bag and some boiling water.

"That was nicely handled. Thanks for that." I can tell from a quirk of her lip that she is withholding a smile and laughter. She hands me the steaming mug and we both sit down at the small table in the breakfast nook.

"You have learned nothing, Naveen. And don't think I

don't know the part you have played in this whole thing."
I spin to face her, listening and looking for any sign that
Celeste would overhear us.

"Keep it down. You don't know anything about me." Pru
shrugs and takes a sip.

"I am just saying, better she finds out from you than
from-"

"I am perfectly aware. And I will handle it when the
time comes." I cut her off, no trace of any humor in my
gaze. "If you take that chance from me, make no mistake,
you will not like my revenge."

When she does not look affected in the least, not even
pulling her gaze from mine, it is me who is the first to look
away, irritated that I was not intimidating. *Wow I must
really have lost my touch. That or time has faded my memory of
how intense this chick is!* Begrudging, I listen as she beings to
talk again.

"Our main priority is to keep the *Princess* safe. So
nobody can know she is still alive, unless it is a dire need."

"Obviously." I bite back. "Where is she now, anyway?"
She points with her chin to the stairs. "Upstairs. I would
presume from the lack of footsteps that she is taking a
nap."

We both fall silent and not another word passes between
us until the empty bottom of the mugs were both visible.

"Do you think her plan will work?" I ask, trying not to sound as worried as I feel. It takes a bit for her to answer, but when she does, it is far from reassuring.

"I don't know. But it is the best option we have right now. If she seems to think it will work, we have to believe her." Pru thinks a moment, "You know best how we didn't particularly get along in school-"

I snort derisively, "Yeah, I remember."

She rolls her eyes, but continues her train of thought. "What happened after I... well, died? Nothing I saw in her would have lead me to believe she would completely abandon her life. Her parents were so convinced, but I was *not*."

"It was you." I answer.

"What?" Surprised, she watches me, trying to catch a trick of some sort.

"After you died, everyone including the Stone's, told her to move on, that it was an accident and one that was an eventuality for you." I look at her apologetically, but when she doesn't stab me or stop me, I continue. "Your death caused her to see the lack of value we place on a life, that our world has to see. She realized that is not what she wanted. She wanted to have a long happy life." I sigh and run my fingers through my hair, distressed. "And I ruined it. I dragged her back into it all."

Pru doesn't move to reassure me, just lets me stew in my guilt. That in itself was comforting in a way. I didn't need anyone to make excuses for me. And I am sure in her own way, she felt similarly. After all, her one job had been to protect her and keep her unaware of the dangers all around her.

As if echoing my thoughts, she says quietly, "We both let her down. All we can do now is to help her."

I was in the process of making late-night omelets from the remaining eatable items still in Celeste's fridge when Celeste finally comes back down to join Pru and me. Pru is lounging in a chair pulled out from the table, feet propped up on top, and is flipping through a magazine. She had been running a steady commentary the entire time I had been in the kitchen, but I quit listening after the comment, "Huh.... if I were a type of Mexican food, I would be a taco! Cool..."

She joins us in the kitchen, sleep still filling her eyes, puffy from apparent tears. My heart melts at the sight and I want to pummel everyone responsible for everything happening to her, including myself. I tried to not let it show how much of what Pru said to me earlier were things I was already telling myself. *But if CeeCee ever finds out I doubt she will ever speak to me again. Now that I have her again, I don't want to let her go.* I turn back to the stove and scrape plates full of eggs for Celeste and Pru. As Celeste joins Pru at the table, they both dig into them and before I can even join them, they are done and looking at me with their eyes pleading, hungry for more. So I fill their plates up again and finally join them at the table. After all of our plates are emptied again and the mandarin colors of sunset shine through the window, Celeste breaks her silence.

"Okay. Here is what we are going to do." Looking at me, she continues. "We are going to pay a visit to work. I have something I need to grab from my computer. Pru, I need you to get us tickets to London. From there we can get a cab to Wales. It will be pricy fare, but sell my tv or something for cash." Pru and I exchange a look of uncertainty but don't dare to interrupt. The look in Celeste's eyes borders on maniac and it makes me extremely wary. But neither of us can argue with that plan.

"I just have a few questions." I finally ask. "How do you plan on getting to work without being noticed? You are dead remember?"

Pru adds in. "Yeah, and by us and we, who do you mean? Which us?"

Celeste gaze bounces between Pru and me, all business. "Both of you. I am going to need both of your resources. And V, you will distract the receptionist that you are so fond of, and I will slip in. Plus if we go in on Friday right before 5; hardly anyone will still be there." She waves off the unenthusiastic look on my face. I turn to Pru, hoping for her to cut in and point out how flawed this plan was. But quite the opposite, she has already on her phone and is pulling up the Denver Airport flights.

"When do you want to leave?"

Celeste doesn't even have to think. "Tomorrow night."

My jaw drops. "We are going to need weapons, and clean phones, and you will need a new passport! Do you plan on getting all that tonight? Because I don't know anyone *that* fast." In response, Celeste glares at me. "Are you done?" She asks. Out of the corner of my eye, I see Pru choke down an unexpected laugh at my shock of Celeste's sudden confidence switch. She waits with her arms crossed over her chest, leaned back in the chair just watching the whole exchange.

Shocked, I say, "Um.... I guess so."

She stands and struts confidently to the window, the one carved with ornate swirls and flowers. Pru and I look on as she presses a series of the flowers and with a soft whirring noise, a thick jet black screen descends over the window, shutting out the view. Next, the glass top of the stove slides seamlessly back and from below rises up a large locked chest. If that was not enough, next the pot rack hanging from the ceiling descends all the way down to the countertop. Above the pots and pans, what was previously hidden in the ceiling instead reveals itself to be a polished gun rack filled with six different variations of large guns. She strides to the chest that opens; ejecting multiple drawers full of blades, handguns, what appeared to be a variation of poison darts, then finally a drawer full of passports and foreign currency. With expert hands, she loads a couple of empty magazines and throws them in a black bag she had pulled out of the bottom drawer of the chest. She rifles through a couple of the passports and chooses one, throwing it and a few wads of cash into the opening alongside some already included guns and daggers, all holstered into the lining of the bag.

Pru is as thrown as I am and stammers, "How?? Where did you get all of this?" Celeste slams the chest shut again; causing all the drawers to slide back into place before she shoves the pot rack back into the ceiling. While she moves to the screen covering the window, she looks at us over her shoulder, so pleased with herself for throwing us both for a loop, her smirk rivals Pru's best.

"You seriously think that I was that dumb to leave my

family's protection with zero back up plan?" She presses another pattern of buttons and the screen slides back up; all back to normal.

CHAPTER 32

<u>Celeste</u>

I can't help but feel satisfied at the look on their faces. Part of me feels insulted at the fact that they thought that this was pulling me so far out of my comfort zone. *After all, we all were trained together.* But the pleasure of seeing them, this surprised for once, makes it all worth it.

"Alright, how? How did you do this?" Naveen is even more astonished than when he first saw Pru back from the dead. "I thought when you left, that meant you lost all of this." He gestures to everything hidden.

I sit down and pull the locket back out from under my shirt into their view. "Remember this? Combined with the name Stone and a large chunk of my savings, I reached out to some old family contacts that, for the right price, wouldn't ask questions and wouldn't say a word."

Pru looks at me with a whole other level of respect. "Nicely done, Stone."

Stifling a yawn, Pru asks. "I think I am going to call it a night. Is it okay if I take the spare bedroom tonight?" I nod in consent and she vanishes up the stairs, leaving Naveen and I still sitting at the table.

"Is it okay if I stay here tonight too? I can crash on the couch if that works."

This time I shake my head no, and he looks shocked but that mingles with understanding. He gets to his feet and moves to slip on his jacket until I reach out and grab his arm to stop him.

"I meant you can take my room. I slept long enough that I won't be sleeping for a long time. I am just going to stay up and work on the plan for tomorrow."

"You sure?" He asks.

"Of course. Just don't sleep naked, okay?" I joke.

"I suppose I can try, but I won't commit to anything." He responds in turn, calling over his shoulder, following Pru up the stairs. He pauses on the third step, still in view of the kitchen. "CeeCee? You alright?" He steps one stair back, and I jolt my gaze up to where he was watching and force a smile.

"Yeah, I am fine. Just a hard day. But it is good to finally have some answers, I guess." I wave off his concern, and Naveen slowly starts back up the stairs, only to stop again when I call out to him.

"V? Hey, thanks for being there for me. It's good to know I have at least one person who hasn't lied to me." He gives me a sad smile.

"I would do anything to protect you, CeeCee. I just want you happy and safe." With that he turns and disappears up the stairs, shutting the door behind him with a click.

Now finally alone, I look down at the bag I had packed, thrown on the ground next to my feet. I hear the familiar sound of a car pulling up in front and take one last look around my home. Tearing myself out of the chair, I throw the bag over my shoulder, without looking back. I exit my house and climb into the taxi that I had called for earlier, for once right on time. I get settled in the backseat and ignore the churning anxiety in my stomach.

"Denver Airport International, British Airways, please?"

I turn to watch my house grow smaller, as we pull down the street and around a corner. I try not to let myself dwell on the monumental decision I had made and instead let my head fall back to rest on the seat back. As the houses and buildings fly by, staring out the window, I let my thoughts drift.

The blaring morning alarm sounds, and I shove my face into my pillow and groan as I stretch out my bruised, raw skin, and my tender, aching muscles. The first two weeks of school had been, in a word, torture. Literally. One of my classes was Torture 101. Before that, we had what is loosely referred to as Physical Education. What it actually was, was boot camp. Starting at 0500 the alarm would sound and we had fifteen minutes to get up, get dressed, and run the mile across the grounds to the training area. Oh, and if you were late you had to do ten laps for every minute late. That was just the penalty, then the warm-up would start.

Margo was not joking about a lot of girls not making it very long. After the first two days, three girls had quit. Then by the end of week one, four more were gone. Now at week two, so far only one had not shown up to breakfast one day. The Professors did not seem worried at all about this. "Culling the diseased herd." That is what a few of them called it. Much to everyone's surprise, the scholarship girl was not just surviving, but thriving! *After the second day,* no one *called her Charity anymore. Her real name was Pruscilla Denis and if there was anyone I needed to watch my back with, it was her.*

"Get up idiot. You are going to be late." I look up to see her standing in the doorway, fully dressed with her cocky smile. "Seven minutes, roomie!" Then with what can only be described as a maniacal laugh, she took off at a sprint.

"Shit!" I muttered and launched out of bed before I can remember that my muscles are gasoline and sudden movement sets them on fire. I cry out in pain. Any more of this and my muscles will explode! *Grimacing with each step I take, I throw on my pants and hastily pull on my shirt as I run out the door, my shoes in my left hand, a hair tie in my right.* Alright, time to set a new personal record, Celeste.

I barrel on to the training field to where the rest of my classmates are waiting for me. As I reach the group I hear the familiar beep of the stopwatch as our head trainer, simply known as "Burke" stops the time.

"Five minutes." Burke spits out in his rough Ukrainian accent. "Fifty laps. Go."

"What?" I protest. "I was only three minutes late!"

"Yes. But you still have to put on your shoes. So I rounded up."I look at the shoes still in my hand in defeat. Sighing I yank them on, ignoring the look of pleasure plastered on Pru's stupid face. Finishing up my laps I return, already sweating, to the group gathered around

Burke. Well, those aren't girls... *Some additional, and*

noticeably handsome, men had joined the class. Cursing again under my breath at my shitty luck so far this morning, I try to smooth the crazed, windblown mess that my hair had become on the runs and pray that their sense of smell was lessened out here in the openness of the field.

"Right, now that this slacker has served her morning punishment, we can begin. Ladies, these are the boys from Invictus, the brother academy to ours. There are certain ops we will coordinate with them, so Headmistress Hansen has organized some events to get you used to each other. So pick a partner, and behave!*" He looks at us with annoyance when he sees the girls preening and shooting coy looks at the attractive young men, all who look like they could not be more bored. All* except that one. *I freeze as I meet the eye of one of them, staring me down with a smile on his face that catches me off guard. With a spark of attraction that* had *to have been noticed by both of our classmates, I knew I had found my partner.*

CHAPTER 33

<u>Celeste</u>

I close my eyes at the familiar feeling of the plane lifting off the tarmac and into the dark sky. Only now do I let my thoughts return to the hours before I found myself boarding the plane by myself. Everything I had planned came together, all from a single phone call.

I woke up from my heavy sleep to a sole thought. A

plan. *I reach for my phone resting on the nightstand. Lucky for me, after everyone thought I had died, no one had deactivated it or even moved it from where I plugged it in all those days ago.*

"Miss Stone?" A bewildered voice answers after I dial their number with shaking hands.

"Hello, sir."

"You sound quite alive for someone I thought to be dead." I wince at that reply.

"I know. It has been an interesting couple of days. But I need your help if you are willing.

A pause. I can practically hear him thinking on the other side of the phone.

"How can I help you, Miss Stone?" I release my breath with a puff of air and I feel some of the tension of the short wait relaxing from my shoulders.

"First off, can you get me on the first flight tonight to London? From there I can get home on my own. Can you also pull an address of a person for me? I left my laptop on my desk and I don't think I will be able to get to it in time." I hear the sound of him clicking on a keyboard and I send a silent thanks down the phone line.

"What is the name, love?"

"De'monte'. Edgar De'monte'." A moment of quiet passes until my phone dings with a message.

"Found him. I just sent the address to your phone. I will also

get your tickets bought and they will be waiting for you at the British Airways counter. Be there at 2300 and ask for Antoni."

"Thank you, Mr. Bently. Truly." I pause, thinking of how to say my next request."

He is able to catch my thoughts, even from far away. "Is there something else?"

"I don't want V to follow me." I bite my lip, continuing to chew on it and the idea I had swirling around my tired brain.

"I am going to tell them that I am going to slip into the office to grab my computer. They will think when they find me gone that is where I went. And they won't know that you know I am alive. Will you-"

"-hold them up?" He interjects, with a grin evident from his voice.

"If you wouldn't mind, sir." I respond in tone.

"Not at all, Miss Stone. However, who is them? *Someone other than Mr. Lazaro?"*

I chide myself for my slip up. "Just another friend from school who came to find out what happened to me after they heard I died." I lie smoothly; it was becoming as easy as it was years ago. But I can't find myself to be repulsed by it anymore. It was life or death now and I wasn't playing around anymore.

"Ah, I understand. I will do my best to distract Mr. Lazaro and whoever may be with him. Best of luck, Miss Stone, and safe travels." With a click, he hangs up.

I feel a rush of anticipation. Finally! I am no longer just sitting and waiting for something to happen. I am taking the offensive and let's just see what I find out there. *I look at the address on my screen that Mr. Bently sent, memorizing it quickly before deleting it and removing the SIM card; sticking it into a hidden pocket of my left boot. I take a deep breath and stretch, finally feeling better than I had in days. I don't let myself feel the guilt from leaving the other two behind. They had left me out of plenty, deeming what was best for me without even letting me know. Now it was my turn.*

I was far from helpless and it was time the world remembered that fact. I throw open my door and walk down the stairs, all the while repeating my secret plan in my head.

I wake after a few hours of restless sleep to a dark plane cabin. However, despite the late hour, I look around and see not a sole traveler asleep. Two seconds later, I discover the reason as the plane drops about fifty feet, making all of us lurch with the sudden movement. I turn to the passenger next to me.

"How long has this been going on?" The lady looks at me, fear clear on her face. She then responds in urgent

French, explaining that she did not speak English. I try again, this time in the same language. Relief shines for a millisecond, that is until another drop sends her grasping, panicked, for the armrests.

"About twenty minutes." She finally responds to me, after catching her breath. She closes her eyes and begins a stream of prayers, Latin intermixed with French. I decide to let the woman stress in peace and turn to look out the window. Flight or even extreme turbulence was not something that had bothered me ever since Comrade Galina had taken our class out only to leave us; parachuting out the side door of the plane.

Before leaving us all in terror, she had shouted over the loud engine, "Land the plane and you will pass." With that, she left seven fifteen-year-olds, who did not even have driver's licenses', to sort it out. Without hesitation, the other girls looked to Pru and me, pleas stark in their eyes. So with no chance to second guess, we jumped into action, while the five other girls curled up in the cabin; holding on to each other. Pru and I took turns guessing and pushing buttons and pulling what appeared to be a steering mechanism. After about five minutes of trial and

error, we had figured out a decent idea of how not to crash. But now with only about nine-hundred feet from the ground; we had no more time to guess. After the bumpiest ride of my life, we, at last, bounced off the ground a few times before we were able to get the feel of it. Both of us only able to hold our breaths, while the plane slid safely to a stop.

The rest of the girls de-boarded quicker than lightning, and begin to thank God for landing safe and sound. Only Pru and I remained where we sat, both panting as if we had just run twenty miles in one-hundred degree weather.

Once our legs quit shaking and we were able to join the rest of the class outside, Comrade Galina was waiting with an unusual look on her face; respect.

"Well done ladies. You two will continue with this course. The rest of you," she shoots a sour look at the others, who are still rolling around on the ground, sobbing and calling out. "The rest of you will need to find a different elective."

Not one of those girls looked upset at that fact. Pru and I, however, were not so sure we got the best end of this deal after all.

CHAPTER 34

<u>Celeste</u>

After the extreme turbulence and my praying seat neighbor both quieted down, the rest of the trip went very smoothly. Unfortunately, before I was able to get any more sleep, we had landed and I was outside of the airport flagging down a taxi. I am finally successful and give the cabbie the address I had memorized and he takes off without a word. Thankful for the quiet, I do the math and take a guess whether either of my babysitters had woken and realized I was gone yet. If they hadn't woken earlier than eight AM, then they would be doing so any minute now. I glance down at the SIM card still stashed in my boot and picture the angry messages I am sure will be pouring into my phone the second I am discovered. I pull my mind back to my current situation. *I will worry about all that if I survive.* Finally, the cab slows to a stop and I look up at the house we are pulling in front of. Just an unimpressive townhouse with a dry, brown lawn. Handing the payment to the cabbie, he looks around, uncertainty clear on his face.

"You want me to wait for you, love?" I glance around too, taking in the sketchy surroundings.

But I smile at him, "I will be fine sir. Thank you though." I step out and pull my bag out from the trunk. I wave at the man, waiting for him to leave. He gives me one last wary look before finally inching away and vanishing around the corner. Now that I am alone, I at last let my uncertainty show.

Edgar De'monte', whose address I was currently standing in front of, was my family's butler/security guard/doctor. Much to my dismay, he had passed away a year before I had finished school and been cast out of my family. When I came across his name as a current owner of a house here in London, I had a moment of clarity that if my parents were to trust anyone with a location and ownership of a safe house, it would have been Edgar. So here I was, taking a major roll of the dice, and hoping that my intuition was going to pay off. I sling my bag into place over my shoulder and make my way to the front door. The closer I get, the more unsure about this I am. *This place looks abandoned.... But even if I am wrong, I can at least see if there is anything here I can use.*

I hold my breath in anticipation, ringing the doorbell and listen to the eerie chime echo through the empty house. My shoulders droop when after a few minutes, I receive no response. Scanning my eyes around the neighborhood; once determining that no one was looking, or even around, I pull my lock picks from a compartment inside the bag and get to work. After about forty-five seconds, I hear the satisfying click from the deadbolt disengaging. I push it open and see the usually stagnant dust around the door fly into the air and flurry. Picking my bag back up, I tiptoe into the house and have to withhold a sneeze while I shut the door behind me. I let my bag drop to the floor again, this time it sends up a cloud of swirling dust.

Time slows down when I catch the creak of an old wooden floorboard and I drop down, dodging the strike meant for the back of my head. With a thrust, I kick my assailant in the shins, eliciting a grunt of pain. In the next second, I whip an old stained rag from the table to my left, and with my next kick aimed at his crotch, he drops to his knees. Flipping around, I twist the rag around his throat, cutting off the blood flow and oxygen. After six seconds my attacker goes slack and I release the tension, letting him sag the rest of the way to the floor. I don't give myself a chance to relax, knowing that it was not worth the risk to assume there was only one person hunting in that house tonight. I slip off my shoes and grimace at the feel of the dirty floors. *Dirty socks are minuscule in the scheme of things.... but still gross.* I unzip my bags and with steady hands load one of my guns and slip over my head a belt stocked with a dozen throwing knives. All the while keeping an eye on my surroundings, then before I turn away, I slide the bag under the couch. *Not perfect, but it will do for the moment.* With footsteps, I creep through the house, silent thanks to my socks which are already disgusting and caked with dust. I return to the unconscious man and without a second thought I stuff the awful rag into his mouth and duck tape it shut, and his hands together. Then with an afterthought, grab a tiny bell from a nearby china cabinet and duct tape that to his hands as well. *Just in case he wakes up.* I shrug at my handy work, dusting off my hands before I pick back up my gun, and turn back face the rest of the house. I revert back into my training, sweeping the house expertly as any CIA agent. Working my way through the different rooms, I don't see any footprints in the dust or any other sign of life, other than bugs and something furry that was either a rat or a squirrel. When I return to the still unconscious man in the dining room, I let my arms drop a little, only now realizing that my muscles are quaking from fatigue. I roll my shoulders out and holster my weapon. Hands resting on my hips, I nudge the man with my toe.

"Hey. Wake up, asshole." Nothing. My mouth quirks downward into a frown and I drop into a squat; feeling for a pulse. I release a breath of relief when I finally find the faint, but present, beating of the man's heart. *What was that?* My attention catches on a sliver of light slipping through a crack in the floorboards, only visible from this close to the floor. I gasp, then without giving the abhorrent floors a second thought this time, throw my whole body flat on the floor next to my assailant and press my eye to the crack. At first, I am unable to see anything other than a fuzzy glow of the light, but with a succession of fast blinks, I realize shadows are moving within the light. I push upright again and feel my heart leap with victory, though tangled with apprehension. My hope was that, obviously, it was some member of my family downstairs, but life taught me the opposite. *Plan for an enemy. Always.* The rough Ukrainian voice of my old trainer Ivanov or as Naveen always fondly referred to him, the *Russian hitman,* echoing in my head. I hear a tinkling, distracting me from my thoughts for a moment, until I remember what I had taped to the man at my feet. I crouch down beside him and grasp him by his hair.

"Good morning, sunshine. Let's have a chat." The man's eyes fly open, then narrow to a piercing glare. He begins to shout what I can only assume were threats and *not* sweet nothings. I silence that with a yank of his hair, and his glare only grows in intensity, the anger pooling and turning his eyes almost completely black. I rest my finger on my lips, motioning at him to keep quiet before I pull a knife out off of the belt strung around my chest, making my point clear. I look around the room with altered eyes. If there were people below me, there has to be a way to get there. As if struck by lightning, a thought hits me and I remember my grandfather's love of secret doors; all in unusual places. I then pull my memory back to when I first noticed that I was not alone in the house. *A creak of the floorboard. But which board.* I spin around looking for the trace in the dust where the man's footprints had originated from. I follow them back into the kitchen, then let out a stream of curses. I had not been careful or even conscious about preserving the trail when I had walked through the kitchen, marring all but the ones that strode from the kitchen to where he found me. I groan in frustration and move to return to the dining room to see if, after some *convincing,* the man would help me.

On my third step, I halt, and my whole body tenses. I shift my weight from the front foot to the back, then front again. *Yes!* The creak sounds as the pressure forces the old board down against the nail. I was positive that was the exact sound that I had heard, but I shift my balance again to elicit the noise once more, just to be sure. I spin around, trying to think of where he would have come from to land on that plank. *No.... it couldn't be that easy.* I hold my breath and reach for the handle of the refrigerator, only to be yanked back by my hair and thrown to the ground. My head spins and tries to make sense of what just had happened. Pure instinct makes me reach my flexed foot out and cup the knee of the person standing over me, yanking it out from under them. I hear a pop as the kneecap dislocates and the man drops screaming with pain. I recognize the man who was previously duct-taped in the dining room, before pulling my fist up to slam him in the face. But when I see something change in his face, I freeze before I can hit him yet again. Subtle underneath the agony, was recognition. His eyes remain locked on the pendant hanging around my neck. It had slipped into view from where it had been hidden under my shirt.

"CeeCee??" The man's voice says, incredulous. I stumble

back gasping, my turn for recognition.

"Bash?! Sebastian?" He nods, but is unable to speak, just cradles his injured knee. I wince, then similar to approaching a spooked animal, I inch towards him. Looking at him for approval, gently cupping his knee, I yank. He lets out a howl of pain, then panting he goes limp, relief flooding through him. After catching his breath, he flexes his leg, uncertain at first, then, at last, more comfortably.

He finally speaks, "You always could kick my ass. Good to know you haven't changed." I smile, abashed, then throw my arms around him. He cringes in pain at the stiffness of the various bruises that were blooming, a result of our altercations. We break apart and he motions with his head to the fridge.

"Figured it out, huh?" He chuckles. "If there was any doubt, you are for sure a Stone."

There is so much to say, but I don't even know where to begin. So we both sit without a word for a bit. Now that I was so close, I didn't know what to do. Understanding, Bash just watches me sadly. He always was waiting for me to make the first move, my loyal sidekick. It had been a close tie between who I had hurt most when I left this life behind, Bash or Naveen. I try not to think about that and decide it is now or never. I move to wipe off my hands, but then laugh deciding that it is a lost cause when I see that my pants are even dirtier than my hands.

"Well," I finally break the pause, getting to my feet and offering a hand up to Bash. "Let's go find the family, shall we?"

CHAPTER 35

Naveen

I awake to the sound of a car alarm bleating outside. I grumble and pick up an unused pillow, shoving it over my exposed ear to attempt to muffle the sound. *How does Celeste sleep with this much sun coming in?* Now that I finally feel relatively at ease knowing that Celeste is, for the moment, safe, I can catch up on the sleep that I have been missing for the last few weeks. I doze back off, inhaling her scent and letting it soak into my dreams. Minutes, hours, or maybe only seconds pass by. Before a loud bang slams me back awake and I launch to my feet, knife unsheathed and in my palm at the ready. I let my stance relax when I see only Pru in the door, that is until I see how pale and shaky she is.

"What?" I whisper, as if I make too loud of a noise it would make my temporary happiness from that morning shatter.

Almost like she feels she same, she whispers back.

"She is gone..."

Even though I knew that Celeste leaving us both behind was not something that Pru would joke about, I still had to see for myself. I stumble down the stairs and into the empty kitchen.

"Maybe she went for a run, or out to grab breakfast?" I try to come up with a reason for why she would not be anywhere in the house.

"The bag is gone, Naveen."

My stomach drops at that. What she said was the truth; hard and cold it settles into a solid pit of ice in my heart. I stand helpless and see the same feeling reflected in Pru.

"Why?" She asks the question I was not able to. I turn and hurry back up the stairs to grab what little of my things I had stashed here, trying not to give in to the panic of the answer that races through me. I spit it out though, knowing it was what we were both thinking anyway.

"Because she doesn't expect to survive."

Less than five minutes pass before the two of us are dressed and ready to go. Ready to go where? I don't think either of us were quite sure of that yet. We meet back in the kitchen where Pru had unlocked and was going through Celeste's secret arsenal.

"You remembered the code?" Pru looks up from examining a blade at that comment, shaking her head no. I must have looked as confused as I felt because she points at the wall where the buttons to press were concealed. Looking closer, understanding hits me hard.

"That was all part of her plan last night; she wanted us to see all of this and know how to get in." I get closer to see the faint smudges on the buttons she had pressed. Only a shade darker than the rest. I lean closer to tell what she had discolored them with. "Is that paint?"

Pru chuckles. "Foundation. She must have rubbed it on her fingertips before coming downstairs. I only noticed it when I was trying to figure out the pattern and was looking super close." She shrugs. "Like she planned." She sighs and returns to the chest, still stocked with various weapons. "I admit, I underestimated her. I thought she had gone soft."

I let out a soft laugh that blends into a sigh. "It wasn't just you. In truth, I felt the same." I lean against the wall and cross my arms across my chest. "I think we need to follow Celeste's plan. I bet she is still going to do what she told us last night, if not that, then something similar."

Pru agrees and returns the kitchen to its normal state.

"Alright, let's go. We are already ten hours behind and every minute counts."

After that helpful comment, Pru did not shut up about it. After the first hour in the car, the whining started, and for every minute after that, my agitation only continued to grow. When we finally pulled up in front of Sentinel Security, I was ready to strangle her. *How did Celeste even make it through school with this chick as her roommate?* Pru didn't waste any time jumping out so I take a few deep calming breaths, lingering in the joyful silence once the door shut behind her. I knew that once we got any information on where Celeste next went I would have to be completely focused on Pru and my game. I was aware that she would have no problem leaving me behind in an instant, ditching me and going to find Celeste on her own.

Once I was no longer able to provide her additional information, she would slip away the instant I turned my back. *Or put a dagger in it.*

At that comforting thought, I look up through the windshield to see Pru standing there with her hands on her hips, toes tapping, radiating her impatience. Remembering the thought about a dagger in my back, I wince and step of the car to join her before her anger turned to violence.

"Sorry to interrupt, but can you get your ass in gear?"

I shoot her a death glare and stalk to the building, not bothering or caring to check if she is following me. I don't even bother flirting with the receptionist. She looks bewildered; at the change in our routine or the look on my face, I can't tell, but buzzes me in any way. I was not leaving an opening for a conversation. Not today. She looks at me, only for a second for approval, seeing if she should stop my shadow. But when I sigh and hold the door open for Pru, she relaxes, pulling her hand from the alarm trigger. Thankfully, neither of us say a word as the elevator descends, it's soft whirring a relaxing sound in its familiarity. When we step out on my floor, I have to withhold a groan when I see Mr. Bently approaching us, a big grin on his face. I look for a way to dodge him, but when nothing comes to mind, I brace for the inevitable.

"Mr. Lazaro," he greets me, patting my shoulder. "What

brings you in today?"

"Just a quick trip. I need to grab some things, then I will be on my way." I try to slip past him, avoiding the trap of conversation. It fails. His voice halts me before I take two steps.

"I am glad you are here actually. I need your help with something. I wouldn't trust anyone else." His eyes dart past me and land on Pru. Something in his look changes; what exactly, I can't say. Attraction? Confusion? Whatever it is Pru just rolls her eyes in response. "This way Mr. Lazaro." He has me follow him into an elevator and Pru and I both end up realizing there is no way to brush him off without an explanation. One that might put Celeste in danger if we reveal her.

So we trope after him, albeit reluctantly. He leads us to a dark room, lit only with a single fluorescent light fixture flickering over a card table placed in the center of the room. Surrounding the ominous table were stacks of boxes full of... *papers?* I look to Mr. Bently for answers, but he avoids my gaze. *Weird.*

"We are having trouble locating a target that a client wants *taken care of.* I have had everyone I can think of looking into this, but can't pin it down." He gestures to the stacks. "We believe that his next movements are somewhere in this, but..." His voice fades to silence. "I need your trained eyes on this." I begin to interrupt, trying to come up with any reason to get out of this, feeling the clock ticking each second by like a death chant. He cuts me off, "I know, I am sure you are in a hurry to get to London, but I need you on this." Pru freezes, and I look at her, trying to convey with my eyes. *What the heck is wrong with you?* I look down at my watch. No, it's not our flight, we still have thirty minutes to spare before we have to hightail it back to the airport in Denver.

"Mr. Bently, I honestly am in a rush and distracted at the moment. I am afraid I will not be much help at this moment. But I will assist the second I get back." I start for the door but end up having to stop when Pru doesn't follow me to the door. I turn to find her striding towards Mr. Bently, a deadly look in her eye.

"What-?" She silences me with her palm held up, not taking her eyes off of Mr. Bently. Her voice is like the calm before the storm, and her words chill me to the bone.

"How did you know we were going to London?" My mind races, going back over everything all of us said since entering into the building. He, at least, has the decency to look abashed.

"Damn, I told her I wouldn't squeal."

"Her!?" Pru and I share a panicked look.

He sighs, "Celeste. Yes, I know she is alive. Although I

will admit I am ever so offended neither of you trusted me enough to include me on that little tidbit." He holds up his hands before either of us can say anything. On my part, I want to know how he found out, but Pru just looked like she wanted to rip him a new one.

"She called me last night and asked me for three things. First, to get her a ticket out to London. Second, to provide her with an address. Third, to delay *them*, I only understood a little more when you and this young lady exited the elevator today. Other than that I know nothing and will say nothing." Neither of us can think of a reply but I know both of us are having the same dismayed main thought. *How could Celeste do this to us?*

I try not to dwell on that and instead decide to be productive. My tone shifts to one that gets both of their attention and leaves no room for arguments.

"Sir, we are going to need a helicopter, and your private jet." He thinks for only a few seconds before nodding, reluctant but understanding.

"I will have the jet prepped for the two of you at Denver Airport." Pru interjects once again and I stare in surprise, but I don't question it at the moment.

"Three of us."

If Mr. Bently is curious at all, he doesn't show it. "And the helicopter is on the fifth floor. I will let them know to expect you." He begins to walk away, but I stop him one last time.

"What was the address you gave CeeCee?"

"It was for an Mr. Edgar De'monte'." He spits out the address after a second of delving into his memory. This time when he turns to leave, neither Pru nor I stop him. After the door closes behind him, I finally turn to Pru, at last able to ask the question I have been trying to puzzle out ever since she made the comment.

"Three of us?"

CHAPTER 36

<u>Naveen</u>

"Absolutely *not!*" I state, pulling up in front of the address the Pru had typed into the GPS after our quick helicopter trip back to Denver.

She rolls her eyes in response. "You have no idea, do you?" My jaw snaps close and I try to think of what she could be talking about. Exasperated, she massages her temples. "How much do you know about Keirion's job?" My mind races trying to catch up with whatever Pru seems to think I am missing.

"He.... he is an insurance salesman for large businesses?" I feel my anger starting to rise when I glimpsed her amused face humored at my confusion. "Well, what then??" I snap at her.

"Yeah, he is *not* in insurance. At least, that is not his real job."She pushes open the door and steps out, evidently not waiting for me. I try to rack my brain for everything I had learned about Celeste's most recent ex-boyfriend, yet nothing stood out to me to give me any ideas of what Pru was talking about. I look up to see her already standing on the doorstep, eyebrow raised and her major attitude basically screaming at me, *get over yourself.* I groan and open the car door, joining her at the front door, despite all of my better judgment. She gestures, now with a victorious smile, for me to knock. I take a deep breath and remind myself that other than being exceedingly irritating, I had no real cause to pick her up and drop her in the ice-cold pond across the street. Without letting myself dwell on it any longer, I knock loudly.

I am not quite sure what I honestly expected when Keirion's face appeared in the door's small window. Maybe for him to punch me square in the jaw or maybe walking away without even bothering to open the door to hear what I have to say. But Keirion was clearly the better man, a fact I already knew, but was solidified and proven to me yet again when he opened the door and extended his hand out for me to shake. I meet his gaze, trying to catch some sort of trick, but from the sorrow plain in his eyes I know it is genuine. *He is a wreck...* Before the thought can even finish inside my head, it hits me again; this guy still thinks his girlfriend is dead. *Well, aren't we are about to make his day and shake his whole world.*

I take the extended hand and try to think about how to start when his eyes land on the familiar woman standing beside me.

"Ann?" He looks reasonably confused and tries to connect the dots between how the two of us would know each other.

"Hey, Keirion. We need to talk. Can we come in?" She looks around, clearly paranoid, and is taking special care to ensure we were not followed. Keirion doesn't respond, he only moves aside to let us come in. We shuffle into the condo and I can't help but be impressed at the bright open rooms, cathedral ceilings, and huge windows with an amazing view of the mountain range.

"Nice place man." Everything is meticulously cleaned and organized; reminiscent of my military school days. Pru and I sink into the large black leather couch. I nod to her to start the story since she had a plan already in mind. After all, she was the whole reason we were here in the first place and not already on a flight to London. Keirion sits across from us, watching and waiting.

Pru clears her throat, "Keirion, you know me as Ann; Naveen, however, knows me as Pru. All three of us grew up in different places, but our lives are more tied and related than we ever could have guessed. Keirion, I took a position at your work to keep an eye on Celeste." He looked pained at the name, but his confusion shines through stronger.

"How do you - did you - know CeeCee?"

"We went to school together. We were... trained together." His eyes perceptibly widen, but he doesn't interrupt this time.

"I know what you are, Keirion. I know who you are, really are." He glances first at me, then back at Pru.

"I don't know what you mean." Pru rolls her eyes and huffs with impatience, seeing that she is going to have to spell it out for him.

"I know you are CIA."

Keirion and I both jump to our feet. He pulls a gun out from a hidden side pocket of the armchair at the same time I pull my own, concealed in my jacket pocket.

"Wooahhhhhh...." Pru steps between the two of us, arms

extended in an attempt to calm us both. She motions with her eyes to play nicely- I make the first move to holster my gun again and raise my hands. Keirion keeps his pointed in our direction; I can see him trying to figure out what to do with this unexpected revelation.

"Hey man, it's cool okay? I was recruited by the CIA but I ended up going the private route. Neither of us are going to say a word, I swear."

That seems to, at least partially, reassure him for the moment and he point the gun down to the floor, but still keeps it at the ready and in his hands. Pru and I take that as a good sign and return to the couch.

"If you would continue with the rest please, V."

When looking at him, I simply ignore the gun and can only pray that with my next few words don't make him decide to shoot me just for causing the pain I already have inflicted on him.

"CeeCee is alive, man." Despite being a trained professional, like the rest of us, the words hit him like a truck, even causing him to stumble a few steps back before sinking into the chair again. He gapes at me, eyes begging for more information, so I oblige. I fill him in on everything, and I mean everything. Pru encourages me to continue when I pause, unsure of what all to reveal, and fills in what I forget. By the end of an hour, Keirion is sitting, literally, on the edge of his seat; absorbed completely in what we were saying. Once done, his brain is working overtime, yet the first comment he makes was the one that changed his life the most.

"CeeCee is still alive...." He shakes his head in disbelief. "I can't..." He inhales deeply. "Okay. So what do you need from me? I assume it is something since you told me all of this and came here." This time I look to Pru for the explanation, still not sure myself of why we were here.

"Where is she anyway? Can I see her?? I know she is probably still mad at me, but I just need to see her..."

"Well-" I start, but Pru helpfully cuts in.

"*That* is why we are here. She is gone. She took off last night to go find her family and try to get to someone who can help her find Chen Feng and the people who want her dead."

"Unbelievable," Keirion mutters, and we all fall silent for a few moments, each of us lost in our thoughts.

"Okay." He breaks the silence and begins pacing back and forth in front of us. "We have to go after her. Do you have any ideas where she would have gone?"

"We have an address. But nothing else after that." He nods before pulling out his phone.

"What is the address?" He types it in as we recite it to him and a grim look of satisfaction dawns on his face. No longer haggard, he looks hopeful for the first time since we arrived.

"De'monte'." He whispers when his search yields results. He looks to us, clearly hoping for more answers. "I remember CeeCee saying this name, one of the few names she did mention. A family friend or something. She said he was the closest thing to her family she had left after her parents died... or didn't die, I guess?" He runs his fingers through his hair, clearly overwhelmed by the information we had just dumped on him. Despite this, his training was thorough and he was keeping his cool pretty well.

"Alright well, let me pack and I will be ready to go. Do we need flights booked?" He starts typing into his phone again but halts when we shake our heads no.

"We have a jet waiting at the airport. It is ready when we are." He tries to hide how impressed he was, then vanishes into a bedroom at the end of a hall. Pru and I look at each other, our exhaustion reflecting in each other's faces.

"Well, that went pretty well."

I wince. "You didn't just find out that the man who thought I was stealing his girlfriend, is as capable of killing me without notice, as I am him." Pru's laugh echos through the room, bouncing off the windows and making me laugh along with her for the first time all day.

CHAPTER 37

<u>Naveen</u>

The perk of being able to simply board our waiting plane was unfathomably valuable; however, once in the air, there is only so fast the plane can go. So once we all were aboard and the flight attendant had poured us all drinks, the three of us fall into an uncomfortable, impatient silence. Pru separates to her own corner after pointedly making eye contact with us and sticking a pair of earplugs in. As usual being as passive-aggressive as a person could get. The threat of what would happen if either of us shattered her sleep lingers in the air; the plane quiets. Keirion and I are humored, yet still lower our already soft voices. It doesn't take very long, but still longer than I expected, for him to broach the topic of Celeste again.

"So you two met at school? What about the school she went to?"

"I don't know a whole lot; they kept all the secrets that you would expect for an academy of its type. But every great once and a while, we would be privileged enough to be allowed on the campus." My thoughts drift back in time, trying to find the word to describe the school.

"It is called Amethyst Academy - picture a Renaissance castle... complete with sweeping grounds, hedge mazes, and stained glass windows everywhere. Now slap all the modern amenities throughout inside. That was just what I was able to see. Even throughout all the years that CeeCee and I have known each other, she has never spoken any more about it, and I never asked. It's the same for her and my academy, Invictus. Some secrets are ingrained into you from day one and they put too much fear in you to slip them out." I take a swig of the warm cup of coffee before leaning back in the chair, waiting for Keirion's next questions.

"And how long *have* you known, CeeCee? I knew you knew each other for a long time, but I guess I didn't get the whole picture." I swirl the steaming brew, reveling in the bitterness and deep down uncertain about my walk down memory lane with Celeste's new man. When I don't answer right away, he must sense my hesitation, and asks a different question. Unfortunately, this next question was not any easier to answer.

"What happened between the two of you? I saw her face when she first saw you at the door, and it wasn't happiness."

I peek at Pru's now sleeping form and take a deep breath, then down the rest of the coffee before answering.

I first try to laugh off the second question, "Well I showed up with some real bad news... of course she wasn't happy to see me!" He doesn't take the bait of humor, his only response a deepening frown. My nerves cause me to start to tug my ear and wince at Celeste's voice echoing in my head, giving me grief for the stupid nervous tick.

"Okay, but it is not a story I am proud of." Sighing, I run my hand over my face, then grimace at the voice that chimes in.

"You know I have been curious about this myself." My eyes jerk to where the Pru is now sitting up and watching us. I respond with a venomous glare. "You two were so hot and heavy in school." She shoots an apologetic look at Keirion, but he thankfully doesn't appear to feel the immediate urge to kick my ass.

"We met a few weeks after school started and the two

academies put our groups together to coordinate, in preparation for us working together in the future. It is a long time tradition for them to blend us and start making connections in our world early on. Anyway, I rigged the partner selections to get CeeCee as my partner and after the first few days of her being completely irritated by the annoying boy she was assigned with, we hit the turning point where we became best friends." I let out a sigh and gaze into the dregs of the mug and look around for the suddenly vanished attendant, only to find that Pru had moved from her previous spot to the chair next to us. My now captive audience begs me to continue with their heavy silence. "It wasn't until our third year together that things changed." I look, uncomfortable, at Keirion, but his gaze remains merely curious. "I think we both knew that attraction had been there since day one, at least I felt it... but once we did cross that line, nothing had felt more natural. We saw a future together and couldn't imagine anything different. Then you died," I look to Pru, and the blunt comment causes Keirion's jaw to drop, visibly shocked. It is only then that I realize that we had neglected to mention that little fun fact. "Well... we know *now* that you didn't die, but CeeCee's parents went to extreme lengths to convince us all that you had. That is when everything changed. Over the next few weeks, I could tell she was really upset and something inside her had shifted. I-I didn't take it truly seriously, I guess, when she began ranting about how upset she was that the school and her family wanted her to just brush off Pru's death. Then other little things that I think always had bothered her now only boiled over and piled on to each other. It continued to plant more and more seeds of doubt. Until one day, she didn't want this life anymore, that was when she told me point blank that she was done. She wanted to live a life full of compassion and happiness, not stressed day to day if someone was going to threaten herself or her family." I stop talking, a lump in my throat grows and sticks, I try to swallow it away, but only manage to feel more nauseous by the second. "She asked me to go with her. She said she couldn't picture life without me, either way. I was thrown..." I glance at Pru who is watching me, surprisingly, without judgment in her eyes. That is the only thing that gives me the courage to continue talking. Talking about all this for the first time was cleansing, but also made me want to find Celeste right this second. So I could- I don't even know- but just to even see her again would ease the pain that had grown every day since I had watched her walk away. "She knew what she was asking of me and how much it would change all my plans. She gave me until that night to give her an answer. I think she thought, and reasonably so due to everything I had ever told her, that I would choose her. That I always would." I try to ignore the shame that starts to choke me. "To this day, I don't know what I would have chosen without outside influencing." Comprehension fully hits Pru and she pales a shade. "An hour after CeeCee left me to my thoughts, with a promise to return that night at seven, her mother walked in and sat down across from me." Exhaustion sweeps over me and I rub my eyes, but now that I have started to tell the whole story, I can't stop. "She told me that it was going to be best for Celeste to just get a clean slate along with a clean break. If I wanted to do what was best for both of us, I would just let her go. I was a stupid kid and it seemed like an easy alternative. Plus I was conceited enough to not even contemplate that she would go through with her plan if she found out that I would not be going with her. Each of us were counting on the other not to let us down." I shrug, feigning a nonchalance that I had perfected through the years. "I guess she was stronger in her conviction than I realized she was.... If I had just *listened* when she had talked those last few weeks." Pru leans in and puts her hand atop of mine.

"You know it was not your fault, V. Her parents had been orchestrating that, probably from day one." I slip my hand from under hers.

"I know that now. But I still left her, when everything I had said before that was the opposite. She showed up that night, bags packed, excited for the long future she was sure we were going to have together. Instead, I crushed her; it wasn't my intention, but I did. I told her that if she didn't want this *awesome* life, that there were plenty of other girls out there that were cut out for it if she wasn't." Pru's eyebrows shift into a deep v, anger spilling out of her now. She is not alone, Keirion looks murderous. "Like I said, I was a stupid kid. And whatever you are thinking or want to say to me, save it. Most likely I have said it to myself a hundred thousand times." I look to Keirion now, at last coming to the end of my story.

"The next time I finally saw her face up close was that day I showed up at her door only to find Prince Charming there with the girl of my dreams." The murderous look recedes a little, but he doesn't unclench his fist. After all, I just proclaimed his girlfriend was the love of my life. I hold my hands out, trying to placate him. "You didn't see her face the night you walked away, Keirion." Now it is his turn to pale and he swallows hard but doesn't say anything. "She loves *you* now, and I don't blame her one ounce for it. The better man has won." I once and for all swallow my self-pride and extend my hand out for a truce. He takes a deep breath, obviously thinking still about punching me, I am sure, but he accepts.

"Let's just get her back and see if she still wants either of you." Pru says, regular attitude returning, stretching with a yawn.

Keirion copies her and looks between the two of us. "I think it might be time for all of us to at least try and get some sleep." He checks his watch. "We have about seven hours until we land." At that, we all disperse to our separate corners of the jet; all lost in the thoughts and memories of everything we learned today, coupled with the past.

Instead, I allow myself to think about the days before my happiness was shattered and the thought of Celeste in my arms that lulls me into sleep.

CHAPTER 38

Celeste

Bash holds the refrigerator door open, revealing a set of stairs hidden behind. As I step on the top step leading to my family, my heart thumps at the thought of seeing them for the first time in a very long time. Then a whistling noise sounds, causing me to pause my decent, and Bash and I both turn to identify the noise.

And then the world explodes.

The room around me swirls with smoke and flaming debris, only adding to the chaos of my head spinning and ears ringing. I try to blink the disorientation from my eyes but it only makes it worse. The smoke seeps into my mouth and lungs, defeating my attempts to cough it out. I spit out the sticky blood filling my mouth while my mind tries to play catch up. Calling out for Bash, I think I spot a leg sticking out from the wreckage of the cabinets, now just a pile of wood shards. Choking out his name, I feel my panic rising by the second. I start to crawl towards him, ignoring the distant pain of glass splinters slicing my palms as I pull myself slowly across the ground. I fight against the lull of unconsciousness, aware now of forms running up from the hidden stairwell into the sudden hell that had erupted. *I was so close....* I let out a sob as I see one of them take a second step towards me, only to jolt back with a spray of blood. Then like dominos, the same thing happens to the rest of the people arriving at the top of the stairs. One person after another are shot right before my eyes, dropping to the floor like puppets with their strings cut. The ringing in my ears finally begins to fade, only to be replaced by the loud retorts of gunfire. I scream out to whoever might still be alive or downstairs preparing to join the fight.

"Stop! Don't- Don't come up here!" I know I sound frantic and desperate, but my years of training had never prepared me to see the members of my own family being annihilated in this way. I close my eyes against the terror unfolding before me. I had never felt so helpless. *But you are not.* That thought snaps me from my stunned state and I scuffle to one of the fallen figures, I am unable to look at the face, unable to bear it right now. I have to keep my thoughts as straight as I can. I pull the Uzi machine gun from his grasp, shaking from the shock of the amount of blood already pooling and mixing with the dust. I strain my still-ringing ears, and wince at the discovery that I was not going to be able to hear anything definitively for a long time. I look around at my environment, trying to log my available resources. I notice a large, gleaming hunting knife stashed in another prone figure's boot and I slide it out, adding it to my growing collection before moving from one body to the next.

In what feels like mere seconds, I can hear soft voices and the sound of heavily booted footsteps. I try not to dwell on what I am doing as I quickly conceal myself out in the open, laying down amidst the wreckage, bodies, and blood. The copper tang already mixing with the dust has turned into a muddy cake that soaks into my shirt and mats my hair. I let my jaw fall slack, making my body appear broken, just in time for a group of men to pass over me, sweeping the area, and seeing if their initial attack did the job. I count the eleven black shadows that pass by and hold my breath steady in my chest praying that they are not being so thorough as to check pulses. I don't let my relief show when I hear the feet start to move again and begin descending the previously concealed stairwell. I let my eye creak open and see two black figures left behind, one gun at the ready, moving to the check the upstairs. The other one stands waiting at the top of the stairs. I nearly cry out with relief when I spot out of the corner of my eye what looked like the moving foot of Bash. At that moment, I know that I have to move fast before they discover him alive and use a single bullet to change that. Bash lets out a groan and the man standing only feet from me turns at the sound and takes a step closer to investigate. I don't let myself hesitate, jumping to my feet and jam the knife blade deep in the side of his neck, severing his vocal cords and slicing his carotid artery in one go. I catch him as he starts to fall and ease him without a noise to the ground. I wait listening for any indication that someone had heard me or suspected anything. I curse my damaged ears but don't *think* that any alarm had been sounded. I hurry to the pile of debris covering nearly all of Bash and with as little sound as I can manage I try to clear some of the wood covering his head and face. He is steadily starting to gain awareness; by the time I have enough cleared to see his face, his eyes are wide open and it is clear to see he is in severe pain. I shush him gently as I can, while still getting the message across.

"Do not make a noise. Pretend you are dead." I say, straight to the point. Thankfully, he must understand because he immediately stops trying to free himself. I slip a gun into his bloodied hand and with a nod from him, I turn and slip without a sound after the man who had gone to search the rest of the house.

I stalk without a sound through the house and at last find the lone man in one of the upstairs bedrooms, rifling through a closet. He starts, turning to find me standing there, gun raised to his face. For someone who is obviously a mercenary, he is not even remotely trained properly. His gun is slung across his back, goggles are pulled up to his forehead, and he was combing the rooms looking for things to steal.

I take a step closer to him and he watches me, waiting to see what I will do, but doesn't make any motion to fight back or even try to intimidate me. He can see there is nothing he can do, and I almost even feel some sympathy as I slam my elbow into his face breaking his nose. Then I think of the jumble of bodies strewn out on the kitchen floor. With that image stark in my mind, I slam my elbow down again, this time into the back of his head, at last sending the man unconsciousness. In his fall the sound of his weight hitting the ground is softened by a pile of discarded old clothes. I pause and pray the thud, though soft in my ears, was as quiet to the rest of the house. I hold my breath, counting the seconds that pass by me. My heart stops, blood running ice cold when I hear men's voices echoing from below. I hustle to barricade the door to the bedroom, unsure if they had heard me take out the last man just now, or if they had found the body of the one I had left dead in the kitchen. Thundering footsteps sound on the stairs and I slide the magazine out of the Glock in my hand, thankful to see the magazine is full. I reach again around to where I had slung the Uzi over my back and lay it on the bed next to me, then add next to it my assortment of extra blades and magazines. I reach for the Uzi and then wait, aiming it at the door, ready for the first sign of someone trying to get in.

Even though I was expecting it, I still jump at the first attempt to kick in the door. That same second I press hard on the trigger, releasing a steady stream of bullets through the door and into my waiting opponents on the other side. I hear a few people hit the ground and the rest scatter, searching for whatever cover they can find. I grab for my next weapon once the Uzi was emptied and useless to me. Though I brace myself, I am still not prepared for what comes next. The constant pepper of bullets had left a decent-sized hole in the already decrepit wooden door. The rest of the people who had invaded were not the same level of ineptitude as the man unconscious in the closet. I hear the clang before I see it bouncing. *Flash grenade.* With an extremely bright light and loud retort, what little of my hearing I regained was gone again and my corneas were burned with the white imprint that impairs my vision and makes it impossible to see anything. I pull the trigger of the Glock, emptying the magazine, to try and buy myself time to at least be able to see shapes. But the toll of the numerous attacks on my brain was too much and the world around me began to spin again. I bite my tongue, pinch my arm, slap my face, but nothing shakes me back to reality. When my sight starts to return, too late I realize that my opponents had kicked in the flimsy door and surrounded me. Through the fog of white circles, the shadows dressed in black gesture at me with their guns to drop to the floor. From where I sit, I have a prime view down the stairs and to the front door. My stomach churns and I cry out at the sight of a familiar face looking up at me, before being dragged out of the front door and out of my sight. *My mother.*

I am forced to the ground, though it doesn't take much for them to get me there. My knees give out easy and I don't bother to even wince at the burning crack that reverberates through my legs when my knees connect to the floor with my full weight. I do hiss in pain as they rip the now useless handgun from my sliced and glass embedded hands. They ignore my pain and cries, handcuffing my hands behind my back before patting my bruised and battered body for any additional hidden weapons. The few they find are tossed alongside the rest on the bed. I see another face appear at the bottom of the stairs and can read his lips as he yells to his compatriots.

"Hurry. Fire."

One of the men standing around me motions to another to grab me, then pats his gun. A clear sign of what he will use, should I give them any reason. But I know I won't. My fire had gone out. I gave all that I could even just get to this point. And all this was my fault. The moment I had regained consciousness after the first explosion had taken out Bash and me, I knew. I was the reason they had found this place, how they had found all of us. Whether they had followed me, tracked me, tricked me... Somehow they knew that I would lead them here and I had fallen right into their trap.

Only one thought stopped me from completely caving in on myself. *At least Naveen and Pru are safe. That is the one thing I did right.*

I let them yank me to my feet, the metal of the handcuffs slicing my wrists with the sudden motion. The group escorting me descends the stairs at a rapid pace, the smoke billowing from the kitchen grows thicker and thicker. We exit the house, all of us coughing from the haze, and I see four large black SUVs waiting for us. I look desperately for any signs of familiar faces. Maybe to see my parents again, or Bash, or even a distant uncle, but all I see are the faces of hateful strangers before being shoved into an open seat. Before I can resist, a needle is stuck in my neck, its cold contents injected. This time I am grateful for the darkness that envelopes me.

CHAPTER 39

<u>Naveen</u>

My gut churns with anticipation with each of the seconds that pass by. It grows with each step we take through the expansive airport and everything seems to take even longer. But even I know that I can not take on this beast solo, so I wait for Pru and Keirion, despite every urge to take off running and leave them behind. Anything to get to Celeste as soon as I possibly can. Time ticks by, however, stretching the separation between us and Celeste wider and wider. I can feel my irritation and urgency reflected in both of the others, but even if we all took off at high speed or hell, even if we could teleport this instant to

Celeste's side, it still wouldn't feel fast enough to us. Pru seems to be the only one of us that is relatively sane and not chomping at the bit; so she has taken the unspoken lead. From the plane steps to the cab it only takes a mere four minutes, but it still feels like an eternity. Every person walking in front of us was an obstacle that I felt the desire to shove out of my way. And from the anger brimming in his eyes, I can tell Keirion has a similar mindset. Somehow we all make it through the airport and drive away in the cab without knocking anyone unconscious. Pru watches us with a combination of unease and humor.

Her face suddenly transforms after a while in the cab, shifting to a sharp frown that lodges a lump in my throat. I turn to follow her gaze and feel my face drop. Even quite a distance from the road we were on, a large cloud of smoke billows and furls into the night sky, one that is beginning to turn to dawn light. I turn to the others, speechless for a second, then gather my thoughts to try and rationalize, for all of our sakes.

"Come on. What are the chances that in all of London, that is where we are heading? Probably just a house fire." I feign a nonchalance I do not even remotely feel. From the faces of Pru and Keirion, I know that they are not convinced any more than I am, but we all pretend, for our remaining sanity. The closer we get to the address we had given the cabbie, the less we were convinced that the origin of the plume of smoke was not our destination. We pull up to the dilapidated wreck of what we could only assume used to be a house. We pile out of the cab, none of us speaking a word, only trying to take in the sight of what now appeared was a dead end. A few remaining firemen were still there cleaning up what they could and putting their supplies away. Keirion approaches one and begins to grill him on what had happened. No flames or even smoke spit out the house now. Only soggy ash drips from every surface that could be seen. Keirion returns to us and fills us in on what he was able to gather from the man as they pile in the truck and leave us standing on the now emptied street.

"They said there was nobody home; that no one has lived here in years. They are putting the fire down to an electrical anomaly, but that was all he knew. He said we could go in if we wanted but he wouldn't advise it. I guess it was not the most stable structure, even before the fire." Keirion shrugs and turns to look at the charred building in front of us. The first rays of sunlight gleam through the nearby trees before any of us speak again.

"I am going in." Neither looked shocked at that, just resigned. Pru nods.

"I'm coming in too." We both start up the cracked

sidewalk to the open front door and from a crunch behind us, I know that Keirion is following as well. We share a dubious look then each take tentative steps into the house. If there was any sign that Celeste was here, it is going to be an absolute miracle if it survived the inferno. I step gently, testing the first few stairs that lead to the second floor. With a nod, Pru vanishes around the corner to the left, Keirion the same to the right. The three of us move methodically and carefully through the house, looking for any sign that Celeste, or anyone, had been there. *Why would she come here? Keirion said he had heard the name mentioned by her before. So it had to have some meaning....* *Think, Lazaro.* I pause next to a wall between one of the bedrooms and the hallway. *That hole looks familiar.* I bend to get a closer look and my breath catches. *That is a bullet hole.* I look around at the rest of the walls and begin to spot more and more of the same hole puncturing the house. I feel a brief surge of elation. *There was a gunfight here. Maybe that is why the house was on fire? To hide that!* Then I realize what that might mean for Celeste and my elation turns to nausea. After studying the holes I decide that they originated from the bedroom straight off the stairs. I push open the remnants of what used to be a door and it pops off the hinges, crashing to the floor. I wince and freeze, waiting for the whole house to collapse at the sudden movement, but when it doesn't I yell back to the others who are calling up to me.

"What the hell??"

"You bringing down the house up there?"

"Yeah, I'm fine. Thanks for checking." I retort, resorting back to my comfortable sarcasm. I study the room and spot something in the closet. I get closer and terror clutches me.

"That's blood." I mutter to myself, then move back out to the bedroom when I am not able to see anything else. That is when I spot a shiny object hidden partially under the bed. Dropping to my hands and knees and I reach for it. *It can't be.*

I call out to the others. "She was here. For sure." I hear the running footsteps of Keirion and Pru, the fragility of the house now forgotten at the news. They surround me and I let the object I had found under the bed dangle from my fingers in front of them.

"The Stone's locket..." Pru whispers, snatching it from my grasp.

"There is blood in the closet and bullet holes in the walls too. Something happened here." I say, my voice mirroring how grim I feel. Pru wears a similar look.

"You think that is bad? You should have seen the kitchen that Keirion and I came across. It is completely destroyed, and blood stains everywhere under the ash.

Something really bad happened here."

"Thanks, Captain Obvious." Keirion snaps at her and the tension in the room skyrockets.

"Listen, guys. We have to assume they have CeeCee." My voice cracks and they both look to me, pleading for some kind of reassurance, even though there is none. "Keirion, who can you contact that would have any information on the Yoshitomi Group or Cheng Feng? If we can track them down, I have no doubt we will find CeeCee too."

He nods, pulls out his phone, and heads outside to make some calls. I look to Pru now, "You are the only one here who knows anything worthwhile about the Stones. This was their safe house, wasn't it?"

She grimaces, but nods. "I found a secret staircase in the wall. Before it was blown to shit, I would assume it was behind a fridge or cabinet. But I went downstairs and the walls were decorated with the Stone sigil. It had to have been them. Everything else is gone though: computers, weapons, files, all of it cleared out." I sigh, not pleased, but unsurprised.

"They must have followed her here somehow..." My thoughts race, only to keep coming back to one idea. I can't fathom it at the moment, however, so I push it aside to deal with later. With nothing else to do, we trudge out of the house and find Keirion, ending what looked like an intense phone call.

"My handler is not pleased I broke cover and left the country." He explains. "But I know where they took her. Cheng Feng owns a large chunk of land just outside Ealing, in Park Royal. I had a friend check surges in electric use and they said just two days ago a warehouse on the property went from not being used at all, to full power." I clap him on the back and see a light of hope gleam in his eyes, and Pru shines a wicked smile.

"Let's go pay him a visit, shall we?" Pru says, shining a wicked smile.

CHAPTER 40

Celeste

I wake to a loud cacophony of sounds that could loosely be referred to as music. I groan and try to sit up from where I am sprawled out on a stone floor strewn with what looked like dirty clothes intermixed with torn up blankets. My head pounds unbearably and I press the back of my hands against my eyes, failing in my attempt to clear my eyesight. No luck as it is still mostly filled with bright swirling lights and I feel like my eyes are going to burst in my head. *I definitely have a concussion.* I try to gather what I can, through my sensitive gaze, about my surroundings, but see nothing aside from walls of metal keeping me in the room I have been thrown in. I don't dare call out, fearing what will happen to me when they realize I am no longer unconscious. Even if I had been brave enough, I doubt I would hear any response back, thanks to the 'music' reverberating off the metal in an eerie echo. I take note of what parts of my body aren't bruised or damaged and I fail to find anything. *Concussion, damaged eardrum in at least my left ear, maybe my right too. My index finger is for sure broken.* I look down and wince at the clotted blood that has congealed around the large slice just below my right hip. *Oof forgot about that guy with the knife....* I take a deep breath and search for some distant memory of what I was supposed to do. I come up blank and don't bother to withhold the sob that wells up out of me. That was the crack that breaks the dam. It's not even so much that I *let* myself break down, more accurately, I am no longer able to hold it back. I wail and tear at my hair, completely overwhelmed by the hopeless situation I had found myself in. Despite all my best efforts, I came to this end. I fit in an unbecoming shrieking laugh amidst the crying at the irony of it all. If I had just stayed and become who I had been trained to be, I doubt I would have been vulnerable enough to end up in this situation.

The attack of laughter and tears finally subsides, transforming into hiccups; my body trying to return my breathing to normal. Once quieted, I feel slightly better, even though my body and brain still pound with throbbing agony, made worse by my recent convulsion of sobs. I stare into the distance, trying not to think about anything at the moment, and just pray that I might get some sleep then maybe try again tomorrow.

How much time passes? I have no idea. I let myself drift in and out of consciousness until I see movement, barely enough to even catch my attention. It's more out of irritation at being drawn out of my stupor that I glare at the source of the movement. The second I realize what it is, I shuffle on my hands and knees until my face is pressed as close against the bars holding me in the metal cage that I can get. *It's a hand!* Around the corner and across the room, someone had reached their hand far around that edge so that they could enter into my view. I scold myself for being so dense and taking so long to realize that they were trying to get my attention. I see blood trickling down their arm and dripping thickly onto the floor from where they had repeatedly sliced their forearm on the sharp metal barrier between us while trying to catch my attention.

"I see you!" I say, loudly as I can risk, and the dirty hand gives me a thumbs up, then launches into a rapid, but noiseless tapping on the metal wall. *Morse code!* I think excited for a mere second and dive deep into my memories of when my mother made me learn it alongside English, back when I was a child.

D O. N O T. G I V E. U P. D O. N O T. G I V E. U P. D O. N O T. G I V E. U P. D O. N O T. G I V E. U P.

The unidentified prisoner continues the message over and over again a total of ten times before finally tapping out, I. L O V E. Y O U. just once before the hand vanishes back around the wall and out of sight. A knot tightens, almost unbearably, in my chest when I had a lightning strike of suspicion of who is the other person in here with me.

"Mom...?"

CHAPTER 41

I tap my fingers, my impatience obvious, and wiggle my feet propped up on the old whiskey barrel hidden in a dark corner of the previously abandoned warehouse I now find myself in. I huff and look at one of the guards who stands by, waiting, and monitoring me. *Making sure I am a good girl.* I cackle wildly and the man looks on with fear at the sudden crazy outburst. He shares a look with another standing a few feet away and they both shift on their feet, uncertain. I roll my eyes and let my head fall back limp with boredom, just staring at the ceiling and feeling the hours drag by. *This all should have been done the night I shot her in the neck.* I add tracking down her savior onto my to-do list. I crack my neck and then slam my feet to the ground with a *clack* when my jet black heels connect with the concrete floor. I grit my teeth and feel a surge of satisfaction as the man assigned to watch me starts to visibly tremble.

"Where the hell is he? I delivered, now I expect the *payment!*" The music that has been playing at ear bursting level, is the only response I receive and I snarl at the man. "I demand the money now," I get to my feet and his eyes bulge. "or I will just take them back and be on my way. I am *sure* I can find another buyer that would pay handsomely for a set of Stone's." The man opens his mouth to respond but doesn't get the chance to offer an explanation or plead for his life before footsteps start to approach us and he nearly wilts with relief. A squad of guards in matching uniforms stomps into the separated part of the warehouse I have been kept waiting in. A bunch of men in stuffy suits follow them closely and keep their distance from where I stand. *Fine by me. A dose of fear may increase their chances of survival.*

They stare at me for a few seconds, longer than my fraying patience can handle, and I snap at them, shattering their strong external appearance. They all jump and I smile, wicked to match my tone. "Well, who is going to pay up? Or shall I just be on my way with my cargo?" A man, apparently the one in charge of this group, steps forward and wipes his sweaty brow with shaking hands.

"We-We are just waiting for confirmation that these are, in fact, the people that my employer has been looking for."

"Should I be offended that he doesn't trust me?" I respond, my irritation clear, hand on my chest as if I was wounded.

He smirks in response, looking around at his comrades. He seems to calm a bit as if bolstered by the people surrounding him. *Like I could not take out all these idiots and remove his head in ninety seconds.* But I don't interrupt, and let him believe he is safe.

"Without causing offense, the last time you informed us the job was completed, she turned up yet again. And on a doorstep here in London, no less."

I grind my teeth in fury. "It should have been completed. When I left she was as good as dead." I reply, my anger overflowing. "I shot her in the neck with the Revenant toxin. How the hell would I have even guessed that she would get the antidote, which is *extremely* rare, by the way, just in the second before it hit her heart."

"You should have made doubly sure," is his only reply. Out of the corner of my eye, I see the guard go still in the corner, gulping hard, his Adam's apple bobbing noticeably. *Good. At least one person in this room is not a complete idiot.* That changes when I take a step closer to the men opposite me, and they all take a step back with trepidation, their grins vanishing in the blink of an eye.

"Oh, don't you worry your little heads about that." I lower my voice to a whisper, reveling in their complete attention.

"Everyone I want dead always will end up that way. If only eventually." I gesture to where the deafening music continues to beat and where I had deposited the unconscious bodies of the Stone women.

While obviously shaken, the man decides to disregard my statement and nods to three of the men who separate from us and head in the direction I had just gestured to. The man then attempts to placate me and calm the mood shift in the room.

"However, she ended up leading us to the rest of them, so our employer is generous enough to still compensate you for delivery. Once we have confirmation from Mr. Feng, we will then wire the money to the account you previously provided." I sigh, but return to the chair, propping my heels back up on the barrel top.

"Whatever, just hurry. I have things I need to do." I force an uncharacteristic smile that doesn't reach the rest of my face. They don't look reassured a bit and begin muttering to each other in rapid Chinese.

After listening briefly and determining that their discussion wasn't relevant to me, I ignore it and pull out my phone;\, looking for any messages about new targets available. *None worth my while on this continent right now.* Before I can slip my phone back in my pocket, it chimes with an incoming message.

2:07pm Ash, did you do a job in Denver a few nights ago? I have had some people reaching out trying to identify a shooter who used Revenant toxin. If it was you, LAY LOW. They are dead set on finding whoever did it.

The number comes through blocked, but I still know who it was. The only person who knew that I had as a toxin in my arsenal. I try to think of what to even respond. I know the person wouldn't snitch on me, and only said anything out of concern of an approaching threat. But I wasn't too worried. So I click out a quick response as I hear the three who had split off earlier to verify the occupants in the metal cells, finally returning.

2:09pm Kay, don't worry. Just tying up the loose ends then I will vanish. Couldn't turn down the money. All in a day's work. Same place, same time?

* * *

I get a thumbs up this time and withhold a smile before returning the phone into my pocket. I school my features back into stone before turning to face the three rejoining us. He slides a phone back in his pocket and nods at the others.

"Our employer has confirmed that these are who we were searching for. He will arrive tomorrow evening and wants us to remain here and keep them where they are for the time being." Now he turns to me. "I have transferred the money and you should see it arrive in your account now. You are free to go."

I don't check before striding from the room knowing, just as they did, that I knew exactly where they would be if that money did not appear in that account. Leaving the warehouse, the music finally muted from the outside, I smile and step into the waiting car. *Sorry, CeeCee. Hope your death is quick. But I doubt it.*

CHAPTER 42

Celeste

There had been no further communication from my mother, or at least who I suspected was my mother, on the other side of the wall. Unable to think of anything else to do, for the time being, I take to rolling a semi-rounded piece of concrete I had found in the corner, back and forth across the chipped, filthy floor. It rolls out of my reach and clatters to the ground. Sighing and rubbing my aching temples, my head is still irritated by the unending thumping music. Suddenly, I scurry to my feet at the sight of three men standing an arm's length away from the bars of my cell. I cross my arms, glaring hard at them, but if they are intimidated it doesn't show. Their only motion is to hold up a phone, camera pointed in my direction. I look in confusion as a voice sounds over the phone speaker; someone was watching on the other end of the line. I watch them, bewildered, as they point at me, like I was an animal at the zoo.

I strain my hearing to guess what is being said but am unable to catch anything before they move on to the other cell. This time through a momentary pause in the music, I manage to hear a faint Chinese accent say, "That is both of them. Send the money." That is all that transpired before the three men left, none of them speaking another word. I take a deep breath, feeling my shoulders droop, exhaustion only being shuffled to the side by the direness of my situation. I lean my back against the metal wall and my thoughts race with a million different things.

If they were looking for confirmation that we were who they were paying for, that must mean it wasn't Chen Feng's men who hit the house. But then who could it be?? One of the thousands of freelance mercenaries or hitmen, probably. I shake myself before I can get lost in that deep hole of possibilities. *First things first. I need to figure out where the hell I even am.*

Silence washes over me with such suddenness, I sway in relief. Sliding down the wall, I disregard the filth that is for sure now coating the back of my shirt. *Thank god the music stopped.* I then remember the other captive and shoot back up, hurrying over to the bars, pressing close against them. I whisper across the now silent space.

"Hello? Can you hear me?" No response and I dig my finger into my ear, wincing from the evasion into the already sensitive hole, coupled with the worrisome amount of blood that coats my finger. I bite my lip and pray that the earlier explosion did not cause permanent damage. *I need to focus first on living that long.* I shudder at the unsettling thought and scan the floor for anything that I can toss to try and catch the attention of the person I was suspecting/hoping was my mother. I spot the small chunk of concrete discarded on the floor again. I ignore my sensitive hands, still sliced and embedded with glass and wood splinters, and start trying to break the chunk into smaller pieces. I began chucking them over to where the hand had appeared earlier. After the fourth throw with no response, I curse with frustration when I hear footsteps sound, heading towards us. I look around to make sure there were no signs of what I was attempting before throwing myself back on the ground. Plastering a dull look on my face, I glaze my eyes over and feign staring up at the ceiling with disinterest.

This time, it is a different group of men, and only two instead of three, that approach us now. One who is carrying a tray full of what smelled like soup. I inhale deeply and my mouth already begins to water when I calculate how long it had been since my last meal. They yell at me something in Chinese and I feign incomprehension. *Never know when they may slip up if they don't think I understand what they are saying.* So I just continue to stare blankly back at him. After trying one more time and then realizing that I was not simply being rude, I just didn't understand them, the man repeats it for the third time, now in English.

"Back to the wall if you don't want this poured on the ground in front of you." I appease him and follow the instructions to the letter. He then sets the bowl on the edge of the cell.

"Good girl." The insolent man says and I have to bite my tongue, literally, to stop myself from retorting something that would not have been good news for my next undetermined amount of meals.

The other man accompanying him and delivering the other bowl to the second cell shouts sharply at the one antagonizing me. It is then I see a look of fear wipe the smirk off his face. He rushes over to the other cell to the side of the second man and yells, in Chinese, "Get the physician and the key!"

My stomach drops when what he says processes and my

head starts automatically jumping to the worst-case scenario; which is reasonable seeing the direction my life has continued to go these last few months.

I wrap my hands around the bars and slump to the ground, weak with helplessness. The other man returns with a set of keys and a be-speckled older man. They all rush into the cell and I can do nothing but wait. *Please let this just be a ploy to get them to open the door.* The others in the warehouse must have the same thought process, because not two seconds later a group of about fifteen men file into the space dividing the two cells and the AR-15's they brought along are pointed directly at the door, now swung wide open. Voices continue to shout from inside the cell. Whether my brain wasn't computing appropriately due to shock or fear, or the echo of all the noises in the small metal space was too much to differentiate who was saying what; I can't even see much as all of the men pack in and surround the open door, blocking any potential view of who or what was going in and out of it.

I watch the men come and go for the next thirty minutes, all in a panic.

I can't help but feel a slight urge to laugh at the irony of the fact that they were rushing to keep one of us alive, only to simply kill us in the near future at their choosing. I had no illusions about what they were going to do with me by the time they had their fun. What I was concerned about, was what they were going to do to me in the interim. I had sat in many courses at the academy, drilling into us, no pun intended, on how to inflict maximum pain, should the need arise.

I never was drawn to those types of classes, preferring instead to choose other electives that would widen my knowledge of the world, leaning more to the subtler side of espionage. I shudder at the memory of the few girls who were mainly interested in the darker side. *They always seemed to have dried blood underneath their fingernails.*

A shout sounded from what I would assume was down the hall, and from the extreme echo, came from the main part of the warehouse. It snapped me back to the present and I pull myself back up to standing. A squeaky wheel proceeds the gurney that comes flying into view. I watch, unable to do anything else, as they roll the crisp white-sheeted bed into the cell of my mystery co-occupant.

I have mixed thoughts of who I want to be on the gurney. On one hand, I pray that it isn't any member of my family, or even anyone I know. But the other part of me selfishly longs for it to be my mom, so as not to feel so alone and to give me back some hope. *Parents are invincible, right? That is the magic of moms and dads: they are stronger than anything. Especially mine. Even as a little kid, they were always the superheroes, defeating the bad guys and walking away without a scratch.*

Tears fill my eyes and I feel my bottom lip start to tremble when the bed reemerges, starting with the feet. I hold my breath with anticipation, fingers white from gripping the bars. My knees buckle and I have to hold myself up when the face emerges. The men take off running out of the cell to wherever the closest medical ward was, but the glimpse was enough to answer the question.

Mom...

This time it is not hope that fills me at that word when I see her pale face, her fingertips dripping with blood. It is despair.

CHAPTER 43

Naveen

We each take off to our separate corners of the yard, pulling out our phones and reaching out to any resources of contacts. Desperately calling in all favors and help, we give ourselves only ten minutes to do so. Then it would be time to call it, one way or another, we had to decide on what to do and how to do it. We now had a solid guess where Celeste was, but the questions now were: How many guards were we up against? How were we going to get in and get out with no more holes in each of us than what we went in with? And finally, once we did get her out, what were we going to do next? We had no idea how far her attacker's hands reached and what would be safe. My phone vibrates with an incoming message. I read it, wide-eyed, three times before deleting and walking back to the other two. The look of disappointment is clear on both of their faces, obvious there was not a huge amount of success if any. Before we can share our results, however, an intense cough comes from the direction of the dilapidated and scorched house. All three of us turn, stunned, to see an ash and soot-covered man stumbling out of the ruins. We all rush to help him, and Keirion darts to one of our bags for a bottle of water for the man. I recognize him, despite his charred hair and ashen face. Pale underneath the black smudges with scratches all over, he coughs, trying to expel what he can from his airway.

"Sebastian? Bash?" I ask, incredulous that he had, somehow, walked out of that house in one piece. He nods, exhaustion clear in his glossy reddened eyes.

"Who made it out?" He croaks, with a tilt of his head, his thanks to Keirion for the water before draining the full bottle.

All of us wear the same solemn look as Pru responds.

"We don't know for sure.... The firemen said they didn't recover any bodies, but we all know that doesn't mean much. It looks like a shootout happened from an upstairs bedroom. But too much of the house was damaged when we arrived... We can't tell much more than that." Her gaze narrows, eying him quizzically. "How much do you know of what happened? And how did you make it out?"

He blinks slowly, clearly on the verge of passing out. "Everyone that I saw was either shot or taken." If Bash had not been so dehydrated, it was clear he would be weeping. He sinks on to a stone bench that is partly crumbling with age. "You are looking for CeeCee, aren't you?" The three of us nod in unison.

"She was here. That was her destruction upstairs. Someone was following her, or at least they knew she was going to be here. I think they wanted her to lead them to the rest of the family. The second we opened the door to the concealed stairs, the whole place exploded. I lost consciousness when the first explosion hit and when I came to, CeeCee was standing over me telling me to stay where I was. She moved out of my sight, but soon I heard a thump. That was when a bunch more of the men in black came storming up the stairs. Three of them were dragging Aunt Beverly, CeeCee's mom. But the rest of them headed to see what the thump was, at least, I assume. The place started to go up in flames and they began taking away the bodies that were in the kitchen, the rest of my family that was there..." He drops his head into his hand, completely distraught and unable to continue. "Everyone else is dead.

I managed to slip downstairs before they could pull me out too, and realize I was still alive. That is the only way I survived. I found an old oxygen tank and there was just enough for me to survive the smoke." He coughs some more but doesn't say anything else.

Keirion steps forward now, looking more upset than I ever had seen him; and that is saying something considering the events of the last week. He clasps Bash gently on his shoulder and looks him dead in the eyes.

"I know you don't know me, and I don't know anything about you and your family," he takes a deep breath. "But I do know CeeCee. We all love her and will do anything to protect her and your family. That includes getting CeeCee and her mom back safely." Bash looks back up at him, clearly trying to decide if he liked this guy or not. His only reply though was the only one I expected.

"I am coming with you. Whatever you guys have planned." Pru and Keirion look unsure about it, given Bash's unsteady appearance. But neither of them argue, all of us thinking the same thing.

"We need all the help we can get." I extend my hand out to him, pulling him back onto his feet. "What help did you guys get?"

"I got us a ride in and out of the warehouse." Keirion says.

"I have a contact who will provide us the weapons," says Pru, smug at her success. I nod to both of them and begin to put together a plan in my mind, pulling my phone back out of my pocket at the chime of another incoming message. I grin, for what feels like the first time in years; and the three look at me, their curiosity peaking.

"And what exactly do you look so thrilled about?" Pru cuts in, not bothering to hide her irritation. I wish I could have taken a picture of her face. I retort very matter-of-factly.

"I have someone inside the warehouse and she has found CeeCee."

CHAPTER 44

Celeste

I spend the next hour kneeling crumpled on the ground up next to the cell bars. Listening, intent for any information I can catch about my mother's condition. Time passes slowly until I hear footsteps and voices approaching my cell once again. One of them catches my attention and I can't place why, until I hear the accompanying swish of skirts. I withhold any sign of recognition when Hecate walks into view. It takes every fiber of my self-control to not start screaming at her. I have a confusing combination of feeling betrayed, but for some unknown reason, I was also reassured that she was there. Despite the fact that I was shocked that she was there in the first place; in my head, she was my friend even though we had just met. Plus if anyone was going to save my mom, it would be her. Hecate's gaze brushes over me but doesn't stop walking down the same hall that they had taken my mother.

"Your employer is okay with the payment I requested for my services, correct?"

"Yes ma'am."

"Good. Now explain to me why a woman that was in a deadly attack on her home was just thrown into a cell without any checking that she was wounded?" Her clipped accent grows stronger with her apparent irritation. I feel my hope surge slightly at that tone. Is she here to help me? But that thought is doused the second my rational thoughts catch up to me. There was no way that she could have known that I here. Naveen and Pru didn't even have any idea where I was, so how could she? *But maybe she could at least get a message to them.* These thoughts race through me as the man stammers an inadequate response, but they vanish out of eyesight and hearing range before I can hear any more.

Time continues to pass and the pool of blood outside my mother's barely used cell has dried before I again hear the soft sound of approaching feet and two figures appear in my limited view.

"I must check on the other girl. Seeing as you are incompetent enough to let the other one sit on death's doorstep, who's to say you wouldn't let this one too."

The accompanying man looks suspicious suddenly. "Why would you care?" His finger drifts to the trigger, but Hecate doesn't lose her cool composure.

"I simply do not wish to be dragged out of bed at an ungodly hour and have to come all the way back here for something as simple as a few stitches." Stone-cold and unfeeling, her answer breaks a part of me; her act is so convincing. Too convincing.

"Fine." The man responds with an annoyed sigh, plucking the key from a bundle on his hip and unlocking the door. I prepare myself to kick the door into him, steal his gun, and run as far away as I can. But he points the gun at me and I know that will have to wait.

"Back of the cell. Hands above your head. Move!"

I obey, begrudgingly, but not willing to fight too hard at this moment. I could use some of Hecate's remedies; ones I had felt first hand. My head throbs constantly, my eyesight is still marred from the flashbang at the house, and my eardrums are still bleeding from the first explosion at the house. Not to mention my sliced and glass-filled hands, the broken finger, a continuing-to-bleed knife wound on my right hip, and what I assumed were a few cracked ribs. I fail to withhold crying out when the man approaches me, yanking my hands behind my back, tying them tight and painful. His rough hands then press and pat me down from head to toe, making sure that I was not concealing anything that I might use against them. He turns up nothing and steps aside for Hecate. She starts pulling various jars and items out of a big black bag and gets to work, her hands moving with her practiced rhythm. She pauses only to dismiss the man with a wave of her hand, before untying my bonds with quick fingers yanking me free.

"Some of her wounds will require her to undress. Please leave." The man snorts in reply, but Hecate stares him down, unyielding.

"Whatever. I will have to lock you in. Yell down the hall when you need out; the cameras down here are busted."

My attention snags on that, but I conceal it, narrowing my focus to my body pulsing with the torture of the day. *I won't be able to do anything or even think about it until I get some help.* The man leaves the two of us alone and we stare at each other for a moment before Hecate starts digging in her bag again.

"What the hell were you thinking, Celeste?" She slams down a jar she has pulled out, then begins palpating my sides and stomach, not gently.

I hiss with discomfort and she gestures, with clear anger, for me to take my shirt off. I attempt, but can't lift it past my shoulders without excruciating pain. She sighs before helping me, gently lift it over my head. She gasps, unhelpfully, at the amount of torture my body had gone through. Dark purple, green, and red bruises color my entire left side and she mutters a curse in what sounded like Greek. I bite my lip to keep from crying out when she pulls a light green yogurt-looking substance from the jar and begins to massage it on the bruise, ignoring my moans of pain.

"Three cracked ribs. You are lucky they did not splinter into your lung." Her frown was darker than I had ever seen on her usually calm face. Neither of us speaks for a moment while I try and regulate my breathing. Sweat pours down my face from the agony, but she only moves from my side to the knife wound on my right hip.

"My mom," I manage to spit out in between my ragged breaths. "is she going to be alright?"

A cloud crosses her face and she looks back down to the stitches she is sewing into my body. "She is alive, for the moment. There is only so much they would let me do. They plan to deliver her, and you, to Cheng Feng tonight. After that, it does not matter what her condition is." She responds under her breath, glancing behind her, worried that anyone might be listening to the information she was giving me.

She finishes up stitching my leg closed and moves to my hands. I have to stop myself from laughing, despite the situation, at the look of admonition that she shoots me. She removes a pair of tweezers from the side pouch of the bag and the urge to laugh vanishes.

"Brace yourself," is my only warning before she starts to dig into my sensitive palm. It is then that I fall into blessed, peaceful unconsciousness.

I wake to Hecate humming as she continues to work on me. My first realization was that I could see normally, and my hearing had improved as well. I look down just in time to see her wrapping up my now splinter free hand. I exhale with relief at the already subsiding pain. It was still present, just not overwhelming anymore. I could focus again.

"Thank you." I whisper, and she returns with a smile.

"I have cleaned out your ears; there does not appear to be any permanent damage, so long as you avoid any extreme noises for a while. Your hands are now splinter-free and I numbed the skin so you will be able to get some use out of them. Just be aware that they are still cut up pretty badly and you won't have the pain to stop you from opening them up more. I have given you an antibiotic to stop any infections." She continues down the list but begins signaling me with her eyes. I follow her gaze and understand immediately when she moves the gauze a bit to the side and I see the line of syringes and needles she had expertly hidden in the wrappings of my bandaged leg. Hecate then motions to my hand with my splinted finger; alongside the inner band of the splint was a length of a metal bar the size of a paperclip. *She has armed me as best she can.* A wave of affection washes over me and I grip Hecate's arm in silent appreciation.

"Thank you." I mouth. She returns with a sad smile and a nod before getting to her feet and calling to one of the guards down the hallway to let her out. She turns to me one last time.

"They are coming." She whispers before turning back to face the cell door.

A jolt of electricity seems to flow through me at those three words and I have to make sure to conceal that when the guard walks into view. Not bothering to hide his annoyance, he opens the cell and Hecate walks out, ignoring his huffing and puffing. I watch her go, vanishing through the same door she had come from - the same door the three men with the phone had come through earlier. *Okay. That is my way out.* My thoughts clear for the first time since being dragged into the SUV outside the De'monte' house. So I begin to formulate a plan.

CHAPTER 45

<u>Naveen</u>

Pru, Keirion, and Bash all launch into questions, the summary of each being who, when, how, etc. In as few words as I can, I explain about the first text I had gotten from Hecate and then the one I received just now.

"They are at that warehouse, but she said they are being moved or killed tonight. There are about 120 guards there right now, but more arriving tonight along with Cheng Feng and his men." I look around at the already worried and upset faces around me and decide how much to actually share. *You need them to know exactly what we are all walking into.*

"They are both in real bad shape." I share and run my filthy hands through my hair before I realize it, wincing at the grime now coating my head. "That is why Hecate was even there. She heard word yesterday through the 'underworld' grapevine that something was going down here in London and she hopped on the first plane here, suspecting what we all know now. Someone spilled on where the Stone's were and they were going to be taken out today. She got the call two hours ago that her services were needed."

Keirion interrupts. "Who are we talking about?"

Pru explains, "The healer that a lot of us non-government-funded assassins use. She is a medical genius, but the cost to go to her is rarely just coin. She is ruthless and word is, some of her deals can cost you a piece of your soul." She attempts to meet my eye, but I dodge it.

"Either way, she is there and is able to help us however she can." Pru doesn't look satisfied but is not stupid enough to keep pushing me right now to talk. I continue, falling into a routine I have many times before. "We have two extraction targets. No hostages, no surrenders. We have one goal and that is to get CeeCee and Beverly Stone out alive. Eyes on the inside report Beverly is unconscious and strapped to a medical gurney with oxygen and an IV."

I turn to Pru and she has switched into mission mode as well. "Pru, you will extract Beverly. Roll the whole damn bed out with her on it if you have to. Keirion, you will get to CeeCee and get her clear of the cell. Bash, you and I will lay down cover fire and will take the heat away from the other four. You will be outside near the car, keep it running, and be ready to leave when we are. I will take the main part of the warehouse. Hecate says that right off the main warehouse area, at the far south end of it is a set of double doors to go through. That takes you right to the cell area, that is where it also connects to a hallway. Go down the hall and the fifth door on the left will be the makeshift medical room. That was where they had Beverly the last time Hecate saw her." A large nondescript van pulls up the road behind us and Keirion points at it with a nod.

"That's for us."

It is clear that this plan was not very well thought out, but it was the best we had with only four of us against at least one hundred and twenty fully-armed men.

"We have three hours, roughly, before Cheng Feng arrives. We have to get them out before he kills them both."

Silence follows that statement, an ominous countdown starts in each of our minds. Pru breaks it in her oh so charming way.

"Well, if you boys can keep up, we just might make it out of there in one piece." Each of us smile at that, though hesitant at first. "Let's go get some guns!" She calls over her shoulder sauntering off to the waiting van.

We pull up in front of a dusty RV and I can't help but feel what little hope I had wilt.

"Is this the right address?" I turn to ask Keirion who sits in the driver's seat; his own wary face questions the same thing. We both now turn to face Pru who just rolls her eyes and slides the van door open. She jumps out without waiting for us before reaching the door and pounding loudly while shouting obscenities at the occupant.

A man with a bushy beard, red eyes, and a beer gut throws open the door with a bang and starts to lay into Pru, freezing only when he takes in her face.

"Prusilla??" Awestruck, he starts to tremble, then pulls her in, enveloping her in a hug that we could tell was not enjoyed much by Pru. We both watch from the front seats of the van, waiting for her to throw the man to the ground, or maybe start kicking him. When neither happens, my eyebrows rise of their own accord due to my shock.

When she finally maneuvers out of the hug, we have exited the van and stand a few steps behind her. She straightens up as if daring us to question her.

"Keirion, V, I would like to introduce you to my father."

Our mouths drop open; that was not what either of us was expecting. The man, Pru's father, ignores us entirely and only has eyes for his daughter.

"What are you doing here?" He finally asks, his voice thick with emotion. "I thought you were dead."

"It is a long story, Dad. But I left some things here that I need. Can we come in please?"

He doesn't respond, only steps aside to let us pass. We all pass the scattered beer cans, take out containers, and full ashtrays without comment. Pru leads us back to what I would assume is the bedroom and we cram into the small space. She shuts and locks the door behind us. Turning with a sour look she wrinkles her nose at the smell, but doesn't comment other than to order us to help her move the mattress. The three of us manage to lean it part ways against the wall. When Keirion and I turn back, Pru is kneeling on the floor, ripping up the tiles glued to the floor. Watching as she peels more tiles away, what appears to be a trap door is revealed underneath. It is pulled open, with a creak and a puff of dust, and I can't help but laugh at what we see there. Stooping down to help her, the three of us pull up ten trays lined with foam and filled with guns.

Pru dusts off her hands, "It is not as elegant as CeeCee's arsenal, but it works in a pinch. Let's just take all of it back to the van. Now that the old man knows it is here, it isn't safe anymore." She snaps the door back down over the now-empty hole and I help her replace the bed, covering what we can of the removed tile and the now visible trap door.

Each of us take a few of the trays and shuffle again past the precarious piles of trash that cover nearly every surface in the RV. But we make it back outside where the man waits for us. In the middle of a long drag of the cigarette perched between his lips, he takes a sharp breath when he sees the contents we are carrying out of his mobile home. This sets off a coughing fit and we hurry to stash the trays in the back of the van, taking care not to wake the sleeping Bash who lies sprawled in the third row. We had convinced him to get at least some well-deserved sleep before we barreled into what was sure to be an ordeal. The man finally catches his breath and stops coughing, launching into questions about where we had gotten all the weapons, what was going on, why we were taking them, all while growing more and more red from his boiling anger.

Pru looks at him sharply. "Don't worry about it, Dad.

Not your problem anymore."

With that, she turns and climbs back into the van; her father is now stuck speechless. Unsure of what we were supposed to do, Keirion awkwardly thanks the man and returns to the driver's seat. I just wave, uncomfortable, and join the others back in the van. As we pull away, I see in the mirror the man pull out and light another cigarette before we drive out of sight.

I turn to face Pru, eyebrows raised, questions clear in my gaze.

"Let's just say Celeste is not the only one with Daddy issues. Forget it, okay V?" She dons on a mask of indifference, hiding a real hurt. I decide this was not the moment to push it and turn back to face the front.

"Okay, well we should wake Bash. We are twenty minutes out and need to gear up." A wicked grin mixed with relief at the topic change flashes up on Pru's face.

"Now let's have some fun boys!" Keiriron and I can't help but groan at her enthusiasm, yet our adrenaline starts to kick in and we join in her excitement.

CHAPTER 46

Celeste

I wait an additional fifteen minutes after managing to work the metal piece of the splint loose from where Hecate had expertly slipped it in past the guards: sewn into the splint itself. Whatever she used to numb my wounds was a miracle and I send a silent thanks to her for that gift. After waiting for the minutes to pass, giving Hecate a chance to be far from anything that was about to happen, I get to work on the lock of the cell. I flashback to memories of sneaking through the Stone estate with Bash. We had been unlocking and sneaking into forbidden rooms ever since we were kids. Those memories are now painful when I think about the condition I left him in and I knew it wasn't good news that he wasn't stashed in a cell near mine. I blink the tears away that cloud my eyes and draw my focus back on the task at hand. *Shit. It is harder than I remember.* I chew my lip and have to recenter myself a few times as my hands start to shake with exertion. Any minute I could be discovered. The knowledge that the cameras were down over in this area was a slight reassurance, but after the comings and goings I had witnessed in my time here, I knew the double doors just feet away from me were the only way from the main part of the warehouse to the medical unit down the hall. *My only way out too.* I had no idea about what all would be waiting for me on the other side of the doors, nor did I have any optimistic delusions that it would be an easy escape from there.

From the number of men I saw pass me and the different faces each time, my rough estimate was there would be at least one hundred men between myself and my freedom. I feel the tumblers click inside the lock and I exhale sharply with relief. Not wanting to just toss the life-saving piece of metal aside, I slip it into my bra and roll my neck to loosen it a bit. I also do some jumping jacks, doing whatever quick activity I can to wake my deadened, bruised muscles. Once I was as ready as I would ever be, I push open the cell door, helpfully oiled on its hinges, and take my first step of freedom. I turn down the hall and count my steps. Everyone before me that was heading for the medical unit had taken between thirty-two to thirty-six steps before the squeak of a door sounded, so I match them. I start down the empty hallway, passing a few doors on my way, but I mostly ignore them. None of them have windows or even any light shining underneath the door, so I don't fear anyone spotting me or that someone will come flying out from them. I hit thirty-four steps and turn to face the door to my left; this one does have light shining through its cracks when I push it open and hear the familiar telltale squeak of the door. I spot my mother laying on the same gurney I had seen before, about twenty feet from me. Before I can take any steps closer though, a man in scrubs turns around from the counter on my right, where he had been jotting down some notes. He gasps, but his reaction time is slower than mine. I grab a shiny silver tray full of tools and slam it into his head. It makes a metallic clang when it hits him and he drops like a rock.

"Sorry, sir." I say, not truly feeling sorry at all, and drag him by his feet a little out of the way.

I rush to my mother's bedside and inspect her with quick eyes. It appeared that Hecate had worked her magic on my mother too. Despite being covered with bandages and scrapes on her pale face, she looked better than when I had saw her just hours before. She looks older than when I had seen her outside of the Stone estate eight years ago, but then again, so was I. I slide my hand into hers, cool and limp, and simply allow myself a few moments to hold it, reassured by even the simple touch. I freeze when I feel her fingers twitch, and with the slightest pressure, she squeezes mine. I gasp and stroke her face gently. I whisper, even though there was no one else around.

"Mom, you are going to be okay. I am going to get us out of here." She doesn't respond but her fingers tap out another message to me.

C A M E R A.

I freeze at that word and curse loudly, whirling around while looking toward the ceiling. Sure enough in three of the corners, active cameras hang, all blinking green. I rush to the adjoining room where the man in scrubs still lies in the corner unconscious. I scan for any weapons that may have been left with him and spot nothing but more medical equipment. I shrug and make do with what catches my attention. I grab a handful of scalpels from a tabletop, luckily still capped with plastic to aid in protection, and slide them into my back pockets. An unused IV pole lingers in the corner and I yank the main pole out the socket that attaches it to the wheels. I slam the hooks off the other end and am left with a rather sharp, though not particularly elegant, metal spear. I close the door between myself and the room with my mother placing myself as a human barricade. I grasp the pole and ready myself at the sound of footsteps approaching. The door flys open and I yell, swinging the pole over my head and aiming for theirs.

"Holy shit!" A voice screams before ducking my hit and falling to the ground in shock. I stare back them, then nearly faint with relief.

"Pru!!" She smirks in return and clambers back to her feet.

"Well, look at you throwing our plan into chaos! You were supposed to be waiting in your cell like a good little girl."

"You and V came alone? Are you crazy??" I ask. She pushes past me and moves to my mother with purpose.

"Well, yes and no." She starts yanking wires off my mother and I have to fight the urge to shove her away. "Yes, we are crazy. But no, we did not come alone - sort of."

"What do you mean, sort of?" She motions for an empty syringe from a tray, and I hand it to her automatically, my head simply trying to get caught up with this turn of events of her being here.

"It is V, Bash, Keirion, and me. So not much better of a rescue squad." A wash of different thoughts and emotions hit me all at once. *Bash? Keirion? KEIRION??*

I sputter incoherently but she ignores me, turning her focus back on the unmoving form in the bed. She fills the syringe with a mystery liquid that she had pulled from a bottle out of her pocket and inserts it into my mother's IV with practiced hands. I must have had confusion written all over my face because she answers my unasked questions.

"Bash is alive; he is waiting at the car. Yes, Keirion is here because he is a secret CIA operative. And yes, I just shot your mom up with a mystery liquid that I have no idea what it is or does. But that is only because Hecate told me to."

I struggle for a response to any of that, but thankfully I am spared responding at that moment. My mother's eyes fly open, her eyes darting back and forth between the two of us.

"Sorry, ladies," Pru halts the waterworks that are seconds away from starting with a raised hand. "We have to go now. Talking is for later when the bullets aren't flying." I nod and help her pull my mother to her feet, thrown seeing her so unsteady for the first time in my whole life. Pru pulls one of the multiple guns from a boot holster and passes it to me along with a full magazine belt that she unclips from her waist.

"I will get her to the car. You help lay down cover. V is out in the main area waiting. Keirion should be somewhere out there too. He was supposed to find and rescue you, but someone wore her big girl pants today and got herself out." Despite the sarcastic tone, I can tell the begrudging respect that she now had for me.

I clip the belt around my hips and check the magazine already inserted in the gun.

"Okay. Let's go." We start out of the medical unit, and the second the doors are pushed open, the sound of gunfire echos down the hallway. The three of us limp down the corridor and I chide myself for not grabbing any pain medicine while I had the chance. We reach the double doors outside what had been my cell, with no sign of Keirion.

"Ready?" I turn and ask Pru. She nods in return and I can see the strain of carrying my half-awake mother is beginning to take a toll.

"Just get outside and stay with Bash. I will find Keir and V and get out as soon as we can. No use in having to try to find you too." I don't give her a chance to argue before pushing open the doors and, crouching bent over, the three of us hobble over to a stack of pallets. I don't let myself linger, only pausing to plant a kiss on my mother's clammy white forehead before running off in the direction of the thunder of gunfire starting to sound deep on the other end of the warehouse.

CHAPTER 47

Celeste

I slam my back into a pile of barrels, throwing myself past an onslaught of bullets zipping past me. My chest heaves from trying to catch my breath and I give myself ten seconds to recollect my senses. I then try to lean around the wall of protection but have to immediately pull back when another round of gunfire is shot in my direction. So I try something else. I catch sight of an empty discarded wine bottle, dusty from its years of being discarded in the corner. I lunge for it and scramble back to the pile as fast as I can. I use my shirt to dust it as well as I can before setting it back on the ground, then rolling it gently from out from the behind the barrels. I smile with relief when my idea works, a little. I can't see very far, only reflections of my immediate surroundings. But it is a good thing, because only fifteen steps from where I sit, semi-protected, were three men slowly and without a sound surrounding where I sit. I have only one thing left to do; pray that there is no one around that will shoot me.

I jump to my feet, the top of the barrels reaching only up to my chest, and press the trigger three times. Each shot echos around me and all three of the men drop dead. I collapse back to the ground myself and listen in for any returning shots. I hear nothing however and a drop of relief reassures my rapidly beating heart. I push back up on all fours and get ready to run to the next source of protection I can see: an old overturned wooden desk about fifty feet away. I take off at a hard sprint and looking up to the metal walkway that crisscrosses the warehouse about thirty feet from the main floor, I finally see the two who are causing all the chaos. *V and Keir!* Elation courses through me when I see, for a fact, that they are both alive and well. Or at least, as well as any of us could be at this moment. Looking surprisingly at home with a gun, Keirion fires his gun, taking out his own slew of men below, matching Naveen hit for hit. Some other guards notice me and turn their shots in my direction. I make it to the desk, barely, taking cover just as Keirion and Naveen both spot me in return. I can see the nearest exit door now, all of us are only minutes away of freedom from this whole nightmare. I lean out from behind the table, looking again for the two men. I catch a glimpse of them slowly working their way to the stairs. I lean around the other side to see what stands between us and the outside. About another sixty men stand, ready and riled, all armed and most of them already taking shots in our direction. I spot the stairwell that Keirion and Naveen are working towards and gasp at the sight of another exit door. *If I can just make it to the stairwell!* I look around for anything that would make this a terrible idea and can't spot a thing; other than the large group of men shooting to kill all of us. *The concrete wall surrounding the stairs will protect us from whatever they shoot at us, once we all make it there, that is.*

A smell catches my attention, and I sniff trying to identify it. *Is that... Jaegermeister??* I have a sudden recollection of a not so pleasant hangover due to the alcohol and I can't help but gag at the memory. But it sets off an idea. I peak around for the cause of the smell and finally spot it. A stack of barrels close to the door had been damaged due to the shooting and some of the holes had begun to leak the liquid all over the floor. My mind races putting together a risky plan. I pull the metal piece I had stored in my bra and grab for a discarded piece of concrete and a piece of wood that had been leaned up against the nearby wall. I also pull out two of the syringes that Hecate had stored in my leg wrappings and, taking a hopeful guess, jab one in my leg and the other I set aside. I exhale with relief when the morphine hits immediately, and I send yet another loving thought of thanks to Hecate. I then squirt the contents of the other syringe I had removed onto the piece of old wood. I also pull out the scalpels I had snatched and one by one remove the plastic piece protecting the blade; then, with an expert throw, lodge them each into one of the barrels full of Jaeger. I hold my breath, hoping that my foolhardy idea will pay off. Finally, each one is pulled downward by the heavy handle of the scalpel, popping free and leaving a hole spewing even more of the high-proof alcohol onto the floor. I don't let myself feel any sort of victory yet and I turn back to the piece of wood now soaked with the highly flammable morphine. Moving with fast hands I strike the metal bar against the piece of cement, trying again and again to create a spark. Nothing happens and I flip around again, looking for Keirion and Naveen who are still taking a majority of the gunfire. My breathing catches slightly when I don't see Naveen, but Keirion is near the top exit of the stairwell. I turn back to try some more, knowing that this is going to be our saving moment if I can get this *stupid, hunk of god damn wood lit!* Finally a spark lights and hits the wood. I cry out with my success and before the flame can take over the whole thing, grab it, and chuck it to the ever-growing pool of alcohol. The explosion hits and throws everything within fifty feet into the air with its force, including me. I land on the cement floor in the center of the room, the air knocked from my lungs. I cough and try to catch my breath, screaming from the pain on my already battered body. I spit the blood that has poured into my mouth from when I had bit my tongue as I hit the ground, but that pain secondary to everything else. I realize that I am just a sitting target and try to make my body move to somewhere more protected. But then I realize that there is no one left *to* shoot me. Bodies lay scattered around the warehouse, thrown by the explosion just like I had been. *It worked!* I can't help but think, as everything begins to blur. My concussion from earlier made only worse from my second head knock in less than twenty-four hours. I am aware just enough to see two figures running towards me. I search for my gun, but it is nowhere to be seen. But the hands that grab me are not violent. No, they are gentle and loving.

I look up to see Keirion, and my heart beats even faster than I ever thought possible. I also see Naveen kneeling beside me and the two pull me to my feet and press another gun into my hand. With their help, together we all run for the stairwell exit.

The fresh air hits my face and I laugh out loud, close to collapsing from the happiness of seeing the night sky; though cloudy, the moon shines bright. That snaps me back to sanity and I can stand on my own again.

"Bash is over here with the car. Let's get out of here." I hear Keirion say and we follow his lead as we begin working our way to the right around the outside of the building. As we turn the far corner I see the van waiting for us, Pru and Bash standing outside of it. Naveen and Keirion take off at a sprint for the car, and I follow closely, until I hear a strange noise coming from behind. I stop and turn as a sharp retort sounds from a sleek black car that had just pulled up and I feel something slam into my side. Blood spurts out and I hear all four of my saviors at the van screaming out my name.

CHAPTER 48

<u>Celeste</u>

So... I have just been shot. I know if I keep standing here, staring stupidly at the blood pouring out of the wound in my side, that I will probably get shot again. As everything moves in slow motion, I think back to a large Ukrainian man yelling at me.

"Pain clears the head girl. Keep your wits about you. Even if it hurts, you need adrenaline." I shake my head as I brace myself for what I am about to do. Gritting my teeth, I shove my thumb deep inside the bullet wound, just above my right hip. But everything starts to clear as a scream slips out through my dry, raw throat. *Man, this is really going to ruin my day.*

Logically I know that I should run for the protection of the van, but instead, I pull back out the gun and do the opposite of what anyone would do. I take off at a sprint at the man standing outside of the car. At first, he looks shocked, then terrified when it dawns on him what I am doing. I get closer and see the face of the man who had haunted my days and nights for the last few months, the man who had completely overturned my whole life. By the time he lifts his weapon and reaches for the trigger, it is too late. I lift my gun, still running, and open fire. I unload the remaining shots into his chest, stopping to walk the last fifteen feet. An icy calm washes over me when I reach him, lying dead at my feet. I don't feel joy. This was a cycle of death that I *never* wanted to continue. *He left me no choice.* I remind myself, then turn back and walk to my friends. They all watch me with open mouths and solemn gazes. I stop in front of them, not knowing where to even begin with what to say. Pru, thankfully, is the first to break the silence.

"I'm *starving!* What are we getting for breakfast?" We all only respond with exhausted laughter and then, as if he had been restraining himself all along, Keirion pulls me in for a tight hug, and finally a deep kiss. We part and I smile up at him, only then do we notice the others had left us and were waiting, impatiently, in the van. Keirion helps me into the waiting van, and before the door slides shut, I catch a glimpse of flames beginning to engulf the warehouse. Pru reaches over and starts to patch me up. I feel long, calloused fingers slide into my grasp and I turn to see my mother smiling at me. So many words to say, but I don't have the energy for even one. I let my eyelids slip shut and fall into a deep sleep.

We make it back onto the jet waiting to take us back home, staggering, limping, bleary-eyed, and coughing. Once we finally lift off from the tarmac, we all breathe a deep sigh of relief. I break the calm when I begin asking some questions that had worried me the entire time I had been kept in the cell.

First on my list, "Where is my father?" My mother is able to answer that one for me. He had been one of the first up the stairs, those shot right before my eyes. I gulp hard and reach out for my mother's hand. She was coming back to Denver with me and together we would sort through our many scars.

"Okay, now did any of you tell anyone where I was

going?"

"No." They all respond in unison. I can see in their faces that this was something they had each already thought about. I massage my temples with the implication of that knowledge.

"We all know what that means then, right?" Keirion looks lost, but Naveen and Pru nod with their agreement.

"Mr. Bently. He told Cheng Feng, and from what Hecate told you, maybe five minutes after I hung up with him." Betrayal and anger rush through me and I see that feeling mirrored on the others. Keirion leans back in his chair, his thoughts racing and jaw tense with irritation. He looks around at us, thinking over his words with care.

"I know you each have your own vendetta and right for revenge against Bently. But from my view, none of you can act on it without retribution from the whole company, and who knows how deep his contacts run."

"What are you thinking?" Pru inquires.

"I can make him disappear." I had been filled in on the fact that Keirion was, in fact, an agent of the CIA, a fact I still could not come to grips with. He continues explaining, matter of fact and without pride in what he is saying.. "His people can not take revenge on the whole United States government." We all consider the idea, and I look to my mother for her thoughts.

"I never wanted this life for you." She looks at Pru. "I am sure she has told you about the lengths that your father and I went to try and make a normal life possible for you. Doing anything that might spark another flame of revenge against you is not worth it for me." She turns to address Keirion now. "You have my vote. My daughter clearly loves you so it is still, in my mind, a representative of my family repaying the debt owed to my husband's killer." She pats my hand and then excuses herself to the other end of the plane, leaving us to our conversation. I brush past the statement my mother made about my love for Keirion. I had no other comment because we all knew it was true, and thankfully no one else calls me out on it.

"I agree. Please take care of it, Keir." He nods, nothing pleased in this resolution, but only the knowledge that a dangerous player would be taken out of the equation. I then voice my final question that had been rolling through my mind.

"Has anyone heard from Hecate?" Naveen grins.

"I can answer that for you. She said to tell you, when you inevitably escaped, that she would be waiting at your house with tea and soup." I smile and feel a surge of affection for my new friend.

"By the way," Naveen clears his throat. "The price asked of me wasn't that hard to pay." My confusion must have been clear on my face because he continues. "The *deal with the devil* that everyone warned me about, I have to help Hecate smuggle in supplies to a small village in Africa and help smuggle a bunch of orphans back out. " He rubs his head, trying to cover up some embarrassment and he leans closer, lowering his voice. "Might actually be the best job I have ever taken. You know, karma wise…" I reach out and squeeze his hand with thanks and look around at the group assembled before me and my eyes fill with tears.

"I can't thank you all enough. All of you came after me…. Even you Keir, and you thought I was dead!" I laugh aloud at that crazy sentence and he chuckles along with me.

"Oh my god…." I say finally realizing the reality of that fact. "I'm dead!" My laughter grows until its painful; I clutch my stomach and wincing through the laughing as the action shakes my sensitive ribs. "What the hell am I going to do?" I ask once I calm myself enough to catch my breath and speak. "This is probably going to throw even Ridley for a loop…" They watch me with a combination of humor and concern as Keirion responds.

"I have already taken care of that. To anyone who looks into it or asks, you were a member of the witness protection program for a bit and, in order to protect you, the story was spread that you were killed in a freak accident. I already had someone contact your office and got your job back at ST&T if you want it. Or the CIA has a few job openings if you want to keep this excitement train rolling." I look back at him in awe.

"Thank you Keir... You don't know how much of a relief -." I cut myself off, unable to find the exact words to say. I reach out for his hand and he places a kiss on my forehead. I catch my eyes with Naveen's and he nods, his message clear. I don't know what had happened between the two men, but something had shifted and, despite our history, Naveen would be stepping back with no hard feelings. The separation that had always been *there* between Keirion and me had vanished now that we finally knew the actual truth of each of our lives, and our pasts.

Pru chimes in, faking her disappointment. "I guess you can have your house back too..." That comment combined with the exhaustion takes over and we all break out in fits of laughter as the Rocky Mountains come into view of the plane windows. I gaze at them feeling content of who I am, and whole for the first time.

CHAPTER 49

I can't believe that bitch got away. After practically gifting her to those idiots, she escaped. I should have charged way more. Oh well. She is more fun to play with still alive.

I hear my phone ring and huff with annoyance. Then with years of practice switch my personality with ease and answer the call with my preppy and way too irritating voice.

"Hey girl!" Across the line, I hear a reply from a voice I thought I had heard the last of when I shot her in the neck a few weeks ago.

"Hey, Ridley! Did you miss me?"

Acknowledgements

First off, thank _you_ reader. Whether you realize it or not, you have literally made my dreams come true simply by picking up this book and choosing to read it. So from the bottom of my heart, thank you.

Now for my very first fan; the one I sent my very first chapters to, to see if I should even continue writing. The person who has been there for me since day one. My mama. After reading those chapters, her reply was, "What happens next!?" And that was what motivated me to continue telling Celeste's story.

Obviously, I have to thank every single member of my family, because I certainly wouldn't be who I am to where I am in life without their love and support. Grandma and Grandpa Stratton, Granny and Papa, all of my aunts, uncles, and cousins; you know who you are! I am so grateful for each and every one of you. Special thanks goes out to my Granny, an author herself, who was my go-to for random questions about the whole book writing process. She was also another member of my family who was willing to be a first reader of the book; giving me feedback and the final push to see this thing through.

I also have to give a shout out to my favorite local coffee shop, Kitt's Coffee. They have no idea, but a *large* portion of this book was written at their tables and was fueled my many of their amazing lattes and snackies. They also were a huge inspiration for Celeste's coffee adoration.

Now last but not least, my wonderful husband, Slade. He is the one and only reason I wrote this book in the first place. For the last year, he has been listening to obsess, talk and stress over this whole process. He has pushed me constantly to not give up, even the I was exhausted and nervous when it cam time to at last share it with the world.

Thank you again, everyone. *You will forever have my gratitude.*

J.R. Molt was born in Las Vegas, Nevada, but grew up in south central Nebraska alongside her three sisters. She lives there still, with her husband Slade and two adorable fur babies, Odin and Flynn Ryder. Her love of writing and of books spans her entire life. With Daughter of Stone as her debut novel, she is honored to join the legacy of authors before her.

* * *

Follow her on Instagram, Facebook, and Twitter

@jrmoltauthor

Website:

rockingchairsandbookshelves.com

<u>Upcoming Books</u>

To Complete the Stone Trilogy…

Son of Steel

Child of Shadow

And her independent thriller novel…

Devil in the Trees